What Others Are Saying about Dawn Crandall and *The Cautious Maiden*...

"A hint of mystery, a dose of betrayal, and a tantalizing romance—everything a historical romance lover could want! Dawn Crandall yet again crafts a tale that will leave her readers breathless."

—*Roseanna M. White*
Author, Ladies of the Manor series

"Prepare to be swept away with this beautifully compelling tale of romance and intrigue as Dawn Crandall deftly weaves her magic in *The Cautious Maiden*. Set against the backdrop of New England's Gilded Age, this novel of faith and redemptive love, sprinkled throughout with a sense of mystery and danger is a unique story embracing the spirit of Brontë's *Jane Eyre* and a delightful touch of Austen's *Pride and Prejudice*. *The Cautious Maiden* kept me turning the page until I reached a most sublime ending. A must-read for fans of Christian romantic fiction!"

—*Kate Breslin*
Award-winning author, *Not By Sight*

"Readers will be captivated by Dawn Crandall's fourth novel, *The Cautious Maiden*. Emotions run deep and draw the reader in with flawed characters and gentle nudges of romance that flare into a passionate journey of forgiveness and new beginnings. Violet is an innocent woman with a generous heart. Vance is a reformed rogue with the best intentions. Together, they create an amazing story sure to please the hopeful romantics in all of us."

—*Pepper D. Basham*
Author, Penned in Time series and *A Twist of Faith*

"What do you get when you mix a redeemed rake, an innocent maiden, and a determined villain? A tale impossible to put down! A great blend of action enhances characters who are intent on following their instincts: in one case a new call to obey God, in another a long-held trust that God is in control, and in the last a selfish desire to use others for his own good. Many thanks to Dawn Crandall for creating a romantic escape with a wonderful ending!"

—*Maureen Lang*
Author, Great War series and the Gilded Age series

"Dawn Crandall's characters capture your attention in this charming work of Gilded Age historical romance written in first person through the eyes of Violet, a gentle, innocent young woman with a loving heart. Then enter a gentleman rogue with a questionable reputation, who has now become a believer; add a wicked villain stalking around in the shadows, untrustworthy relatives, and the pace is intriguing. The multiple twists of the plot along with the hills and valleys of the romance between Violet and Vance made for a delightful read. Of course we are always so satisfied when faith in Christ and true love win out in the end. Well done."

—*Diana Wallis Taylor*
Speaker and author, *Mary, Chosen of God*

"*The Cautious Maiden* is a deeply absorbing love story—literally impossible to put down. Dawn Crandall deftly infuses the plot with equal measures of intrigue, conflict, heart pounding romantic moments, and character growth to form a captivating page-turner. The depth of honesty and redemption found within *The Cautious Maiden* is as refreshing as it is brave. Readers who enjoy romance, history, and stories brimming with hope will not want to miss this brilliant work."

—*Jessica Keller*
Author, *Saving Yesterday* and *Searching for Home*

"In *The Cautious Maiden*, author Dawn Crandall takes a reformed rogue with a redeemed heart and plants him solidly in the Heroes Hall of Fame. The power of Christ to transform a life; the power of love to transform a heart; the power of grace to transform a rogue into a hero—I have loved each book so far in The Everstone Chronicles, but I firmly believe that *The Cautious Maiden* is Dawn's best yet!"

—*Carrie Schmidt*
ReadingismySuperPower.org

"Time ceases to exist whenever I pick up a book by Dawn Crandall. From the earliest pages of *The Cautious Maiden*, I was immersed in the story of Violet and Vance. How could I not love this sweet, timid heroine with a big heart and her valiant hero seeking redemption from his past? The romantic tension sizzles, and that, along with unexpected suspense, makes this a novel guaranteed to steal your breath away. It certainly stole mine."

—*Savanna Kaiser*
TheEngraftedWord.net

"With a perfect balance of redemption, intrigue, and—as always—romance, Dawn Crandall flavors this story with a delectable journey you won't want to set down. Her unique voice and finesse of human emotions rolls across every page, reminding readers why she's firmly established at the top of the inspirational romance market."

—*Susan Tuttle*
susanltuttle.com

"Readers will connect deeply with Violet, feel the complete range of her emotions, and likely find themselves gasping with surprise or swooning from the romantic moments sprinkled throughout. Fans of Jody Hedlund and Julie Klassen will fall in love with Dawn Crandall's historical romances!"

—*Denise Hershberger*
Book reviewer, fiction411.com

"With a fabulous mix of romantic tension, thrilling suspense, and spiritual truths, Dawn Crandall instantly pulled me deep into the story of Vance and Violet! Her ability with first person narration never ceases to amaze me as it helps me connect with her characters in ways that I never would have imagined. The journey this book took me on is rife with fears and struggles which I thrilled to see these characters overcome."

—*Aerykah*
aerykah.wordpress.com

"In *The Cautious Maiden*, Dawn Crandall grasped my heart and brought out every emotion with an endearing heroine, a reformed rogue, a heart-pounding romance, jaw-dropping plot twists, lurking danger and suspense. She's taken broken characters and demonstrated God's amazing transforming power through grace, forgiveness and redemption within these pages. This book was absolutely amazing! It will be hard to get into my next book now after being so emotionally involved with Violet and Vance."

—*Katie Edgar*
ktslifeofbooks.wordpress.com

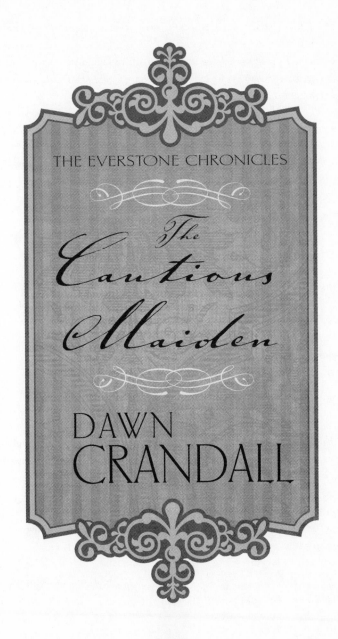

THE EVERSTONE CHRONICLES

The
Cautious
Maiden

DAWN
CRANDALL

WHITAKER
HOUSE

The Cautious Maiden

dawncrandallwritesfirst@gmail.com
www.facebook.com/dawncrandallwritesfirst
www.twitter.com/dawnwritesfirst/@dawnwritesfirst
www.pinterest.com/dawnwritesfirst

ISBN: 978-1-62911-750-8
eBook ISBN: 978-1-62911-751-5
Printed in the United States of America
© 2016 by Dawn Crandall

Whitaker House
1030 Hunt Valley Circle
New Kensington, PA 15068
www.whitakerhouse.com

Library of Congress Cataloguing-in-Publication Data Pending

1 2 3 4 5 6 7 8 9 10 11 ⅅⅅ 23 22 21 20 19 18 17 16

Dedication

For Little Rhett and Baby Blake.

1

The Stolen Crown

*"Forgiveness is the fragrance that the violet sheds
on the heel that has crushed it."*
—Mark Twain

Saturday, March 26th, 1892· Everston, Northern Maine

Hey Vi! You got a minute?"

My brother's voice came to me from the darkness, falling over the safest place I'd ever known—Everston, where I worked the front desk, and where, for the first time in my life, I had any sort of independence.

"Ezra, you shouldn't be here." I had no fear of anyone overhearing me; Everston turned into more of a hunting base than a fancy, high-society resort in the winter, and most of the part-time guests were on a bear hunt.

The newly fallen snow showed no tracks before me as a clue to where he might come from, but I continued regardless. "If Dexter finds out you're here, he'll have you taken to Laurelton and then what? Would they hang you?"

Ezra came out from behind the bushes lining the high stone wall of the veranda.

"Aw, I doubt that, Vi." The stench of the whiskey on his breath assaulted me. "And you don't need to worry none, I won't get caught anyway." He usually was too self-assured, as if convinced he was indestructible. Some days I wished he were right. If he were indestructible, I wouldn't worry about him half so much.

It really didn't surprise me to find that Ezra had been drinking. But that he was inebriated didn't concern me nearly as much as the fact that another man—whom I'd never seen or met before—came out of the bushes behind him. Ezra never did well in the company of others. For some reason, he always needed to out-shoot, out-talk, or out-drink anyone and everyone he could. He was so easily led astray. And so far off the narrow path we'd followed as children.

"Is that her?" The stranger's voice seeped from the darkness like oil, and I wished I'd been able to place him. My brothers' "friends" changed so often. They were not so much friends as carousing companions who usually left Ezra worse off than before.

"Yeah," was Ezra's only reply, and before I could muster an answer, the stranger slid to my side, pulled me to him, and clamped his arm about my waist. He caught my arm and pressed my wrist against my back. Pain shot from my hand to my twisted shoulder. I bent forward with a scream, only to be hushed by the force of my brother's hand against my lips. "Violet, hold still. He won't hurt you."

As the stranger slowly lessened his grip upon my arm, Ezra took his grimy fingers from my mouth.

Trying desperately to believe my brother, I remained silent as they kept me awkwardly hunched over. But Ezra didn't remove his hand from my face. He moved his fingers to my jaw where they tightened and held my head steady before him; his other hand was clamped at the nape of my neck. To my horror, the stranger tore my bonnet off, reached into my hair and loosened the blonde strands from my hair pins until it was pulled taut from my scalp.

Tears escaped down my cheeks as I realized Ezra would do nothing to help me. What all would Ezra allow this man to do to me?

"Ezra?" I whimpered, staring helplessly down at his wet, muddy boots.

Before he could answer, I felt the cool blade of a knife against the back of my neck, then the release of the stranger's hold. Ezra's grip on my jaw lessened, and I whipped my head up, savoring the freedom, too focused on getting away to realize what that freedom had cost me. As I stumbled toward the steps of the veranda, I felt the difference. The soft edges of my hair tickled the same tender skin which the cold metal of the knife had made contact with moments before.

I reached to my ears with both hands in disbelief. My long hair, my gorgeous blonde hair—my pride—was gone, chopped off at my chin. With the fingers of both hands grasping at the ends, I turned around; positive they had done all they had desired. Ezra was crouched down over the bushes, vomiting into them while his friend stood beside him holding the wavy lengths of my golden hair. My tears returned with an intensity that made my head hurt, blurring my vision.

My fingers combed through my shorn locks until reaching to the back of my head where they were even shorter. Dreadfully short! Only a few inches in length! I felt sick, as though my right arm had been severed from my body.

Bringing my hands to my face, pulling what strands I could with them, I covered my eyes, half wiping my tears and half wanting to hide in shame.

"Ezra?" I whispered.

He'd stood from his bent posture, wiping his mouth with his sleeve. His friend had vanished...with my hair. Not that it mattered. It wasn't as if I could truly have it back. What would I do with my hair, cut in such a dreadful way? How long would it take until it was presentable again?

"Don't blame me, Violet. I didn't know what else to do."

"But why?" I fingered the material at the shoulder of my dress. Not a single strand was left behind.

"Don't ask questions. You don't want the answers."

"But I do! Why did you have to cut my hair?"

"I didn't know what I was doing. I was too drunk to think, and I said things, promised things I shouldn't have, and now I've got to fix it. And I don't know how. Just trust me, I'll get you out of this mess I've made."

"You want me to trust you after what you just did?"

"You don't need to know any more. You just need to do as I say—and right now, stay close to your friends."

"I don't have any friends; at least anyone who would be able to help me."

"Come on, Vi, you have friends. What about Dexter and his new bride? And her brother? Vance Everstone has been around a lot lately. I've heard you have dinner with them at times. You're lucky to have a connection to such a—"

"But they won't understand. What am I supposed to tell them about my hair? How will I keep my job?"

"You have more to worry about than that stupid job of yours! Just get in good with the Everstones. They seem to like you." Ezra turned away and without another word, walked down the snowy path toward the lane headed to Laurelton. He must have hidden his horse somewhere in the pine trees outside Everston's front gate.

The thought of using Estella and her brother in any way to better my own situation turned my stomach. Not that I thought they truly cared anything about me. Why would they when they knew that my own good-for-nothing brother had burned down their beloved Blakeley House? And what would they think of me when they found out my role, that he'd put a stronghold on me that cold, autumn morning until I'd confessed I knew his favorite girl had been staying there, hidden away with them, which had induced him to start the fire in the first place?

As I walked the long trek back toward the front steps to the veranda, the icy cold wind suddenly cut straight through my hair to my scalp. Ignoring the wisps that the wind blew into my face, I flipped the collar of my coat up. A sob bubbled up from my chest. Ezra always had the upper hand, it seemed, and letting him know just how terribly upset I'd been; it would have given him too much knowledge of my heart.

Although, while taking part in this violation against me, he seemed a little sorry once it had been done. What did he mean by all he'd said?

I sat on the steps with my face in my hands, ignoring the fact that they hadn't been swept of the snow that had fallen. What did it matter now? How could I go into Everston as I was? How could I face Dexter and Estella? They would ask what had happened— and what could I say without lying? If I told the truth, they would wonder at my continued association with my brother who was wanted for committing arson against them. I would surely lose my job. And without my job I'd lose the privilege of living in the employee dormitory. I didn't have anywhere else to go besides back to The Hawthorne Inn, to my brother.

I had an aunt in Massachusetts, but I didn't know where. Going back to Ezra was my only other option. Was that why he'd done this? Did he not like the fact that I worked at Everston instead of staying to help him with what he'd made of my parent's beautiful home?

I hadn't stayed around long once it was clear that Ezra's plan was to make it into a brothel; only long enough to see a few of the first overtly confident girls show up and take residence. Later, after I'd started working at Everston, I'd heard that more had arrived— and that they weren't always willing.

It made me ill to think of what kinds of things were happening in the only home I had ever known. And that there was nothing I could do about it.

The most pitiful sound I remembered ever making escaped from my chest. Would I eventually become just as helpless as those women?

I'd certainly never be invited to dinner with Dexter and Estella again. Not that dinner was the most important thing to think about just then, but it had been something I valued.

Dexter and Estella had taken up the habit of inviting me to dine with them when Estella's brother was around, but I didn't know why. I knew it had nothing truly to do with Vance Everstone's presence. They likely wanted to keep the numbers right, and that was all.

To dinner on the sixth floor of Everston was actually where I'd been headed when I'd heard Ezra's voice from the bushes. I'd put on my best dress—which was the one I always wore to dinner with them—and done my hair into the most elaborate of coifs, lacing my yellow ribbon through the elaborate coils. I felt around the edge of my collar and scanned the sidewalk.

Even my ribbon was gone.

I felt the tears striving to return where I'd sufficiently stuffed them since seeing Ezra walk away. I closed my eyes. I'd been fooling myself for the last few months. I didn't know why they'd been including me until then, but they wouldn't anymore.

"Miss Hawthorne?"

My eyes startled open, and I jumped to my feet at the sound. I quickly wiped my fingers across my lashes, trying to contain my shock at having to face anybody in such a state.

Vance Everstone. Even through blurry, tear-filled eyes and at a distance of about ten feet, he looked too good. His black eyes and brows were perfectly situated; his mouth, nose, and jaw so amazingly sculpted and proportioned. Ever since the moment

I'd first seen him at the end of October, I couldn't help but think of him much too often...as ridiculous as it was to entertain such thoughts. I couldn't help it, but every time I saw him, he unwittingly captured my attention. And it was beyond annoying that he did so, because he seemed to want nothing to do with me.

And why would he?

Vance Everstone was primed and ready to take over his successful father's empire of a few dozen hotels and a lumber company which covered almost half of Maine. I was just some girl with the misfortune of having a gambler and drunkard as a brother.

Vance knew my background. It was probably the reason he never spoke to me beyond politely contributing to dinner conversation that floated around the table. Which, I supposed, was for his sister's sake.

"Miss Hawthorne...Violet, are you all right?" Vance came up the walk Ezra had just vacated.

Hearing my given name upon his lips shocked me into silence, even if I'd wanted to answer him. I gripped the collar of my coat to my neck, hoping to hide my shorn hair and my tear-stained cheeks.

"Are you crying?"

"No," I answered, revealing only my eyes from behind my lifted coat collar.

"All right then...were you crying a few moments ago?" He'd come closer and now stood only a few feet away. That was when I realized he held my bonnet in his hand and probably wondered why it had been on the ground so far away from where I'd been sitting—if the fact that I'd been sitting on the snowy steps outside Everston's warm, dry lobby wasn't something to question already.

Without giving a verbal answer, I lowered the corners of my collar from my face.

He stood stark still, staring at me as if I'd grown another head. "What happened? Who did this?"

It was an odd way for him to ask; as if he already knew I'd had no say in the matter—but perhaps my tears had been clue enough on that count.

"My brother…but I'm not sure why." I swallowed hard and felt my blood turn hot with embarrassment. For what else could I say if he asked for more details?

He took a moment to gather his next question. "Did he hurt you?"

I shook my head, my loose hair tickling my jaw as it swept by my face. "But this"—I grabbed the ends of my hair—"this is humiliating."

"Now, I wouldn't say *that*. It isn't conventional, but it'll grow back."

"But my hair…."

"You still look as pretty as ever."

My eyes shot to his, my disbelief overshadowing his shocking words. They couldn't be true; not from someone like Vance Everstone. But why would he say such a thing, especially considering he'd hardly ever said a word to me when he'd had ample chance?

"You're to dine with Dex and Stella upstairs with me tonight, are you not?"

"I can't. I don't want to go looking like this."

Vance paused, chewed his bottom lip and stared up at Everston, as if looking straight through it. And then to my surprise, he quickly took my hand and steered me back to the veranda. Leading me up the stairs and down the length of it until we came to the doors to the reading room, he guided me inside. Removing my coat, he led me to one of the chairs in the corner and made me sit. Then he pulled another chair from a few feet away and set it right in front of mine, handing me my bonnet. Without a word, he sat studying me with his amazing black eyes, in a way that could only be described as intimately.

Was this what it felt like to be the aim of a scheming flirt? I'd thought I'd be able to withstand such blatant tactics, but now I wasn't so sure. Vance was far too good-looking for his own good; so much so that just the thought of him thinking anything at all of me sent my heart racing.

Could he tell?

"Do you happen to have any hairpins left?" Vance's words broke through my thoughts.

"Why, no, but there might be some on the ground outside—" I moved to stand, but Vance stopped me with a gentle hand at the cuff of my coat sleeve.

"I'll go look. You stay right here, don't go anywhere."

"I was about halfway to where the path bends around the hotel when…it happened," I whispered.

With a sympathetic glance, Vance stood and left the room by the way we'd come in.

While he was gone, I imagined him searching the ground for a few minutes, every so often collecting a pin here and there. This little service, and the fact that he cared to stop on his way up to Dexter and Estella's to help me, did dangerous things to my already overly active imagination.

I didn't know why I'd felt some strange connection to Vance upon our first meeting—as if he'd in some way recognized something about me upon hearing my name. And no matter how I tried to convince myself that no good could come from my associating with the black sheep of the Everstone family, he kept surprising me. Yes, he would probably be labeled a flirt for the duration of his entire life. But could a man really help it if, at the sight of him, women practically wanted to kiss his feet?

Yet, he wasn't good or heroic. No true gentleman would amass the rumors that Vance had, unless he was guilty of at least a few of the accusations. I had to keep reminding myself of that.

Upon returning, Vance took a seat again and held most of the pins out for me to take.

I did so, but answered, "I don't understand. My hair is too short—"

"I think we can figure something out. I wouldn't want you to miss out on having dinner with us on account of feeling unpresentable." He studied my hair once again.

I forced myself to breathe and averted my eyes as he focused on me so completely. How was it that he could make me feel so reassured, and yet on edge at the same time?

And then, without warning Vance took a lock of my hair, deftly twirled it about his fingers and pinned it above my ear, causing me to sit up straight, wide-eyed. "What are you doing?"

"Making you look presentable. Not that this daring new style doesn't look darling on you. I had the impression you weren't happy—"

"I'm not happy; my own brother would—"

"Yes, about that," Vance uttered, tight-lipped. He now held a few of the pins between his teeth, readying them to be of use. He didn't go on, but simply continued to silently pin the strands of my hair into place. I tried my best to ignore how wonderful it felt. Never had I wanted any man to touch even my hand, and yet there Vance Everstone was, practically running his fingers through my hair.

I closed my eyes. It was far too enjoyable, feeling his hands caress my scalp as he seemed to know just where to place the pins.

"Was anyone else with him?" He must have used up the pins held in his lips, for he reached into my open hand for more, brushing my palm with his fingertips. "As you likely know better than anyone else, Ezra never does much on his own. There's always someone leading him farther astray than is good for him."

"Do you know Ezra?" I asked; my eyes still closed, almost as shocked by his words as I was by how comfortable it felt to have him pin my hair. I really didn't want him to stop; it felt so calming.

"We've been acquainted. And you didn't answer my question. Was anyone with him?"

"He had a friend with him."

"Anyone you recognized?"

"No."

"What did he look like?"

"I don't know, just like any other lumberjack loitering about Westward...and now The Hawthorne Inn. What does it matter?"

"You're right, it doesn't. I'm sorry for grilling you—"

"Ezra was drunk," I uttered, almost to myself. "And he told me I wouldn't want to know the details of why he'd done this."

"Of course." Vance said the words under his breath.

I opened my eyes and directed them to his, but his gaze was still focused on my hair. I hadn't paid much attention to what he'd been doing with the pins. I'd been too amazingly relaxed and then distracted by our conversation. Just having Vance help walk me through my feelings of hurt and betrayal concerning Ezra made the idea of facing Dexter and Estella that much easier. Surely I wouldn't lose my job. Surely they would understand my predicament.

"Do you know why he would want to cut off my hair?"

Vance didn't answer, and I had a feeling he knew something about it but wouldn't tell me. He silently handed me the leftover hairpins.

"Is Ezra truly an acquaintance of yours?" I asked.

"I've seen him around."

"He probably knows who you are."

"Doesn't everyone know who I am?"

"I didn't know who you were when we met. I'd never heard of you before; just your father's name because he'd sold Everston to Dexter."

"How refreshing." Vance gave me a sly look from the corner of his eye, stood, and helped me to my feet. "How odd it is that it was *I* who knew of *you* before we met, and not the other way around."

"Me? How would you know me?"

"Your brother has a rather loose tongue when it comes to bragging about his beautiful yet staunchly moral little sister."

I cringed at the thought. If Vance Everstone knew of me from Ezra, how many other disreputable young men also knew about me? And what had Ezra said? Was that the explanation for how Vance responded to me upon our meeting?

"What exactly would Ezra say about me?"

"I wouldn't fret about it, Violet. He has a big mouth. You must know that. I suppose talking about you to his friends is his twisted way of being proud of having such a beautiful sister."

"Even if anyone considered me beautiful before, they wouldn't now. My glorious hair was my only true beauty, and now it's gone."

"Oh, I wouldn't say that."

"No respectable young lady would have her hair cut like this. I think Ezra wanted to humiliate me for some reason."

Vance helped me to my feet and led me to the hall, still intent on taking me up to dinner, apparently. I let him lead me willingly, one hand on his arm, the other holding my bonnet by the ribbons. I didn't know when I'd changed my mind about attending Estella's dinner.

"Ezra might be up to something, but believe me, as long as I'm around—and I'm sure Dexter will agree to protect you as well—we will make sure you're safe. But that means no more lingering about the deserted veranda at dusk; especially when a certain outlaw brother is around." Vance caught my gaze.

"I wasn't lingering about. I was just about to go inside when—"

"Violet, I'm only joking. You didn't do anything wrong, besides possibly being too sympathetic to your no-good—"

"I should have headed inside the moment I knew he was—"

"You should have called up to Dexter and told him Ezra was—"

"You think I should turn him in? My own brother?"

"I can understand your dilemma. I'd have a difficult time doing that as well…but even now, after what he's done to you, you're still sympathetic," he stated frankly.

"After what Ezra said, I can't believe he wanted to hurt me. He said he wanted to keep something worse from happening. I didn't really understand what he was getting at."

"Hopefully you won't have to find out."

I looked up to Vance again; his eyes were focused on the elevator, still a ways down the hall.

It had felt so good to talk to someone about what had happened; it had been so long since I'd had anyone to truly confide in—ever since my parents had passed away. I hadn't made many of what I would call true friends while working at Everston for the last nine months, and was well aware of the reason: no one wanted to associate with a young woman whose closest relative ran a brothel.

I'd thought I could be friends with Estella, but not when her true identity was revealed. Instead of being a simple girl named Elle Stoneburner who might understand my predicament, she was a member of high society. I couldn't be presumptuous and expect too much from her, not when she was an heiress to a fortune, and I the sister of a brothel owner. Even if she and Dexter invited me to dinner sometimes, and I politely accepted, I couldn't think to actually form a friendship with her. Especially not now.

And Vance, her brother—the "heir apparent" of the majority of the Everstone fortune and empire—despite being so surprisingly helpful to me, wasn't my friend. Even if he wanted to be, I didn't think I could allow it.

"You look rather like a careless Shakespearean nymph, now that I think about it," his smooth voice broke through my thoughts, and I looked up catching his eye for just a moment.

"I'm not a careless…anything."

"I can tell. You're quite the opposite of your brother, you know. Just as he's described." Vance cocked an eyebrow over a suspicious look. "What were you just thinking about a few minutes ago?"

"Oh nothing. You've done enough to help me, Mr. Everstone—"

"Please, call me Vance. It's long overdue."

"And you've done more than was needed already...Vance."

He stopped our progress down the hall toward the elevator, motioning me toward a mirror hanging on the wall nearby.

"And really for nothing, for I'd much rather you make my excuses to your sister and her husband than show up to dinner like—"

"Nonsense, you look perfectly acceptable."

"How can you say that?"

"Just look." He gave me a little push toward the mirror.

I faced it, hating to do so in his presence. But what I saw startled me. Yes, my eyes were slightly puffy from the tears I'd shed, but my hair looked amazing. And I was used to doing the most extravagant styles I could manage...back when I'd had an abundance of hair to work with.

Vance Everstone, somehow, with expert skill, had pulled each and every golden strand of my hair and twisted the ends into a lovely roll that circled the back of my head, from ear to ear.

I almost asked him how he knew to do such a thing, but just as quickly realized that I probably didn't want to know.

"Ready to go up?"

"What will I tell them if they notice?"

"Why not tell them the truth, as you've told me?"

"I wouldn't want to worry them. They wouldn't understand."

"You thought I wouldn't worry about you?"

"Well, not exactly that, but I knew you'd understand, somehow. And you did, probably better than anyone else could ever try."

"I'm sincerely happy I could be of service." He placed my hand back upon his arm and escorted me to the elevator. We'd never met before dinner in the lobby; I was usually there early, and Vance was usually late, just as he'd been that time.

We stood silently next to the ever-present elevator attendant on the way up to the sixth floor. For as calm as I'd been while he styled my hair, my heart now beat erratically in my chest just standing near Vance Everstone. And yet I wished to run; I *needed* to run as far away from him as I could get, not exit the elevator onto the sixth floor to have dinner with him and his sister.

But Ben Whitespire would be there as well. He was probably already upstairs, for he was usually early too. Yes, I would focus on Ben. Even if he hardly acknowledged me as I wished he would, he was good, and good to be around.

And Vance, no matter his charm, was most certainly *not*.

It didn't matter how wonderful he'd seemed during the last twenty minutes. He was a rake, and even if one of the rumors I'd heard circulating through Everston about him were true, it would be one too many.

2

Dinner at Everston

"Let men tremble to win the hand of woman...."
—Nathaniel Hawthorne

Upon exiting the elevator and then immediately entering the front hall of Dexter and Estella's sixth floor tower apartment on Vance's ever-steady arm, I was not surprised to see Ben Whitespire and Roxy Blakeley sitting and chatting together on one of the sofas flanking the ornate marble fireplace at the end of the front room. I forced my gaze from lingering on them for too long, setting my heart against the slight bit of jealousy the sight provoked.

Vance helped me out of my coat, took my bonnet from my hands, and gave them to the butler, who hooked them onto the wall tree nearby.

"Hello, Violet! Vance!" Estella greeted us with unconcealed enthusiasm, stealing my thoughts away from Ben and Roxy. I was still amazed she genuinely seemed to offer me her friendship.

"It's so nice you were able to come up together. Did you happen to meet downstairs?" she asked with a sly glance my way.

"As it happened," Vance answered. "We did just that."

"How wonderful. I always knew you two would get along." She turned to Dexter, who had silently greeted us with a smile and then stood off to the side in all seriousness, looking as if he intended to snatch his new wife away from us the first chance he had.

Vance's answer had apparently satisfied his sister's curiosity about us coming together, for she immediately excused herself and disappeared down the hall with her husband.

Despite the warm welcome, I was still terrified of what any one of them might think of my hair once they sat down and had a good look at it. I'd only had that quick glance in the mirror downstairs, and for as amazing as it looked to me then, would it be enough to hide the atrocious truth?

I scanned the hall for another mirror, almost desperate to prove to myself that my hair wasn't, indeed, falling from the pins Vance had so diligently secured. But when I spotted one, I couldn't make myself go near it. My doing so would only draw more attention, when really, I wanted and needed the very opposite.

Every time I thought back to my brother's actions, I felt like crying. It would take years to grow my hair out to an appropriate length again. I could still hardly conceive that it was gone, replaced with masterfully placed pins that did an acceptable job of hiding the truth.

Vance led me into the front room, though I didn't know why he continued to bother. He'd never shown any particular interest in guiding me about on any other occasion.

I reached up to finger a short strand I felt escaping the pins just behind my left ear, but then I stopped, in case anyone might notice.

"See?" Vance whispered, leaning toward me ever so slightly. "No one even notices the difference. And when they do learn of it, I promise you, they will not think any less of you or your hair."

As he finished this secret sentence, Vance stepped away from me as if he'd not said a word. I stared after him. I felt as if a new man had been unveiled to me—that this couldn't be the same Vance Everstone who'd practically ignored me for months. What had caused him to make such a change in his treatment of me?

Why—just because of my unfortunate evening—did he act so differently now?

As I was about to head toward Ben and Roxy, Estella again came up to me. "Vance continues to surprise me every time I see him these days."

"Oh really?" I asked, for I couldn't think of anything else to say.

"He's much changed, even from last summer. If you'd known him then, I dare say you wouldn't recognize the man here tonight."

Estella took my arm and led me to the couch facing the one Ben and Roxy occupied. Their lively conversation still seemed to be going strong, though all I could tell about it was that it involved something to do with the strange behaviors of their pet cats.

I looked toward the dining room and saw that Vance and Dexter spoke together near the entrance which we'd soon be converging through. Vance stood with his arms crossed over his chest and a frown on his gorgeous face, as if stubbornly defending something to Dexter. He didn't look happy, that was for sure. A moment later, Dexter looked at his watch and dismissed Vance, then came further into the room to inform us that dinner would soon be ready.

Vance walked off toward the large wall of windows overlooking Half Moon Lake and the Appalachian Mountains in the distance, and looked as if he was doing all he could not to lose his temper.

When Estella moved to join her husband, I stood as well. And then I found myself walking across the room toward Vance. I didn't know why. He wouldn't likely want my company, not if the severely disturbed look on his face was any indication. But my feet would not obey what I knew to be best, and I ended up standing before him. His discomfiture did something to me, and I just wanted to try to make him feel better. He hadn't seemed that out of sorts before speaking with Dexter. What on earth could he have said that would put Vance in such a temper? Was it about me?

I didn't know what to say, so I didn't say anything. I just stood there with him…trying to figure everything out.

"What are you doing?" he asked, still not letting up on his disparaging mood.

"I'm trying to decide what to say to you."

"Why bother saying anything?"

Taken aback a little, I didn't budge. Although his sister had just reiterated how changed he'd seemed lately, all of a sudden, there he was, acting like a bear.

"I don't have to say anything. I can just stand here." I insisted upon staring out the window as I said the words, though I could tell he watched me closely. "It's quite preferable to sitting alone on that sofa over there across from—"

"Is there something between you and Ben?"

I shouldn't have been surprised by such glaring frankness. Not from Vance Everstone.

"I wish him all the best in whatever it is he sets his mind to."

"And what about his heart?" He looked almost suspicious, but I could hardly imagine why he would be. What would it matter to him if there was something going on between Ben and me?

"It's really none of my concern what he does with his heart."

"Miss Blakeley seems to fancy him, quite a lot."

"He's a likable fellow."

"Would you say that I'm a likable fellow too?"

"Not especially."

He smiled. "Good—you shouldn't."

I gave him a questioning look, for he did puzzle me so.

"You shouldn't seek out my company." He turned his face from me, suddenly interested in the detail of the carved doorframe. "Even amongst friends."

"Because it isn't safe?"

"For your reputation."

"Says Dexter Blakeley?"

His eyes met mine again, narrowed shrewdly. "And any other person who would—"

"Well, we need not be friends."

"That's probably best."

"Is that why you're so firing mad right now? Because people would assume there's only one reason a man like you would want to associate with a young woman whose brother runs a brothel… because…because what other reason would there be than to—"

"That's not why."

Taken aback yet again, my hand involuntarily went to my chest. "I'm delighted to hear it, Mr. Everstone."

"You should be. I have only the most honorable intentions when it comes to you, Violet. I need you to know that above all else."

The conversation had taken such a turn; I hardly knew what we were speaking of, or why. How had things become so confusing? And what on earth did he mean by the little he'd said?

"I suppose it would be best that we not be friends. There would likely be too many complications; especially if the rumors I've heard are true." I took a step away, which he allowed. He even took a step back himself.

"Exactly, Miss Hawthorne. It is for the best."

"Well, thank you very much for having my best interest in mind, Mr. Everstone." And with that final sentence, I walked away.

⌒

"You'll be going to Boston soon, as well? Maybe we could all travel together." Dexter looked down the table, right past me, to direct his question to Ben Whitespire.

"It might be possible. I'm not sure of my plans as of yet, but I do plan to visit The Boston Inland Mission Society eventually.

Crawford always had such good things to say about it, and I feel that God has been calling me to move on from the church in Laurelton."

"Really? You're going to leave Laurelton?" I asked.

"Not any time soon, I don't think, and maybe not at all." His gaze dropped to his plate, avoiding having to turn directly toward me while he answered. "I'm just open to the idea, if my meeting with the mission society goes as well as I hope."

Ben Whitespire hadn't exactly professed any feelings for me in the last few months as our acquaintance had deepened, but we had a certain kind of camaraderie that had given me hope for something more.

The thought of him leaving Laurelton created a hollow feeling in my stomach. He must have sensed my discomfort because when I glanced up next, he caught my eye with an apologetic smile.

What did that mean? I swallowed and determined not to let it bother me. I had much bigger things to worry about concerning Ezra and his treatment of me earlier that evening than to dwell on what Ben's ultimate intentions were regarding me. Although I'd put on my smile and bravely attended the dinner, what had happened was never far from my mind.

No one had mentioned my hair, which surprised me. Perhaps I really was just someone to fill a seat and make the numbers come out right, and not someone anyone genuinely wanted to get to know. Maybe it was best that Dexter, Estella, and Ben would go off to Boston together soon. I'd been too hopeful, thinking I belonged in such an elite crowd, when I really didn't.

From across the table, Vance cleared his throat, capturing my attention away from the most decadent chocolate cake I'd ever tasted. He locked his dark gaze to mine for a moment and then shifted his eyes toward Ben in question.

As if I hadn't already given him the answer.

"When will Nathan and Amaryllis head back to Washington?" Vance asked his sister.

"Oh, not for a few months. Not until little Rafe gets bigger, and after father's wedding in June. Why? Are you going to come down to visit them too?" Estella's tone grew more excited. "We'd love for you to join us; you'll have to come down eventually, you know—"

"Possibly. I've been needing to get down to Everstone Square in Boston for a while now. But I'll have to see. Miss Hawthorne, have you ever considered possibly moving to Washington?" Vance asked abruptly. "Our family could provide you with plenty of connections."

"Um, Washington state? Why would I—?" I asked, momentarily confused by the turn in the conversation. "I've never considered it before."

Vance lifted a brow, eying me suspiciously.

Indeed, why would I *not*, considering what kind of shenanigans my brother could be up to concerning my safety and well-being?

"I know Nathan would love to see more of you before they leave again, Vance. You should come with us." Estella reached her hand down the table toward her brother. I couldn't blame her, but Vance Everstone definitely didn't seem like the kind of man who would welcome such displays of affection and concern from anyone; even a sister.

"And if when they do leave, and Violet wants a chance to move on, I'm certain they would love having her help with the baby."

"Are Lawry, Meredyth, and Wynn still around, by chance?" Vance's words, although they were simply said, sounded forced and empty, just as he'd sounded while talking to me before dinner. As if he'd hated uttering every single one of them.

"They've already started on their journey back to Washington." Estella pulled her hand back. "If you'd wanted to see Wynn before they left, I'm sure I told you multiple times over the last few months what their plans consisted of; that they were heading back in early March."

"I suppose I—I've been busy." And he left it at that.

"Why would you need to see Wynn?" I lifted my eyes to meet his across the table, my curiosity getting the better of me. But seriously, what connection did Vance have to Meredyth's adopted daughter that he would want to see her?

Estella gave her brother a questioning glance, and then answered, "Wynn is Vance's step-daughter. His late wife's little girl from her first marriage, I believe. Isn't that right, Vance?"

My mind raced at the thought of Vance married. He definitely didn't seem the marrying type. And how long ago had his wife died? Why had I not heard about *those* rumors? And what about all of the ones I had heard—were they from before he was married, or after? He hadn't been in active mourning when I'd first met him in October. Why hadn't anyone ever mentioned his wife before?

"Giselle—my wife—passed away during our voyage from France to America last spring," Vance answered my unspoken question. "And yes, Wynn is my daughter, but we all thought it would be best if Lawry and Meredyth adopted her. And it is. It is best she be with them." He still seemed to speak with the same forced nature as when he'd first brought up Wynn, and it made me want to know more. About everything.

Truly, what a conundrum Vance Everstone was becoming. Would he ever allow anyone to solve the puzzle of a man he obviously enjoyed presenting? But then again, perhaps it had been only his wife who'd been able to break through to the real man underneath it all, and now that she'd been taken from him, he wasn't too keen on letting anyone else in. Ever again. That's how he seemed. So closed. So aloof.

But then my thoughts traveled back to when he'd pinned my hair, so tenderly and carefully. Had it been his wife who had taught him—?

Oh! Why were such outrageous thoughts even invading my mind?

New, startling opinions of Vance pushed their way into my heart. He had acted the hero down on the steps of Everston. He'd come upon me at my lowest, and he'd done everything he could think of to make me feel better. He'd convinced me to come to dinner and even persuaded me that I had nothing to worry about concerning my job.

And he'd been right.

When I lifted my eyes from my meandering thoughts, I found him silently watching me. Even if he'd insisted that not being friends was best, the look on his face said so much more than any of his words ever had. It displayed quite the opposite of what any of his overly protective sentences had suggested. The look in his eyes seemed almost *interested*, which caused all kinds of strange emotions to bombard my chest.

Dexter and Estella were speaking about their ultimate plans to rebuild Blakeley House someday, and Ben turned to speak to Roxy who had hardly said a word through all of dinner.

It was amazing how quickly a glance from Vance could make me forget all about my wishful thoughts concerning Ben.

Ben Whitespire really was the best man I'd ever had the chance to meet, and he deserved my thoughts and attention a hundred times more than Vance Everstone did.

He was a preacher, lived an upright life in Laurelton with his two sisters, was tall and handsome enough, and treated everyone—even me—with the utmost respect. He'd gone away for his pastoral studies and returned home to Laurelton when his father had passed away, for the benefit of his sisters, and also conveniently just in time to take over his father's pastorate.

But now he would possibly be leaving again.

"What will become of your sisters if you turn to missions?" I overheard Roxy ask.

"Georgiana has become engaged," Ben replied. "She'll be married soon, and they plan to move to New Hampshire to be nearer her fiancé's family. Lanie will go with them, of course, though the thought of doing so has her seriously considering her options. She's recently finished her teacher training and is considering taking a position, possibly not far from where I'll end up."

"And where is that?" Roxy asked. She could have been reading my mind.

"Tennessee or Kentucky. But again, only as I feel the Lord's guidance."

"There seem to be plenty of people around here who need you." Roxy spoke up again, which surprised me. She wasn't usually so persistent. "How are we going to find someone who wants to come and replace you way up here in the middle of nowhere?"

"He calls us all to do different things, Miss Blakeley. I'm sure someone will answer God's need in Laurelton if I'm called elsewhere."

From the pale, starched look on Roxy's face, I could tell the prospect of Ben leaving Laurelton was something that bothered her—maybe even more than it bothered me. Had Ben been just as friendly to her throughout the months? Maybe his friendship with me really hadn't meant anything. Maybe he was interested in Roxy, instead. Really, he was so genuinely friendly, it was impossible for anyone to tell what he meant by anything.

I turned my attention back to what little chocolate cake was left on my plate. Dinner was almost over, and I again found Vance Everstone studying me. He'd done so on a number of other occasions throughout the months, but now that he'd actually spoken to me and made me feel as though he'd cared about what happened to me—which was ridiculous—the look did something peculiarly new to me. Something even Ben Whitespire, with all his genuine candor, had never quite been able to accomplish before.

3

The Hollow

"*A new heart also will I give you, and a new spirit will I put within you: and I will take away the stony heart out of your flesh, and I will give you a heart of flesh.*"
Ezekiel 36:26

Sunday, March 27, 1892

The next afternoon, after church in Laurelton with Estella and Dexter, I decided to walk to Leightner Hollow, the location in the woods where Dexter provided summer church services for his hotel guests. It was a special place for me, for I hid away there to write on my days off.

No one knew about my writing, and honestly, the children's books I'd started creating when my parents had passed away were really just for my own amusement, something I enjoyed doing. I'd saved up my money from my first months of working at Everston and purchased a writing box, which helped keep me focused. Were anyone else to come across the stories, drawings, and paintings, I would have been simply mortified. That's why I pursued it on my own, in the woods.

I knew it wasn't exactly proper to walk out into the woods on my own, even if there was purpose to it. It was something I'd been used to doing while growing up in Westward before the lumber camps had come to the area, before my parents had passed, before Ezra had taken over and my life had become so dramatically altered.

I'd missed those walks dreadfully. When I'd had the good fortune of meeting Dexter Blakeley and was offered the job at the front desk of Everston, I couldn't help myself from exploring the grounds and falling completely in love with Leightner Hollow.

The walk wasn't long, and the beautiful hills were covered with dense pines and birch trees that reminded me of home. When I finally came to the barren clearing under the giant bonnet-shaped stone formation, my feet were cold and my boots and the hem of my skirt mud-soaked. But despite the chill in the air, I was warm from the exertion of the walk.

I hadn't bothered making my hair presentable that morning, opting only to tuck as much as I could up into my bonnet, keeping it on during church. The night before, I had tried to sleep with it all pinned up in order to keep it for the next day, but decided after a few hours of discomfort that starting over would be worth pulling every well-placed pin out and getting some real sleep.

But I'd been wrong. I should have kept them in and dealt with the lack of sleep. When I awoke, my shortened locks were twisted and flattened and sticking straight up in all directions. No matter how I tried, I could not get the strands into any sort of semblance of order. And I couldn't ask for anyone's help. Francie, who also worked at Everston, would have surely helped me, but I hadn't gained the courage to tell her about it yet.

Once I'd returned to the Everston employee dormitory after church, I'd traded my bonnet for a warm white woolen hat my mother had made me for Christmas once. It covered most of my hair and wasn't at all stylish, but it was warm and that's all that mattered.

I never saw anyone at the hollow, anyway. I knew if I had a room at Everston instead of my stark little room in the dormitory, I would probably have stayed there, sitting by the fire to write, but that wasn't an option. Nor would I ever have such opportunities. No, I had either my frigid room or the blustery beloved hollow.

When I neared the stone platform at the deepest part of the shelter, I stopped in my muddy tracks, startled at the sound of a masculine voice reading quietly, almost to a tune. I stopped swinging my reticule carelessly beside me and stood still, sure that it was Dexter. I hadn't seen any tracks in the snow—whoever it was must have come from the direction of the north end of Half Moon Lake where Blakeley House used to stand.

Not really wanting to find out who it was, I turned around and walked back in the direction I'd come, trying my best to not shuffle through the leaves and melting snow quite as loudly as when I'd sauntered into the makeshift chapel.

"Is that you, Violet?" It was Vance Everstone's voice.

I kept walking, now not caring whether I made much noise as I left.

"Violet, where are you going?" Vance asked when I didn't answer.

I stopped, begrudgingly, and turned around. Vance had stood so his torso was now visible from across the top of the tall stone platform. I watched as he leaned over and set something down, looking at me shyly, as if he were hiding something. I took a step back, in the direction of Everston.

"I'm going back. We shouldn't be out here together. Alone."

"But we already are. And there's no harm in just talking."

"We shouldn't—"

"I'm not going to eat you, Violet." The most amazing smirk crossed his lips as he uttered those words.

I took another step backwards. "Of course not, but—"

"And I'm not going to hurt you, either."

Oh, but he could. Even without actually *doing* a blessed thing.

"What are you doing here anyway?" I asked. "You weren't at church; I thought maybe you went back to Bangor."

"I wanted some privacy." He'd ceased to come any closer, likely because of how many times I'd already stepped away from him. He wasn't exactly close—probably twenty feet away from me, standing near the far corner of the stone platform. "I'm about finished with my business in Bangor. What are you doing out here?"

"Nothing." I swung my reticule behind me, happy my small notebook was hidden inside. "I come out here to get away from work and the employee dormitory."

"Ah, I see. I'm sorry I took your sanctuary without asking. I will leave you." Vance turned around, back toward whatever he'd hidden, and came back around the platform carrying a large, thick book and a small, blue, hardcover pocket-sized one. It looked to be a Bible. He walked up to me, and I thought he was about to go right past without another word, but then he stopped as he came up beside me. "But I find that I can't. And I won't."

"Why not?" I asked, breathlessly. Really, he needed to leave. Being alone with him for as little time as had passed was already causing me to have second hopes that he would stay; that he'd been there hoping to see me; and that he'd, indeed, been there at the hollow reading the Bible, *waiting* for me to show up.

"I cannot, in good conscience, leave you out here alone after what happened to you yesterday." His dark eyes burrowed into me, and I immediately felt ashamed for being completely incognizant of that danger as I'd walked away from the protection of Everston. Not that I feared Ezra, but his friend didn't seem the kind of man who would want to stay away from such an easy target. And that's what I was now. I'd proven it yesterday with my inefficiency at fending them off.

"If you want to head back, I'll follow you at a safe distance."

"But I haven't had a chance to—" I stopped, immediately regretting almost getting into why exactly I'd come.

"To what?" Vance prodded.

"Oh, nothing."

"You really ought not to put yourself in such dangerous situations. What if it had been someone else here, someone else who *would* want to hurt you?"

Although Vance had already urged me to start on my way back to Everston, and I knew it was the best thing to do in our given situation, I couldn't make my feet move. Instead, I asked, "What's that you have there?"

He shifted the books farther to his right side, as if I hadn't already seen them. "Oh, nothing." He smiled, purposefully matching my own vague answer to his previous question.

"Were you reading?"

"I was just looking through some books."

I'd never seen Vance Everstone look embarrassed before, but the blush that crept up his neck after he'd admitted so little, was quite a sight to behold. I forced my gaze from his neck to the books again. Boldly, I reached over and took them from his loose grip.

The small one *was* a Bible, and the larger one, one of the hymnals from Everston that Dexter would bring out for the services during the warmer months.

"I was looking for a certain hymn I'd heard months ago, but it's like searching for a needle in a haystack. I don't remember the title, only a few lines."

"What are the lines you remember?" I turned to the glossary at the back, ready for the challenge, hoping the words would trigger my memory, and I'd be able to find the hymn.

He seemed even more ill at ease than he'd been before divulging the fact that he'd been searching for a hymn.

I smiled. "You don't need to sing the words to me; you can just tell me what they are."

"I couldn't sing them if I tried. I don't remember the notes," he admitted. "That's part of the reason I'm searching for the hymn. I wanted to learn to sing it, for the words I recall are often on my mind." He took the Bible back, slipped a scrap of paper from between its pages and handed it to me. "I wrote them down."

In penciled, block letters I read, "Thy power, and Thine alone, can change the leopard's spots and melt the heart of stone."

I held the paper and closed my eyes, hoping for inspiration. As the words repeated in my mind, I let them sift through my memories. But all the while I couldn't help but wonder why Vance would have had those specific words saved and written, treasured and hidden in his little blue Bible.

That he had a Bible *still* surprised me. Had *his* heart of stone been melted? *His* spots changed? Why else would he—?

Vance took hold of my hand, and my eyes flew open as he pried my gloved fingers from his paper and let go of me. "Never mind." The open manner he'd been discussing the matter with me before was gone, replaced by a wall of stone. "Like you said, we shouldn't be out here alone."

"I'll remember, just give me a minute." I flipped through the back pages of the hymnal.

"You don't need to help me. I need to help you. By following you at a safe distance through the woods back to Everston. Now."

As Vance walked passed me, I stood my ground, still silently repeating the words he'd written down. I knew the hymn. I'd sung it before, probably multiple times; I just needed to remember.

As I scanned the titles, the notes were just barely coming to me. To get them just right, I decided to sing the words to myself, "Thy power and Thine alone, can change the leopard's spots." I stopped mid-sentence and said, "Actually, I don't think it's *leopard's* spots you mean, but rather, *leper's* spots," and then I started over, each note coming back to me stronger than the last, until I got to the final line which I had to repeat, "And melt the heart of stone… and melt the heart of stone…and melt the heart of stone."

I spun around as I recalled the next words—the title of the hymn—and found Vance clutching his Bible in his fist, staring at me, looking as if he were vexed, instead of thankful.

"Jesus Paid it All." I said the words now, instead of singing them.

"Thanks." He shook his head slightly, which completely transformed the vexed look into something ultimately blander, which I didn't at all care for. Then he stepped back toward me, reached for the hymnal and gently tried to pull it from my grasp.

But I kept ahold of it, and we ended up holding it between us.

"You have an amazing voice." His words were surprising, especially after the array of opposing expressions he had displayed before saying as much.

"Thank you." I opened the book, found the title in the back and turned to the page the hymn was on. Then I handed him the book. "There it is. You said you had trouble recalling the notes."

"I'm not likely to forget them now, not after hearing you sing them."

Now it was my turn to blush, and I truly hated that I'd let him get to me with such an easy compliment. He was a flirt, wasn't he? A flirt with a heart of stone—but maybe not anymore? What all did that mean?

"You really have changed your spots, haven't you?" I said, hoping to draw him out.

"You could say that, but it actually hasn't been me doing the changing at all—only receiving the blessings of the change Christ has been doing in me."

I felt something strange melt in my own heart at such unexpected words. Was this really the disreputable Vance Everstone saying such things?

"So, you're implying you're not really as bad as your reputation might suggest?"

"My reputation...you can probably believe all of what you've heard. And you might as well."

"How can you be two such different men? The one I've heard all about, and the one standing before me?"

"There's a verse regarding that, isn't there? I can't remember the reference off the top of my head, but I remember reading, or at least hearing, something about becoming a new creation."

"So, you've only just become a Christian and turned from—"

"The absolute deplorable way I'd been living my life? Yes."

"How did it happen? What made you—?"

"It's actually a long and complicated story, and one your innocent ears are much too sweet to be tainted by hearing." Vance turned, almost as if he now couldn't face me.

"But your heart—?"

"We need to get you back to Everston. You head up the hill, and I'll follow."

I swallowed nervously, a little relieved he'd decided me too naive to hear what he could have said. I spun around without another word and started off in the direction I'd come not twenty minutes before. I had heard rumors enough about how he'd ruined a number of young women over the years and refused to marry them; how he'd been in Europe evading responsibilities at home with his family. Was that when he'd met his wife?

It sounded as if it was a relatively recent change he'd made, and although he seemed entirely repentant of his previous ways, he seemed to struggle with the fact that his past was as awful as it was. Something must have hit him hard to have embraced Jesus as fully as he'd described. And if I were to guess what it was, I would wager it was the death of his wife that had made a difference.

How he must have loved her.

I'd walked a good thirty feet before I heard Vance advance through the leaves. I really hadn't thought it likely that Ezra—or his friend—would come back any time soon after what they'd done the day before, but as I walked back to Everston under Vance's guided supervision, I couldn't help but feel the difference his presence made.

I suddenly wondered if Vance would in fact be going with Dexter and Estella to Boston to see their brother, his wife and their new baby.

By the time I'd made it to the front lawn of Everston, I wasn't looking forward to the coming weeks or months. I hated that all of my new friends would be leaving so soon. Not that I minded working the front desk of Everston, but it was the company of the other employees that I didn't quite fit into very well. I'd been raised to be a lady. Even if we hadn't had as much money as the kind of people who stayed at Everston, I'd had a comfortable life before my parents both died within a week of each other, and Ezra took over The Hawthorne Inn.

How things could change in such a short time! And now... now what did I have to look forward to? I apparently didn't have any pull on keeping Ben in Laurelton, or he would have said something to me, wouldn't he?

I stopped at the steps to the veranda; the same place Vance had found me the evening before. It would have seemed rude to just go on my way after arriving, after all he'd shared with me at the hollow. Vance finally caught up with me in front of the steps, and again, no one else was around. Everston was actually proving to be quite boring during the off season, even in the middle of the afternoon.

It had started to snow on the walk back and I dusted the snowflakes off the front of my long coat as Vance walked up to me. I didn't know why he made me feel so self-conscious.

"I tried to catch up to you once we neared Everston, but you just kept blazing ahead."

"Sorry. I guess I was cold." Which wasn't the truth at all. For some reason I had such an urge to both run away from Vance Everstone and his intense black eyes, as well as run to him for protection.

As if he would *want* to protect me. Which wasn't really the case, I was sure. He was such a quandary. And every time he opened his mouth, he made me want to know more and more about him.

Vance came closer, putting a hand on the railing beside me. "There's something I've been meaning to tell you, or rather, ask you since I found you here yesterday."

When he didn't go on, a million thoughts raced through my mind. What could he possibly mean?

"Yes?" I asked, for he still didn't seem too eager to say whatever it was.

"About Ezra. Do you...do you happen to know how he keeps The Hawthorne Inn going?"

"You mean besides the obvious?" For the first time, I briefly wondered whether Vance had ever frequented the brothel—my degraded home. I shook the thought away; I didn't want to think on those things. It was no good. "Why? What does he do?"

"I'm sure he does any number of rotten things besides the fact, but he gambles quite a lot. And wins."

"Do you think his gambling problem has something to do with what he did to my hair?" I reached up into the wool hat and grasped the strands of my short blonde hair behind my ear.

"I think so. He'd talk about you often when he was drunk—and he was almost always drunk when he was playing poker."

"So, you were there too?" I couldn't shake the thought away this time. "Gambling? Playing poker with Ezra?"

"A few times, but I had my reasons beyond the thrill of the win. I...there was something he'd bet and lost, and I'd been trying to win it back. Without much luck."

"That's very noble of you, Vance," I used his first name as he'd asked me to, although I'd gone back to formalities the night before when he'd been so moody. "But what does that have to do with yesterday?"

"Just forget I brought it up." At his sudden abruptness, I recalled why I'd gone back to calling him Mr. Everstone instead of Vance. As much as I wanted to find out more about him and to keep asking him questions, his brick wall would go up without a warning in the middle of our exchanges, and it frustrated me to no end.

And since that wall usually signaled the end of our conversations, I decided to bid him good day and be on my way back to the dormitory. Which he allowed, of course. It wasn't as if he had anything more to say to me.

4

Mrs. Ava Cagney

*"It is very hard to say the exact truth,
even about your own immediate feelings."*
—George Eliot, *Adam Bede*

Thursday, March 31st, 1892

I spent much of my free time during the following week alone, working at finding ways to make my hair presentable. I had become quite good at fixing it so that its odd length wasn't something anyone would particularly notice.

Dexter had noted it at one point, but he hadn't seemed too concerned about it. And I decided to allow him to assume I'd decided to cut it and sell it, for what other reason would there be? He didn't know I still associated with Ezra on occasion; or rather, that Ezra occasionally slunk in to Everston, badgered me, and then left. If he ever spotted Ezra, I was certain Ezra would be arrested for burning down Blakeley House.

I hadn't seen Ezra since he and his friend had attacked me.

Although my brother hadn't physically hurt me, there was no mistaking the new sense of dread that filled my moments and hours. And although he'd tried to explain that what he'd done was for a good—even if mysterious—reason, what he'd done still hurt me deeply and emotionally.

I'd lived in such a strange state of displacement since my parents had died. Would I ever feel as though I belonged again? Really, only when I had a few spare moments at the front desk, and I could lose myself in my daydreams about the children's books I liked to create, did I ever feel at home. And then again, sometimes I caught myself daydreaming about Vance Everstone.

But I knew, quite well, that although I'd been raised as a lady and had lived my life just as a young lady ought, I was no match for someone like Vance, even if he had changed his ways. He was literally the wealthiest man I'd ever had the chance to meet or converse with. And I couldn't begin to understand why he would make a point to talk to me, especially when he would then, so often, unceremoniously cut off those conversations once they got to a certain depth.

A depth he had usually taken those conversations to himself.

The man was a complete bafflement, and I didn't know why he'd bothered talking to me past seeing me through my bruised feelings the week before.

I huffed out a bit of my frustration. What did any of it matter anyway?

Just as I was about to head out the side door closest to the female employee's resting room where I'd changed out of my uniform, Estella turned around the corner from the hall that led to the elevators and the lobby. I knew by the determined look in her pretty dark brown eyes what she was going to ask of me. And I still wasn't sure I wanted to give her an answer. Because I really wanted to say no, I couldn't come up to dinner that evening. Vance would be there, and everything from the previous weekend would come back to me full force. And what if he ignored me again?

I steeled my resolve and gave her the best smile I could muster.

"You'll have dinner with us tonight, won't you? I meant to ask you before today, but I've not been feeling well."

"I'm sorry to hear that." I nervously tangled my fingers through the strings of my reticule, completely avoiding her question.

"It's the last chance I'll have to dine with you before we leave, and I would so enjoy it."

"Are you sure you're up to hosting if you're not feeling well?"

"I'm feeling well enough right now, and hopefully I'll last through dinner. I'd really like you to be there. It will be small—just you and Ben will be joining us."

"Oh, really?" My relieved response came out involuntarily, and so I hastily added the first thing that came into my head. "You're not contagious or anything, are you?"

Estella laughed softly under her breath as she led me by the arm to the main entrance of the lobby. "No, I'm not contagious."

The stagecoach rolled up the drive, and Estella pulled back the lace curtain. We both looked out the paned window, side by side.

"Oh look, Vance is back," she said, almost to herself. "I didn't know he planned to return. I wonder why...?" Her voice trailed off, and I took a better look down the drive.

Indeed, there was Vance exiting the stagecoach, offering his arm to a young lady with thick, gorgeous blonde hair piled expertly under her ostrich-feathered hat. She wore a black fur coat over a gray striped traveling suit, and I could tell she either knew Vance very well, or wanted to very much.

"I hadn't realized he was gone," I admitted.

"He left for Bangor yesterday morning; he needed to go down for something, but I thought he would travel on down to Boston to meet us at Everwood," Estella explained, and then swept out the door to greet him. I lagged behind her, unsure of what to do. I had planned on accepting her request to dine once I'd learned it would only be Ben attending, but now...now she would insist that Vance join us, and then who would make up the numbers? Would Estella

ask the furred and feathered young lady on Vance's arm to attend?
I hoped not.

Would it be worth it to attend just to see Ben one last time
before he headed down to meet with The Boston Inland Mission
Society? The only other time I would see him would be while he
preached on Sunday. And everyone wanted to speak with him on
Sundays.

Vance's cool, deep voice brought me out of my reverie. "Estella,
you recall Mrs. Ava Cagney of Bangor. Mrs. Cagney, my sister,
now Mrs. Estella Blakeley." His dark eyes just barely grazed past
me standing behind his sister, but then he went on to add, "And
this, if you'll come forward," he urged with a hand in my direction,
"is her friend, Miss Violet Hawthorne."

Thankful that he hadn't introduced me as an employee of the
hotel, I nodded and said, "It's nice to meet you."

"It *is* nice, isn't it?" Mrs. Cagney answered, though her smiling
eyes were still glued to Vance.

"Are you traveling alone, Mrs. Cagney?" Estella asked. "Will
your husband be joining you?"

"Oh dear, no, my husband is gone; not long after we'd wed,
unfortunately. I'm here with my lady's maid, intending to meet up
with my elderly sister-in-law for a few weeks of diversion."

And by diversion, I gathered she meant something very much
to do with the compellingly attractive man standing beside her.

Oh sweet heavens, had Vance actually had something to do
with bringing her there? Or had they merely accidentally met on
the stage? I really couldn't tell from looking at them; only that she
did seem to know him extremely well.

Way more than I ever would, that was for certain.

I couldn't turn down Estella's invitation, and I knew it had
nothing to do with seeing Ben again or wanting to find out how
well Mrs. Ava Cagney seemed to know Vance Everstone.

And I no longer cared whether Vance wanted to talk to me or not; I simply wanted to observe him. Had he truly changed?

~

Vance seemed reserved throughout dinner, even cautious in his treatment of our new guest. I really couldn't tell if he enjoyed her presence. She, on the other hand, glittered at his side and shamelessly attempted to pull him into the conversation.

I'd learned over dinner that her husband had been quite elderly at the time of their marriage and had left her the majority of his fortune.

Ben, seated at my right, could speak of nothing but the upcoming trip to Boston with Dexter, Estella, and now, I assumed, Vance too. Wouldn't Mrs. Cagney be disappointed when she learned that Vance would be leaving her presence so soon! I distracted myself with imagining her reaction when she learned she'd had dinner with the front desk clerk of Everston.

During dessert, Vance kept his eyes on his fruits and sweet-meats just as carefully as he'd studied the stewed mushrooms. By the time we rose from the table, I was fairly certain he wanted little to do with Mrs. Ava Cagney, and that he most certainly hadn't had anything to do with her initial plans of being there.

We all descended the elevator down to the lobby to accompany Ben to his waiting carriage, for he had much to do yet in Laurelton before traveling to Boston.

As the horses clopped down the drive, Estella took Dexter's arm, excused themselves and turned back into the hotel.

"*Won't* you accompany me to the music room?" Mrs. Cagney asked as she sidled up to Vance. "I hear their piano is a fine instrument; I would simply *adore* trying it out for you."

Vance glanced back at me. "Perhaps some other evening," he smoothly replied, taking her hand off of his arm. "I promised Miss Hawthorne that I would accompany her home."

He hadn't done any such thing, actually.

In fact, he'd just spent the whole night acting as if I was invisible. Did he feel obligated to me for some inane reason? That he needed to protect me every chance he had? It was getting dark, but I had walked home from the hotel to the dormitory a hundred other times, just like all of the employees did every day.

But no matter the reason, I couldn't deny the escort, because he did make me feel safe. And I liked that. So I took his arm, and instead of seeming foreign, it was more like the most natural thing in the world. After a few minutes of walking beside me in silence, Vance said, "Ava's made it no secret over the last few months—while I've been traveling back and forth from Everston to Bangor—that she's most definitely set her cap for me."

Vance's candid words shocked me.

I still hadn't given him an answer to his comment after a full minute of walking down the path toward the dormitory—because really, what was I supposed to say to that?

He continued, "She's the kind of young woman who can have her pick of men. And she thinks she wants me."

I still didn't know what to say.

He made a point to turn to me as we walked down the path, his dark eyes trying their best to snag my attention. "And I'm a little tired of it."

"But she's a widow, and you're a widower. Do you not think you would suit?" I finally dared. How had I come to such a place of confidence with him? That he would share such things with me!

"She's attractive, the strong independent type who could honestly survive being linked to someone like me, actually. But I don't want a wife right now, especially one like vivacious, high-maintenance Ava Cagney. No matter how perfect she is for me socially."

Goodness, the questions I had for him! But could I ask them without seeming like a nosy gossipmonger? What would he think—?

"I'm sure you're wondering why. Why not take on the wealthy beauty who's practically throwing herself at me? She's everything I need, everything I could want in a woman, right?"

"Because you're still heartbroken over your wife's death?" I hazarded.

"No," he cut me off quickly. "That is not it. It was difficult to go through, to watch what happened to Giselle, but no, I'm not heartbroken. Love must come before heartbreak."

I stopped walking, stalling him beside me. "You didn't love your wife?"

"I'd been forced to marry her because, you see, she'd found herself in a situation—"

"Oh, you *had* to marry her?"

"The child wasn't mine. It couldn't have been, but the man who was—" Vance took a step, dragging me along with him for a few feet until he stopped just long enough to say, "We shouldn't discuss such things. You don't need to know the details of the trouble I came into while in France." And then he started us off toward the dormitory again. I let him keep his silence, although what he'd said only prompted more questions.

Looking ahead, I was determined not to let my eyes stray his way again, embarrassed that I'd accused him of compromising a young woman, when that hadn't really been the case.

At least that time.

My gaze wandered over the massive wall of windows of the dormitory, shrouded in shadows. The sun had long ago begun to set behind Iron Mountain, which towered above everything on the small peninsula protruding into Half Moon Lake.

I was sure that any number of my fellow Everston employees watched us stroll down the path in the lamplight with baited interest. Why would the owner's wealthy brother-in-law be spending time with Violet Hawthorne? I could almost hear a group of them muttering the words, snidely whispering, secretly thinking they already knew the answer.

Maybe Vance was right, that it wasn't a good idea for us to be friends, if that was anywhere near what was actually happening. I didn't think so, but what else could explain it? He seemed to want to confide in me, even if it was only halfheartedly. And I'd confided in him the week before, though I really had no intention of doing so before it was already done.

"So, you married her although you didn't love her and she carried someone else's child?"

"I didn't have a choice. The man responsible was already married, so she lied and said the child was mine; and she had the kind of powerful family one didn't disobey, no matter who you are."

"Even if you're Vance Everstone?"

"Even if you're Vance Everstone."

"May I ask how she died?"

"The doctors on the ship thought she was having early labor pains, but it ended up being something else. Afterward, they suspected it was appendicitis."

"I'm sorry."

"I don't know how she would have fit in with my family here in the States, but I guess it doesn't matter now."

"How long were you married?"

"A few months."

"When was it that she—"

"Last April."

"But shouldn't you be in mourning?"

"Hardly anyone I know in the States knew that I was married, though the rumors have flown since. Considering the situation, I thought it best that I just move on with my life."

"But not get married again."

"Can you blame me?"

"No, I can't."

We'd made it to the shadow of the building, which caused me to inadvertently grasp his upper arm a little tighter than I had before.

He stopped me about ten feet away from the main entrance. "Look, Violet, I need you to understand that I care for your safety; that everything I've been doing since last weekend has been in the name of protecting you."

I let go of his arm, feeling that he'd done his service in escorting me home, and that I now just needed to get inside—to get away before he said anything too embarrassing. "I understand that completely, Vance."

He reached for my hand as I retreated, but I stepped back too quickly. "I just didn't want you to get any ideas in your head about there being anything romantic between us."

"Of course not. I would never dream—"

"Not that you're unattractive, Violet. At all." He didn't follow me, but stayed where I'd left him. "You're just so easy to talk to, but maybe that's because I've been more focused on your safety—"

"Rather than on seducing me?"

"That's not *exactly* what I was going to say."

"We're hardly friends; I wouldn't imagine thinking you were in any way interested in me romantically. That would be absurd. Just because I wanted to know more about your wife doesn't mean I was hoping you'd—"

"Really? You've never even given it a thought? At all?"

I walked up to the porch, digging into my reticule for my key. "You act so surprised," I said facing the door, trying to hide.

Hearing a grunt from behind me, I turned to see Vance pitch forward. A man suddenly appeared beside him and kicked his knees out from under him. He fell to the ground clutching his middle.

"Vance?"

"Get inside, Violet!"

But by then, the shadow man had come closer—and I still hadn't found my key. Before he made it to me, a strong arm circled my waist like a vice and clamped my arms down. A hand covered my face, pressing a wadded cloth to my nose until all I knew was the sweet smell of blackness.

5

Compromised

"None of us want to be in calm waters all our lives."
—Jane Austen, *Persuasion*

Friday, April 1st, 1892

The next morning I awoke to a pounding on my door.

"Violet? Are you awake?" The pounding continued as I struggled to make sense of the words. "Violet, it's past six o'clock. You're usually out here by now. You're going to be late for your shift."

My shift? What day was it?

Who was calling me?

Oh. It was Francie—we always walked to work together in the morning. How odd that I would forget.

I buried myself farther under my covers; it seemed so much warmer than usual, and so hard to get out of my bed. Surely I could stay there for five more minutes.

More pounding thudded against my door, and I heard the jangle of keys—but then the door opened without the telling sounds of having been unlocked. How strange.

I covered my face with my arm. For some reason the thought of actually moving out of bed made me nauseous.

"Violet Hawthorne! What is the meaning of this?"

My eyes shot open to see the Female Resident Manager, Mrs. Ward, standing in my doorway, her blue eyes wide with undeniable shock.

Francie stood close behind Mrs. Ward, her hands over her mouth. "Oh, Violet! What have you done? How could you?"

How could I what? Sleep in? It was easy when our rooms were so cold, and my bed so warm.

"Violet, what happened to your hair?" Francie asked.

I reached up to finger the ends, "Oh! It's a long story," I mumbled. Is that what was the matter with them? The sight of my hair?

I went to sit up and threw my covers back—only my arm rammed into something warm and heavy. Confused, I turned from Mrs. Ward and Francie and saw for myself what they thought so scandalous.

There beside me in my bed laid Vance Everstone, fast asleep. His bare, muscular arm—which must have been what had kept me so warm while wrapped around me—was now sprawled over my pillow as he slept. I immediately looked down to observe my clothing; I wore only my knee-length chemise. It was no wonder they were shocked! I could barely come up with any words as I again stared down at Vance.

In my bed.

What had happened? And how?

I stood, grabbed my coat, which was uncharacteristically bunched into a pile on the floor with my dress and reticule and hurried it on, desperate for some level of decency. Vance's clothes—his jacket, shirt, trousers, socks and shoes—were dispersed haphazardly about the room.

"This isn't what it seems," I finally stated, knowing they would never believe me. How could they? The situation was obvious—and irreparable. Even if I had no clue how it had come to be.

"I'm sure it isn't," Mrs. Ward said, degradation lacing her every syllable. "Put your clothes on." She reached around for the doorknob and pulled the door closed a little more, silently urging Francie out. "And do wake your *friend*. The two of you have an urgent meeting with Mr. Blakeley, in his office, right now."

"But he's Mr. Blakeley's—"

"I don't care who he is. You both are a disgrace." She slammed the door behind her, but not before I saw a half dozen pairs of curious eyes peeping in, trying to get a look at Vance tangled in my bedcovers.

And Vance had slept on despite having convicted me, with his mere presence, of something I hadn't done. The crowd at my door would ensure that the rumors would begin.

I numbly sat down on the edge of the bed. I didn't know how I'd be able to leave that room, walk down the hall and to Everston, without dying of shame. And Vance would be there right beside me. Stomping my name through the mud with every step.

If I'd thought I would lose my job before, there was no doubt what Dexter would be forced to do once he heard about this.

The thought of meeting with him, alongside Vance and trying to explain what had—and what hadn't—happened made me sick to my stomach.

Shouldn't Mrs. Ward have pulled us out of bed and made a spectacle of us, forcing us to face everyone in what little clothing we'd been found together in? That's what I'd always imagined such a situation would demand, but I was perfectly happy that's not what had happened. Having to get dressed in the same room as Vance and then walk out together would be mortifying enough.

Opening the door to the shallow corner closet, I hid behind it as I dressed.

I didn't care about everyone finding out about my hair now, and I left it as it was, a mess barely reaching my jaw.

Dreading the thought of even glancing at Vance again, I wondered how I would wake him. I almost wished Mrs. Ward had hauled us out of the bed—to save me from having to do such a thing! But perhaps she'd thought—since it looked as if I'd already done so much more—that waking him would be an easy thing for me.

I peeked around the closet door and studied my small disheveled bed. How had I been lying there beside him and not known? But then I remembered the odd heaviness of my sleep, the uncommon warmth, how difficult it had been to get out of bed.

Yes, it was no wonder I'd been warm. I felt my face flush at the thought. Had we been drugged? Gradually the details of the previous evening came back. I remembered that some shadowy figure had pummeled Vance to the ground, someone else had pressed a hand to cover my face, and I'd blacked out. I could only assume that they'd done the same to Vance.

Eventually I stepped out of my closet and made it to the edge of my bed. Vance's bare arm was still draped over my pillow, and honestly, it was difficult to look away. My gaze traveled over his muscles, on and on from his upper arm to his shoulder, to his back.

His blackish brown hair was a mess, which oddly only made him look that much more attractive.

Oh dear Lord, what would I do now? What would Vance do? Would he care that my reputation was ruined? He hadn't seemed to care the many other times I'd heard about, but then again, he'd married Giselle. And he claimed to be a Christian now.

Recalling our talk at the hollow, I had a hard time imagining him having any part in getting us into the situation. He'd seemed sincere and hadn't his last words to me the night before been to dissuade me from thinking anything relational could ever happen between us? The embarrassment I'd felt then was nothing compared to what I had to face now!

And would he ever wake up?

Just then a loud knock came upon the door.

"Miss Hawthorne, I suggest you make haste toward your meeting with Mr. Blakeley," Mrs. Ward bellowed from the hall. "You cannot stay here one minute more. Do get your things and be off."

I hadn't thought of that! That I'd have to move out of the dormitory that instant!

Sucking in my breath, I lightly poked at Vance's bare shoulder, scared of what he might do when his eyes opened, and he saw me standing over him. He didn't move beyond turning onto his stomach and pulling my pillow farther under his head, displaying too much of his bare upper back and shoulders to me. I turned from him, hot with embarrassment and all kinds of strange nervous feelings. I grabbed the rest of my clothing, my writing box, my books and what little else I had and threw them into the small trunk I'd brought to Everston upon leaving The Hawthorne Inn. And because I didn't know how else to wake him, I lifted the trunk and plopped it onto the bed beside him.

"Ow! For all the—" He sat up, twisting the covers, losing them down to his waist.

I spun around quickly, as if I had something else to collect from my empty closet.

"What the...where am I?"

"My room," I squeezed out, along with all of the air from my lungs.

"Your room...your bed?"

Not knowing what to answer, I didn't say anything as I heard him rustle the covers.

"Where are my clothes?"

I bent forward, grabbed the pile from the floor and tossed them onto the bed next to my trunk, which he'd shoved over to one side. "You'll need those. We have a meeting with Dexter." There wasn't a thing of mine left in the room for me to gather, but I couldn't just stand there and face a practically unclothed Vance Everstone!

Another knock pounded against my door. "Are you presentable yet, Miss Hawthorne? Let's do get going."

I stepped toward the door. "Almost, Mrs. Ward." I glanced in Vance's direction for just a moment and realized he'd not moved a muscle since seeing where he'd awoken—how it all must have looked to him! "Do hurry, Vance. We need to explain—" I motioned toward the general space between us, "*this* to Mrs. Ward and Dexter."

"What happened?" he asked the question almost to himself—and with a pained look on his face.

"I'm not really sure. I believe we were attacked on our way into the dorm last night and possibly drugged and then situated into this circumstance on purpose." Another quick glance behind me revealed that, while he still sat in my bed, he'd at least slipped on his shirt.

"A rather compromising circumstance, don't you think?" he added cryptically.

"Yes." I swallowed hard. Would he blame me for getting him into this mess? What if it was some plan my brother had concocted to go along with whatever else he was doing? I opened my closet again and hid behind the door. "For your privacy."

"I'm so sorry, Violet."

I didn't know exactly what he meant by apologizing, but his softly spoken words nearly brought tears to my eyes. I blinked them away, wishing I'd kept a handkerchief handy.

"I'm not sure what happened, but I don't blame you." I spoke from behind the door. "You've been so preoccupied with protecting me—it's not your fault that they've used it against us."

"Who do you mean by *they*?" I could hear him slip on his trousers and sit back down upon my bed.

"Don't you think it could be Ezra? He told me last week to stick near my friends—that I needed to—"

"It very well could be, now that you mention it." He sounded relieved.

Mrs. Ward knocked again, and before she could say a word, I heard Vance open the door. I hurried out from the closet, desperate to stand between them.

"I heard I have a meeting with my brother-in-law this morning?" Vance asked. He carried my trunk and stepped right past her. "I suppose you're the one who's orchestrated this meeting?"

"Well yes, you must answer for—your brother-in-law?" Mrs. Ward's face blanched, but the sudden look of fear in her eyes quickly turned to anger. "It doesn't matter who you are. You should be ashamed of yourself."

"Oh don't worry. I usually am." Vance walked right out of my room, as if he owned the place.

Now that the morning shift at Everston had already begun, there were only a few girls left in the hall to gather what juicy bits of rumors they could.

"And you too, Violet Hawthorne," Mrs. Ward continued nastily, "for sneaking a man in here, inviting him into your bed. You have no place here. This is a respectable hotel, where we have respectable employees, not—"

"Turns out Violet's just like one of the harlots from her brother's brothel!" Someone down the hall called the words, and they stabbed as deeply as any knife could.

Vance turned back for me, switching the small trunk to only his right arm as he hurriedly used his other to take my hand and tug me down the stairs to the front door. "Don't listen to them. They don't know what they're talking about."

"Don't they?" I sobbed. "They might as well be right. I'm never going to be respectable again—not after this morning."

"We'll see about that."

I didn't know how Vance and I had come to be found together in my room, but I also knew it didn't matter. My reputation—despite my strict morals, and despite all Dexter's help during the last year—was ruined just the same.

⌒

"You *what?*" Dexter Blakeley couldn't have looked more stunned. Obviously Mrs. Ward hadn't exactly informed him of why one of his employees needed to meet with him—not even that it was me. She'd left everything completely open-ended, using every detail she'd gathered that morning to incriminate us the moment he realized who he was dealing with.

His own disreputable brother-in-law and the poor girl he'd taken pity upon almost a year ago and given one of the most coveted positions at his hotel.

"Mrs. Ward, thank you," Dexter's voice was more gruff than usual. "That's all I'll need of you this morning. I'll take it from here."

"Are you certain, Mr. Blakeley? They'll likely string together a bunch of lies for you. I'd rather be able to discuss the details—"

"No, Mrs. Ward. That will be all, thank you." And with that, she was forced out of the room by obligation. For the longest time after Mrs. Ward quit the room, Dexter sat with his back to us, facing his small roll-top desk against the wall, his fingers pressed to his temples. I had a feeling his eyes were closed, and that he was either gathering his courage, or perhaps that he was too mad to speak. I didn't know which I preferred. Finally, he swiveled his chair around and looked only at me, ignoring Vance's presence completely.

"I have noticed that you two have been getting better acquainted in the last week, but this…this is definitely not what I expected. Violet, I'm going to ask you first. Please explain to me what happened."

I couldn't tell if he disbelieved Mrs. Ward, or if he simply wanted to, but the way he'd asked the question begged for a different answer than her incriminating testimony provided. And it gave me the courage to start from the beginning, although the truth included my seeing Ezra the week before, which I knew Dexter wouldn't like.

He had his fingers interlocked together in front of him, his elbows resting on his chair's wooden armrests, the entire time I spoke.

When I was finished, he turned his eyes to Vance. "And do you have anything to add?"

After a few moments of silent, dreadful waiting—when I honestly didn't know what to expect from him—he quietly said, "I know Violet won't be able to keep her job after this. She likely has nowhere to go besides back to her brother." Vance still looked at me, but his enigmatic eyes hid whatever emotions he might have been feeling. "Isn't that right, Violet?"

"I guess so." My stomach turned at the thought, but really, besides the estranged aunt I had somewhere in Massachusetts, I didn't have any other option. No one would have me now. Not to employ or to marry.

"So I have a proposition. Actually, it's more of a proposal. I think Violet had better marry me." He looked at me squarely, and I could only stare back.

"Marry you?" Dexter asked. His shock mirrored my own.

Vance looked serious; no cocky lift to his lopsided smile, no glint in his black eyes. He actually looked a bit miserable, to be honest...which sent a dagger through my heart. I would be forced to marry someone who only yesterday had told me he had no interest in marrying anyone, least of all me.

"I'm headed to Boston soon. I was actually supposed to be there yesterday, but I decided to come back because of a strange sense of foreboding that wouldn't leave me. And understandably so."

I'd stopped looking at him by then—it was too difficult. But at that point in his explanation, I could tell he'd turned to me.

"We can all go down together, Violet as my fiancée. And we can have Talia and Stella plan the wedding for sometime this summer, after my fathers' wedding to Madame Boutilier."

It all seemed so straightforward, as if he'd been thinking up these plans for weeks. But when had there been time? On the short walk from the dormitory to Everston? In that short time he'd decided to give up his freedom for the sake of my reputation? When it wasn't even his fault?

If it was anyone's fault, it was mine—for not running far away from my brother. Why ever had I thought twenty miles would be far enough? I should have went in search of my aunt right after my parents died.

"That's probably best, Vance. It says a lot about your character that you'd do so much to repair Violet's reputation when it seems you've been roped into all this against your will." Dexter's heavy gaze collided with mine. "Violet, I think it best you accept Vance's offer. Like he said, you won't be able to stay on as an employee at Everston, but I think it's a fair trade to have you become my sister-in-law. You'll be well-taken care of, at least." He gave me a small grin, though I didn't know how he'd achieved it. Why would anyone be happy to have me forced into their extended family by way of scandals and rumors?

"Will you, then?" Vance scooted his chair back and dropped to one knee before me. "Will you marry me, Violet?"

"I—um…I don't know."

"Violet," Dexter urged, "As surprised as I am by Vance's valiant offer, it is the best option. Otherwise you would be…."

"I know…there isn't anything else to do." I glanced down at Vance—his dark eyes were focused on my face, as if willing me to give him an answer. "Besides going back to my brother, and that's—"

"Not an option," Vance finished for me.

I couldn't believe he still knelt before me, as if he actually wanted to petition for my hand. Which, I was sure, he didn't. He was only being forced into another loveless marriage, and this time, it would be to me.

"Well then," I said. "I guess I don't have a choice."

6

Change of Plans

"No man can sincerely help another without helping himself."
—Ralph Waldo Emerson

A little later, Dexter delivered me to Estella for safekeeping—he'd insisted that I stay in their extra guest room until we left for Boston. Hidden away, of course. It surely wouldn't do to have the scandalously fired front desk clerk seen staying in the company of the owner and his wife—no matter if they had been extending their friendship beforehand.

Vance had seemed even more ill-at-ease when he'd walked into Dexter and Estella's apartment with my small trunk. Had he already wished he hadn't offered for me? Or perhaps that I wouldn't have agreed?

Estella and I sat in the front parlor while Dexter and Vance met in the back study to discuss details about the trip. She'd already assured me that she believed my every word—and that she was more than happy to welcome me into her family. I could also tell that she thought there was much more going on between Vance and I than we'd let on. I didn't feel like bringing up the fact that she was wrong.

I knew the reception I would likely receive from Boston society, including Vance's family, would be far from inviting. Who was

I, after all? And would the event of our engagement really trump the circumstances of *why* we were engaged?

"I never knew Vance well growing up, but he seems to have changed a lot in the last year." Estella took a sip of her blueberry tea, and I remained silent. There didn't seem to be much else to say after such a morning. "He does seem to like you. Perhaps he doesn't mind the idea of being married again."

"Perhaps," I allowed for her benefit. But I didn't think so. And I remembered how miserable he looked when he'd decided to propose.

I hadn't touched my own tea. I was much too troubled to have an appetite. Although everything was seemingly put into order, and I was set to marry Vance, I still couldn't come to the point of thinking we were actually engaged, that I was his fiancée. The idea turned my stomach into knots. Trust him completely? Commit our lives to each other? We hardly knew each other!

When Dexter and Vance finally joined us, we spoke a little about the plans to leave for Boston. We would be leaving that evening instead of Monday, as had been their plan. I would then stay with Vance's wealthy family at their Back Bay estate, Everwood.

After the plans for the journey were settled, the four of us sat and an awkward silence permeated the room.

Vance abruptly stood and walked to the great window overlooking the calm, blue lake and the surrounding mountains. "If you don't mind, may I have a word in private with Violet?"

"Of course!" Dexter and Estella said in unison, and both immediately stood.

"Take your time," Estella insisted as she took my hands in hers. Dexter waited for her by the pocket door to the dining room. "I'm sure you have so much to say to one another."

Once they'd left and securely closed the doors behind them, I turned to Vance, who still faced the view. Allowing myself to study his profile for the first time since he and Dexter had entered the room, I couldn't deny he was literally the most handsome man I'd ever met. And now, I would marry him?

I suddenly recalled the vision of his bare arm and shoulder sprawled across my pillow that morning, and my stomach did a funny flip. The thought of being there again, in his arms, caused a small tremor to race through me. But he wouldn't want me there—it was all just a mean trick, and I had my no-good brother to thank for it.

"There's something I've been meaning to tell you in the last week, Violet. I think it will shed a new light on things now that they've come to what they have."

I waited for him to go on. I knew there had been something he'd only halfway got around to talking about a number of times in that week and that whatever it was had made him eventually clam up each and every time.

"And you'll better understand why I feel obligated to help— even to the point of proposing." Vance turned from the window. The stunning panorama made him look so vibrant and alive, and his gaze locked with mine.

"There's a man named Rowen Steele whom your brother is associated with. I know him too. He's also in the lumber business, only on a much smaller scale than we are at Greaghan Lumber."

I shifted nervously. After so little an explanation, I couldn't help but ask, "What about him?"

"Do you remember me telling you how your brother has learned to be quite the card shark over the years?"

"Yes."

"Well. He seems to have met his match with Rowen Steele. Not only had Rowen been studying Ezra's every play over the months past, but listening with dire interest to everything your brother ever had to say about you."

A chill shivered down my spine.

"I'm not sure what his original goals in bragging about you were, Violet, but last September, Rowen made his move. I watched as he slowly and meticulously cleaned Ezra out of every dime he had. Until he had hardly anything left to offer." Vance paced in front of the window, suddenly avoiding my eyes. "In the final hand, your brother threw in the only thing he had left to bet."

"And you saw what it was?"

Vance only nodded.

"But what was it?"

"It was a photograph of you, Violet. He bet you, and he lost."

"You can't mean…Ezra wouldn't—"

"He did. He's promised you to Rowen Steele, and whether he wants to back out on his word or not, Steele isn't going to sit back and let him."

"So you've been coming around Everston…for my sake? To protect me from Rowen Steele?" I leaned into the nearest seat before my knees collapsed beneath me.

Vance came to kneel before me once more, taking my hands in his over the arm of the chair. "Violet, the Bible says that you are more precious than rubies…. I hope you realize that. And I am bound by honor to protect you, and now, because of our circumstances, to marry you."

His words were confusing, though I understood the general essence—my mind was too filled with hurt and betrayal to really comprehend his meaning. My brother thought so little of me, that he treated me as mere chattel to barter and gamble? That he would so carelessly throw my life away to some man who would do with me as he wanted?

I stood, not answering Vance. I really couldn't think of anything to say. I just wanted to cry. He let me leave the room, and I made it to the guest bedroom where my few belongings were still stashed. I sat on the bed, not really seeing anything; only thinking.

Yes, Ezra had most likely been drunk. But that wasn't an excuse. Had he thought stealing my beautiful hair would make me less desirable to this Rowen Steele? Had he—my breath caught at this—had he put me in the compromising situation with Vance Everstone to *help* me? Had he really thought his disreputable actions could be so easily reversed? Why couldn't he have just left well enough alone?

I may have felt a bit misplaced while working at Everston, but I'd had a respectable job at a wonderful resort with a kind owner. And now I had a prodigal fiancé who didn't love me. And what kind of future? Would Vance end up being faithful to me—a wife foisted on him by circumstances? Or would he end up resenting me?

It had been clear from the beginning that he would never have actually considered me for the esteemed position in his life that I now held. He'd wanted to help me, but he would never have *chosen* me for his wife. He was merely stuck with me as his future bride and would have to marry me unless he wanted to completely disgrace me and a ruin my reputation forever. Which, I could tell, wasn't an option he was willing to take.

That evening Estella stood beside me near the front door in the far corner of the spacious, empty veranda, waiting for the last stagecoach to Severville. I had on a black fur coat and one of her fanciest hats in hopes that no one would recognize me. My engagement to Vance Everstone had been circulated to everyone who would care, but I still felt like an outcast.

"I learned this afternoon that Ben won't be coming with us after all." She rubbed her gloved hands together against the cold chill. "He's heard back from the mission society but had a funeral in Laurelton he needed to officiate."

"That's too bad," I answered.

I honestly had hardly allowed myself to give a thought to Ben since that morning. There was no point. It didn't matter what he thought of me now.

Dexter had gone to pick up his sister, Roxy, from the cottage she shared with their mother while Estella and I waited for Vance to come down from his room.

I wasn't sure what I was supposed to say when I saw Vance now that I knew he'd done so much for me. It made me sick to my stomach wondering if he would eventually regret his actions. How could he not? I was hardly worth the trouble he'd taken. He didn't *have* to do anything, and he was doing all he could for me. And would we really marry? Would he want a real marriage? Or was he only interested in repairing my reputation?

"There they are." I heard Vance's voice boom from the now opened door of the lobby. Estella and I both turned to find him approaching with Mrs. Cagney attached to his arm.

"It's such a shame you have to leave so soon; I'd gathered you would be here for at least a few days before traveling down to Boston."

"Yes, well. Plans change." Vance winked at me with a sideways glance, which sent my pulse racing. Why would he do that? And while saying such a thing! Yes, his plans had changed—but was he really so unaffected by the results? Was his engagement to me now just something else to be entertained by? Did he not realize the severity of our situation?

Estella obviously thought it entertaining—by the little smile she had trouble hiding.

When they came to stand beside us, Vance dropped his arm from her hold, took a step towards me and quickly grasped my fingers, bowing slightly before me. "My sweet Violet." He pulled my glove off ever so slowly and pressed his lips into the palm of my hand.

I couldn't help my sudden quickness of breath. I tried to pull my hand away, but he wouldn't let go. In fact, his hand traveled up my arm to my elbow, which he then held securely.

"Mrs. Cagney," he said, still facing me, holding my elbow. "I know you met Miss Hawthorne last night, but now I'd like to introduce her to you as my fiancée."

"Your fiancée?" she gasped, staring at me, almost in horror. "I thought—I thought she was merely your sister's friend?"

"In the last day we've discovered," Vance had looked her way for a moment, but then he turned those intense, black eyes of his to meet mine, "something we simply cannot deny. And I could not go one more day without making sure she was mine."

My knees nearly buckled, and my mouth might have been gaping open for a moment before I realized what he was doing. So this was what I'd been warned of—what I'd heard all about. Yes, he was quite good at layering on the charm for his own schemes and purposes.

Vance still held me by the elbow, though I wasn't quite sure why. I had, perhaps, wobbled a little as he'd said that last line, but surely I was perfectly able to stand.

"Well, I…I suppose…goodness!" Mrs. Cagney fanned her face, evidently a little flushed by witnessing Vance's resplendently amorous declarations. "I suppose congratulations are in order, and you're all headed to Boston to introduce Miss Hawthorne to the rest of your family?"

"We are; and to plan the wedding for this summer, of course."

"My, you don't waste any time do you, Mr. Everstone?"

"Whatever do you mean?" he asked with a cocked brow. It seemed more like a dare than a question.

"Only that you've had quite a number of fiancées to name within the last year or so, don't you think? What is it, three now?"

"Three to be exact, actually." Vance's grip on my arm tightened, and I inadvertently squeaked in protest. "Sorry, Violet."

"What—did she not know?"

I stood as tall as I could—a few inches over her—and replied, "It doesn't matter." Vance wasn't the only one who could play the game. "He's free to do as he pleases now, and he's pleased to have me. And I—" the words almost caught in my throat, "I am beyond honored that he has asked me to marry him."

Vance's hand strayed past my elbow to my waist, where it lingered lightly. He'd hardly ever touched me before landing that kiss upon my palm, and he really hardly seemed to just then, but at the same time, he definitely *was*. So conscious was I of where his hand was, I could barely concentrate beyond noticing Mrs. Cagney's smug, wide eyes glare at me with envy.

"I wish you well, then," she practically grated out.

That's when I realized Estella hadn't said much throughout the interaction. But I could tell her attention was entirely occupied by everything she'd witnessed between the three of us. And that it had delighted her immensely.

7

The Train

"A person often meets his destiny on the road he took to avoid it."
—Jean de La Fontaine

Saturday, April 2nd, 1892

Soon after Mrs. Cagney made her final goodbyes to Estella and Vance, she disappeared into the hotel and Dexter arrived from collecting Roxy, who would be staying with an elderly acquaintance of his family's for the summer.

Our luggage was quickly stowed away on the stagecoach and the five of us were fortunately the only ones in the vehicle all the way to Severville, where our train awaited. When we made it to the train station, I came to the quick understanding that we weren't simply going to take the train to Boston—we would be traveling in a private rail car owned by the Everstone family.

And upon entering this immaculate rail car, I came to better understand just how extravagantly wealthy Vance's family was. And how much I would likely never fit in, no matter how ladylike my mother had taught me to be.

The main sitting room had dark wood-paneled wainscoting and ornately wallpapered walls, gold tasseled tapestries pulled back at the windows, and a fire already burning in the fireplace at the end of the room. Along one side of the narrow parlor was a large built-in green velvet sofa, and facing it were three uphol-stered chairs, the one in the middle much bigger to accommodate two people.

I noticed that Roxy's face radiated a look of awe, and I won-dered if mine did, too.

Estella led the way through the parlor. "Roxy and Violet, you will share the double room." She disappeared through the narrow door next to the fireplace. Dexter and Vance stayed in the parlor while Roxy and I followed Estella to our room. It was late, and after such a day, I looked forward to crashing onto whatever bed would be provided.

"It's perfectly fine if you'd rather retire early for the evening. That's our plan as well." Estella must have sensed how tired we were. But then again, Roxy seemed tired most of the time.

Estella opened the second door down the hall and ushered us into a cramped little room.

The bedroom was small, but the general grandeur of the rail car created the same kind of ambiance that Everston had. There were two beds, one along the windows and the other tucked in sideways between the first one and the wall. There was a built-in dresser and desk to accommodate much longer journeys than just our one night. With so much extravagance fit into a tiny rail car, I had to wonder what Everwood in Boston would be like.

Once Estella closed the door behind her, Roxy immediately sat upon the bed tucked against the inner wall of the train. "Please forgive me, Violet, but I really need to lie down and rest. I don't mind if you want to stay up for a while though." She pulled back the covers to the bed situated along the wood-paneled wall and slipped in fully clothed, silently fluffing the pillows before resting her head upon them.

"I'll likely retire soon too." I sat upon the other bed and pulled at the tie-backs for the drapes to the wall of windows for her, and Roxy was asleep before the train rumbled down the tracks. Knowing that Estella, Dexter, and Vance could likely still be visiting in the parlor, I stayed where I was, getting used to the movement of the train. I'd never been on a train of any kind before.

Unlike Roxy, I changed my clothes before getting into bed. It would be late morning by the time we arrived in Boston, after Vance's family would be getting home from church, and I wanted to make the best impression I could. Not only were my nerves a jumbled mess because of the situation, I had never in my life traveled outside of my little corner of Maine.

When it was much later, and I'd tried to sleep, and then tried to come up with something new to write—failing at both—I decided I'd spend some time in the parlor where I was sure to be alone at this late hour.

After pulling my worn dressing-gown over my nightgown, I quietly left the room. The door from the hall to the parlor was shut, and I heard snoring, over the sounds of the train traveling down the tracks, which I assumed was the men. But then when I opened the door to the main room, I found a small light on, the sound of the fire still crackling, and Vance sitting on the long sofa reading his little blue Bible.

The sight immediately reminded me of our time at the hollow. If everything he'd said there was true, he was a different man now from the man of the rumors I'd heard. Perhaps if we were to marry, we'd eventually have a real marriage; if I could somehow make someone like him fall in love with me.

But then his words from the night before about his wanting to keep everything platonic between us barged in, tearing apart my wishful thoughts. Was that still his desire? Or would he strive for a real relationship with me? Even if our engagement had such an unconventional beginning?

I wanted a husband who would love me. Didn't every girl? And now, I didn't know if that would ever happen.

Vance finally looked up, but he didn't seem surprised to see me.

I swallowed nervously. This wasn't at all what I'd envisioned happening in coming out to the main room. It would be a good chance to talk to him about things, but I was also scared…and hardly dressed for such a meeting! "Perhaps I should go back to my—"

"Nonsense. If anyone were to come upon us, they wouldn't think anything of us talking together in the lounge. And we are engaged, after all. We're allowed some added privacy because of that." He placed a slip of paper—likely the one with the words from *Jesus Paid it All* upon it—back into his Bible and closed the cover.

"Oh, I didn't think of that. I've never—"

"You've never been engaged before, of course."

He read me so well, which terrified me a little. Would he be able to tell how much he affected me? He always had. There was no use denying it now.

"How could you tell?"

"You're too innocent."

"Not after this morning."

"You're still an innocent. True, we shouldn't have been as we were, but nothing happened. And it was neither of our doing. Even I was blameless this time." He smirked for a moment, and then it was gone just as quickly.

"But your arms…they were…" I stalled, embarrassed.

"What about my arms?" he asked with a clever grin.

"They were around me this morning."

"My arms will likely be around you again, Violet, and I do think you'll survive." Vance motioned toward the row of upholstered chairs across the narrow space. "Please, have a seat. We have a few things we need to discuss, don't you think?"

I chose to sit in the middle, larger chair, hoping I'd be up for whatever it was exactly he wanted to speak to me about. It could be so many things.

"Estella's friend Meredyth, you met her at the wedding. Do you remember her?"

"Yes."

"I was engaged to her for a short time last summer."

Shocked that he'd brought the subject up so readily, I couldn't help but ask, "For how long?"

"A few weeks. It isn't common knowledge, but Ava must have gone digging around—"

"Did you love Meredyth?"

He placed his Bible on the table between us, smiling to himself. "You don't mince words, do you?"

"So she's married and lives in Washington now, and has adopted your deceased wife's daughter?"

"That's what most people believe, yes." He actually chuckled. "You're ready to hear everything, aren't you? But there's too much to explain all in one sitting, even for someone as straightforward as you." He looked at me for some time, studying me. And I didn't really mind, because I could tell he was gathering his thoughts. After a little while, he went on, "I didn't love Giselle or Meredyth."

"Do you have something against falling in love, or have you simply never felt strongly enough to understand what it's like?" Not that I did either, but I had an idea.

Before giving me an answer, Vance stood and walked to the end of the small room toward the door to the outer platform. I thought he would leave, but then he surprised me by turning around and taking a seat beside me. He reached over and took my hands. His eyes—so black and mysterious—seemed to beg for my trust before he even opened his mouth.

"No; I've never been in love, though I've done plenty of despicable things in its name." He shifted uncomfortably in his seat, frowning for about half a second. "To tell the truth, I don't know if I ever will fall in love if I haven't yet."

"Oh." I understood his meaning perfectly: he didn't think he would be able to fall in love with *me*.

"There are a lot of complications to this story, Violet, and I want you to know that I'm not ever going to lie to you. But you'll also have to understand that I can't explain everything right now, all at once."

"All right." I let my hands rest in his. It felt natural to let him hold them, after learning so much about him in the last week. And I hoped it meant that his being with stuck with me wouldn't be entirely unpleasant for him. He had said he thought I was pretty, after all, on a few different occasions.

"I thought it best to marry Meredyth because, because I thought she wanted me to. I thought it would be best, for both of us. And so did Mere, for a long time." Vance blew out a long breath. "This is already getting too complicated for tonight. Yes, I married Giselle, which was for the best, and I didn't marry Meredyth, which was also for the best."

"And you really won't mind marrying me? I *am* a complete nobody. And it looks suspiciously as if I've entrapped you into making a marriage proposal—"

"Mind?" He laughed, though I couldn't quite figure out what was so funny. "To be sure, I hadn't planned to marry again for a long time, but a long marriage to you would be a walk through the park compared to my short turbulent time with Giselle. And I know what you're like, Violet. You're the farthest thing from a seductress. Which is one of the things I've come to like best about you."

"Really? But you said last night that you didn't want me to think—that you said those things because you didn't think of me—"

"You're an amiable girl, Violet, and quite attractive too. I probably like you more than I should already, given the situation. It's just, the plans I had for my life, at least as of this morning, had absolutely nothing to do with getting married again... at least so soon."

I pulled my hands from his warm grasp, rubbed them together and then buried them underneath my legs. "Why do you care so much about helping me?"

"From the instant your photograph made it into Rowen Steele's hands, I've been able to think of little else. You ask why, but how could I not?" He moved closer, and I let him without backing away. "You know what I told Ava this morning? About making you mine?" His arm inched around the back of the seat.

I swallowed. "Yes."

"That wasn't entirely for her benefit. It was part truth—in that I will do all I can for you, Violet, to keep you safe from the likes of Rowen Steele." He didn't come any closer, but really, it was the closest he'd ever come to me besides earlier that morning when he'd kissed my hand and practically held onto my waist in front of Ava Cagney—at least, not counting his having his arms around me in my bed. But he hadn't known what he was doing then, had he?

"I really appreciate everything," I said, unable to keep my eyes from the floor—now unusually bashful before him. "But I fear you'll quickly tire of me. If I'm strictly a charity case, you'll—"

"Violet, don't mistake me. Since meeting you—and especially knowing of the trouble coming your way—I've cared very much, and I've come to the point that I'm willing to do all I can to help. Even marry you. I just didn't think it would come to that, especially in such a provocative way as it did this morning."

I finally lifted my gaze from the floor and found him staring intently at my face. As if he'd been waiting for me to look up.

"I don't want you to become alarmed, but I'm going to put my arms around you now, just as I said I would. And like I said earlier, I do think you'll survive."

"Why?" One hand came out from under my skirt in half-hearted defiance. I wasn't exactly against the idea. Just a bit of a coward.

"Because how long has it been since you've been held?" Without awaiting my answer, Vance pulled me to his chest and wrapped his arms around my shoulders.

As he held onto me with my cheek rested against his jaw, my heart flipped this way and that, trying to understand what was happening between us. It was probably nothing, right? He wouldn't want me as his true wife, would he? Not if he'd been compromised into proposing to me. I wasn't even sure what I wanted the answers to those questions to be.

I hardly moved but to bring my arms folded around my middle between us. He sat holding me there for the longest time, his warm arms engulfing me, his chin rested at my left shoulder. I could feel his breath against the loose hair over my ear. At such tenderness from him, I wondered if we could perhaps make this work, make this false start into something real.

"Violet, I'm not going to get into the details right now, but there was a time when I should have married a young lady, but didn't. It's much too late to do anything about that situation now, but doing this for you helps me feel as if I'm making up a little for that." He still held me, but had leaned back so better to look me in the face. "I promise I will make your life better. I'll do all I can to give you everything you could ever want." He squeezed me about my arms, playfully. "What is that exactly, anyway?"

"What do I want?" It had been since my parents had died that this question had mattered. Since then, I'd only wanted to be safe, and taken care of, which the job at Everston had given me, for a time. Now that everything had been ripped from my grasp again, I didn't even know.

But then my thoughts raced back to the one thing I had left anymore that was completely and utterly mine. My books.

Just then the door to the hall opened. I shrank away from Vance and looked up to see Estella in her dressing gown come into the little space from the hall and make it halfway through before noticing us. "Oh, excuse me! I had no idea you were…I'm sorry for intruding. I just wanted to check on the fire. I assume you can do that before retiring for the night, Vance?"

Without waiting for his answer, she backed through the door and closed it with a smile she couldn't hide.

"Well, that was fortunate." Vance reached along the back of the chair, his fingers grazing my shoulder until they came to my shorn hair. He took a strand of it and twisted it between his fingers and thumb.

I caught my breath, wondering why he'd indulged in such an intimacy…and if he would again soon. Having him handle my hair was proving to be fairly addictive. "What do you mean?"

"I'd rather my family believe we've been infatuated with one another for the last week or so, at the least, before what happened this morning. It will make things less awkward for my family, I think." From the way he continued to finger my hair, so close to my neck, I had a hard time thinking we weren't already almost there. Or, at least, I was.

I wasn't sure what *he* really thought, or why he did anything.

"Do you think they believe that we—?"

"To be honest, I'm not sure what Dexter and Estella believe about us right now. But it doesn't matter. Everyone is going to think we're completely and utterly in love before too long."

"Oh? How is that?"

"We're going to convince them that this is what we both want."

"Is that why you held me? Had you heard her—?"

"I could tell you needed a good, long hug weeks ago. But I was far from having the right at the time, and now I do. That's why."

I couldn't deny it had felt good to be held again, even if Vance and I were still practically strangers. It also gave me the added confidence I needed to tell him a little of my dreams. "You asked me what I want. A lot has happened—the last year has been... different."

"I can imagine. From what I've gathered, you lost both of your parents last year?"

"And my home."

"I'm sorry."

I blinked back the start of my tears. Crying in front of Vance Everstone wasn't something I wanted to repeat. "I want to write books for children, but on a grander scale than I do now." I looked up to find a smile on Vance's lips.

"You write children's books?"

"Well, I do my best. It's not as if they're published or anything. They're simply something I like to do to cheer up the children I know who need it. I gave Wynn one when she was here for the wedding."

"Did you? What was it about?" He still had the strands of my hair wrapped around his fingers.

"A little fox that had lost her way, but then eventually found a new home."

"Thank you for doing that for her. I wish I could have seen it."

"I have another one of that same story." Not that I really wanted to show it to him. Or anyone, really, who wasn't a child.

"Do you illustrate the stories as well?"

"Of course. A children's book without illustrations wouldn't be quite as enjoyable."

"I'd like to see them when there's a chance." He let go of my hair, but kept his arm at the back of the large seat behind me.

I knew he meant to insinuate that there was a chance right then and there, but I didn't move, or even give him any clue that I understood him.

"You will show them to me one of these days, won't you? At least the one about the little fox?"

"I will show you that one. Sometime."

"I'd like that, Violet."

I cleared my throat trying to gain the courage to end our late-night rendezvous. It was tempting to stay and talk all night, but of course, he wouldn't think so. "I better go; it's getting late."

"You go. I'll take care of the fire." He stood, taking a step toward the fireplace. "And I'll see you in the morning."

I paused before saying, "In Boston."

He immediately turned and sat back down beside me. "You're not afraid of meeting my family, are you?"

"Won't your family expect you to marry someone like Ava Cagney? Have they been told about our...our engagement yet?"

"Not yet. I thought it best I tell them in person. They didn't like learning about Giselle through a letter in the mail so much." He pulled a folded piece of paper from the inner lining of his jacket and handed it to me. "I forgot, I made a list of everyone you'll likely meet tomorrow. With descriptions."

I didn't answer. I really didn't have any say about how he dealt with his family and this situation.

"I think you'll fit in just fine; they've all met you before. And it's not always the amount of money one has that determines how well they get along with certain people. If that were true, both Giselle and Ava should have been *perfect* for me. Although my family has a lot of money, I don't want you to think that's all that matters to them. We will be equally yoked together in Christ—that's what will matter most—that you're a Christian." He stood, making his way toward the fireplace again, but this time he opened the door to the hall. "Now, go get some rest. Although I'm quite positive everyone will be happy I'm settling down with such a respectable girl, it will be a long and eventful day nonetheless."

Respectable. Was I considered respectable anymore? I knew enough of Boston's high society to know that, were the circumstances of our engagement and my background spread about, I would be considered ill-fit for anyone's acquaintance, let alone fit to be the daughter-in-law of one of New England's wealthiest men.

I stood and joined him at the door. "Goodnight then. And thank you, Vance." I touched the sleeve of his suit jacket. "You really have made what started out being the worst kind of day into something remarkably the opposite."

"And it's been my pleasure, Violet." With those last words, he leaned in, swiftly kissed my forehead and ushered me into the dark hall. "Have a good night."

I closed the door behind me and stood for a moment in the darkness, attempting to calm my erratically beating heart before going into the bedroom.

I wasn't prepared for this charming and vulnerable side of Vance and I couldn't help but be dreadfully—even more than before—affected by him. He had, without effort, the most magnetic personality when he wasn't trying to conceal it—which he definitely *had* been doing the first few months of our acquaintance, and even at times earlier that week.

Vance didn't seem to be concealing anything now. He was back to being as he had been a few rare times that week since he'd found me crying. I hoped he'd stay this way, and not revert to closing himself off from me. The thought of him shutting down now with the same brick wall he'd quickly constructed between us multiple times before made me feel ill.

He was all I had now, and as I stood there, I prayed he'd be the consistent, strong hero I needed.

8

Everwood

*"He is a gentleman, and I am a gentleman's daughter.
So far we are equal."*
—Jane Austen, *Pride and Prejudice*

Sunday, April 3rd, 1892

Vance was right. Meeting his family wasn't that bad. Until someone asked, "And where is Miss Hawthorne staying while visiting town? Is she staying with Claudine too?"

"No, no. Not that I know of," the older lady with spectacles and a cane, whom I recognized as Miss Claudine Abernathy from the list Vance had given me. "The young lady staying with me was a Miss Roxanna Blakeley, Estella's sister-in-law."

"That's right, Claudine. She's here too, I promise," Dexter explained over the commotion in the front entry where everyone had congregated to meet us at the door.

I stood near Vance, but not exactly "with" him, lagging behind a little. Roxy I spied standing in the opposite corner from me, on the other side of the wide, impressive front door.

There were at least a dozen people in the hall—two of them infants held by their mamas—whom I remembered as Vance's sister, Natalia, and his sister-in-law, Amaryllis.

"Have you not made any definite plans regarding Miss Hawthorne's stay in Boston yet?" Natalia asked.

"Oh I've made plans regarding Miss Hawthorne," Vance's voice boomed over everyone else's. "I'm going to marry her."

"What?" A shrill chorus of excitement came from all the females.

"And she'll stay here at Everwood until we are married." Vance took my hand and stepped farther into the hall. "Violet has no connections in Boston that we know of right now. You won't mind, will you, Father?"

"Another wedding!" Natalia hugged her baby girl close, rocking her back and forth. She made her way through the crowd to come right up to me. "Both Vance and Father will be wed within a few months. How wonderful!"

Vance held my back reassuringly. "Violet, this is my sister, Natalia Livingston, and her daughter, Julianna."

"I remember you, though we never spoke. I was quite busy with this little handful. She has a nanny, but it's just too difficult to tear myself away from her."

"I remember you, too. Your sister's wedding was quite the event."

"You just wait until it's your turn!" Her eyes lit up, and she turned to Vance. "We do get to plan the wedding, don't we?"

"Of course, Violet is looking forward to your help."

Behind Vance's sister, I noticed that his father, the formidable Bram Everstone, was waiting to be introduced. When Natalia noticed him there, she moved out of the way for him to come forward.

This would be the hardest part in my mind—convincing Vance's lumber tycoon and hotel magnate of a father that I was good enough to marry into his impressive family. But if I expected a critical appraisal, it was the farthest thing he presented to me. He was the same as he'd been at Estella's wedding—even to me—a nobody from nowhere now engaged to his son and heir. And would he someday know why? I hoped not.

"Father, this is my fiancée, Miss Violet Hawthorne. You might remember her from the wedding in November. I don't recall if you've met."

"We had not. But let me welcome you to the family regardless, Miss Hawthorne. I've learned to accept my children's decisions throughout the years—for there's not much to do besides. Not that I don't think you're likely one of the best choices Vance has made in a long time."

"Thank you, sir." I tried to imagine what I looked like standing before him, with my best dress—which wasn't nearly as fashionable as his daughter's—and my short hair pulled up as best as I could get it. I glanced up at Vance who had a curiously endearing look upon his face. I'd never witnessed it before. Was it amusement? Or something more like gratitude?

But why on earth would he be grateful for *me*?

Once all of the formal introductions were made, Estella and Dexter accompanied Roxy and Claudine Abernathy to her house, which I'd gathered was down the street. Vance, his brother Nathan, and his father disappeared into a room down the spacious hall, and I was herded into a parlor by Natalia and Madame Boutilier while Amaryllis took baby Rafe upstairs. We'd had breakfast in the dining car of the train, but I hadn't been hungry at the time, and I was ready for all the tea and cakes they could spare. Although I'd slept tolerably well, I'd awoke wishing I'd never left the train station in Severville, despite Vance's assurances from the night before.

And now I'd quickly been trapped in an interview with his elder sister and soon-to-be step-mother. Without him.

When our tea was served and I'd eaten as many tea cakes as I could without attracting undue attention, Natalia started with the questions.

"So, you met Vance at Everston?" She took a sip of her tea, keeping her eyes on me all the while. With her blonde hair and green eyes, she looked nothing like Vance and Estella, but just like her twin brother Nathan.

"Technically, yes. We met at Everston. Estella introduced us in October."

Did they not recall that I'd been Dexter's employee? And how was I to clear up any of their misunderstandings without knowing what Vance wanted me to say? Natalia and Madame Boutilier weren't around me much during the busyness of Estella's wedding—but Amaryllis had been. I wished she'd stayed, for surely she would have been able to help me sort out the truth for them. Of everyone at Everwood, I had a feeling Amaryllis and I had the most in common, as she'd married into the family.

"Were you there visiting the area with your family?"

"No, ma'am. I've worked at Everston since my parents both passed away last winter. Dexter knew my father, as he had a small hotel in a neighboring town. He offered me one of the most coveted positions at Everston, the front desk."

"How fortunate it is that Dexter took you in. He does take such good care of Everston." Natalia took one of the last tea cakes. "If you don't mind my asking, what was your family's hotel like?"

"It was my mother's family's homestead from generations ago—a large brick farmhouse surrounded by acres upon acres of woods. With the railroad coming through, business picked up in the area, so my father turned from not only practicing law in town, but also becoming an innkeeper alongside my mother, transforming our home into an inn."

"Was he also from that area?" Madame Boutilier asked.

"He was from Westborough, Massachusetts, ma'am. He met my mother—who *was* from that area—while staying at Everston when the hotel was newly constructed."

"How delightful! So Everston had a part in bringing your parents together, just as it brought you and Vance together?" Natalia's genuine, happy smile helped make up for the fact that Madame Boutilier had hardly said a word throughout the interview.

As if realizing she'd let Natalia handle the entire exchange, she added, "Although we didn't remember that you were once one of Dexter's employees, I do remember that Estella has always been fond of you. That speaks volumes when it comes to…well, when it comes to your being engaged to Vance."

"Even when it came to me giving in to him." Oh, that didn't sound right. I hastened to correct myself. "I mean: he was persistent, and he didn't seem to care what my family's lot had been, or that I now had nothing. He knew what he wanted to do, it seemed, and it has a lot to do with his faith. I know it's extremely important to him to be equally yoked in marriage to another believer—which I am."

What a muddle I was creating! I wondered if I sounded as ridiculous as I felt trying to balance that fine line between truth and fiction. Everything I'd said was true, but in an effort to make them believe something that wasn't real—that Vance and I were genuinely in love. And it was trying! Would they ever believe that Vance would fall for someone as ill-suited for his family as I was?

"He has changed so drastically in the last few months. And partly on account of our brother's death last summer, and then later on, Dexter's preaching while Vance attended services at Everston's Leightner Hollow last autumn." Natalia set her teacup down, and I finished the last bit of my own tea. "I'm so glad he has you now, Violet, and that he's come back to Boston. It's been so long since he's been a part of our family."

So that was the secret to my ready acceptance.

I hoped I'd prove to be worth it.

⌒

Finally, after it seemed I'd passed all of Natalia's tests, I was shown to my room on the third floor of the gigantic brick mansion.

Everwood was like no other house I'd ever seen. On the corner of two popular streets in Back Bay. It was at least six or seven stories tall—taller than Everston, even—and had a stable and a high, walled-in courtyard in the back. I knew this because that was the view from the many windows of my bedroom.

The room itself was more than I could have ever asked for—a full-size wooden-framed bed with a six-foot-tall headboard, all intricately hand-carved; a fireplace across the room made from white marble; and even a bathroom! My very own bathroom!

Madame Boutilier had informed me on the way up to my room that Vance insisted on hiring her Parisian dressmaker, who happened to be in Boston, to fashion me a new wardrobe—and that a fitting was scheduled for that very afternoon.

I now looked ruefully down at my best dress. I was sure I hadn't impressed anyone on that count, but they seemed to still like me well enough.

And it was true; what seemed to matter most of all was that I was a Christian and that Vance loved me. Hopefully, if they ever did find out *why* Vance wanted to marry me so badly, they would believe the truth and still believe my desire to live a godly life.

And his too.

9

The Everwood Library

"I understand the language of his countenance and movements;
though rank and wealth sever us widely."
—Charlotte Brontë, *Jane Eyre*

Estella and Dexter had returned from Hilldreth Manor just in time for Estella to join Amaryllis and me for my fitting. And it turned out that the three of us together had a genuinely fun time picking out the materials and patterns for my new dresses. By the time we were finished, I was beginning to feel as if I'd become engaged to a prince.

Vance and I were allowed to spend some time before dinner together. Even without any purposeful theatrics of being rapturously in love with each other, everyone seemed to take it for granted that we would grab whatever time we could to be alone, which I was grateful for.

The dressmaker had brought a few samples of her creations, and, when she saw the sorry state of my only gown, insisted I keep the best fitting ones to wear until a few of my own gowns were finished.

So, instead of joining Vance in the study as he'd last seen me, I walked in wearing one of the finest gowns I'd ever seen. It was a light green and yellow creation with lots of pretty folds, ruffles, and lace—and a much lower neckline than I was used to, baring half my shoulders and my collarbone. I had hardly recognized the girl I saw in the mirror. Who knew what a difference a whalebone corset would make to my figure?

I assumed it wasn't exactly the kind of dress one wore just sitting around the house, but Estella and Amaryllis both insisted it was perfectly acceptable for dinner. And I did look forward to Vance's seeing me in something besides the few old dresses I'd worn in his presence so far.

Upon coming into the two-story, echo-filled library, I quickly closed the door behind me. The pocket door thundered harder and louder than I thought, and I jumped noticeably.

Vance chuckled from across the long room where he sat.

When I spun around, I saw that he had a finger marking his spot in the same Bible he seemed to take everywhere.

As I walked toward him, he began reading again. I steered around a few tables and chairs and came to stand before the desk he sat at, and he finally glanced up again.

He almost looked away just as quickly, but then couldn't—or wouldn't. He stared at me for almost half a minute, until I felt like hiding. "Well. That's a different kind of gown than you've ever worn before." He still didn't take his eyes from me. "The dressmaker leant it to me." I collected a pillow from a nearby chair and sat down facing him, the pillow covering most of the revealing bodice of my dress. "It's much more form-fitting than what I'm used to, and I don't think it's meant for daily wear." I swallowed nervously. His eyes now wouldn't leave my face. "It is pretty though."

"Yes, it is." He looked down, noticeably less comfortable than when I'd spotted him sitting at the desk when I'd first come in. "It looks good...on you." His words came out a bit more rough than usual.

"Thank you." I arranged my arms from about the pillow to rest upon the top, squishing it down a bit. "Estella said you wanted to see me."

"Did she?" He'd taken his eyes off of his reading momentarily, but when he caught me staring, he immediately looked back down at the books spread out before him on the desk. It looked as though he was looking through a Bible concordance alongside his Bible. At least when he wasn't looking at me.

The fact that he was so devoted to reading the Bible made my chest swell with appreciation. Yes, I barely knew my fiancé, but as he quietly proved to me what kinds of things mattered to him most, my thoughts of him kept shifting. Layer upon layer of my doubts disappeared every time he opened his mouth. He'd been almost irresistible to look at when I'd first met him, but that was nothing to the pull he created in me from the fact that he endeavored to pursue God, despite his past behavior.

"So you didn't ask for me to come find you?"

"No, but please stay."

After a long drawn out silence—I guess neither of us really knew what to say to each other—I said, "Your family is wonderful."

Vance looked up and held my stare, smiling. "I knew they'd like you."

"I really can't believe they've accepted me so readily. I'm nowhere near good enough to marry into such a—"

"Well, don't think about marrying them, but me...and you'll eventually realize that you're the one too good for me, and not the other way around."

I didn't believe him, of course, and simply added, "I've always wished I had a bigger family."

"Do you have any other relatives besides Ezra?"

"I have an aunt who lives somewhere in Massachusetts, but I'm not sure where. She was my father's sister-in-law, and we lost contact years ago when my uncle passed away. My mother asked me to find her when...when it was clear she wouldn't make it. My father had already passed away that same week of whatever it was that killed them."

"You don't know what it was?"

"I don't. They simply both deteriorated before my eyes within weeks of showing signs of illness. And as soon as they were buried, Ezra took over The Hawthorne Inn, making it into what he preferred. Soon after that, Dexter learned of my circumstances and gave me my job. I mean, my old job."

"Would you like me to find your aunt for you?"

"If you'd like. All I know is that her name is Letty Hawthorne and she was married to my father's brother, Robert, who was originally from Westborough. I'm not sure what she's like, but my mother always seemed fond of her from the letters they'd exchanged over the years. Her husband and my father were from a well-to-do Westborough family. They didn't have much to do with him once he married my mother and stayed in Westward, though. He'd met her while staying at Everston when it was first built by your father."

"Is that right?"

"Although she wasn't exactly from his kind of society, she was a gentleman's daughter. He practiced law in town before we turned my mother's ancestral home into an inn when the railroad came through. And he kept practicing until he became too sick."

"I'm sorry, it isn't my intention to bring up such sad events, but we really ought to get to know one another if…if we're to be married."

I almost expected him to fall back on the mild subterfuge we were orchestrating to make his family think we'd made a love match, but I was more than pleased that he'd brought up the actual marriage plans as his excuse instead.

"So we can make everyone believe this is real." I said, as I stared up at the second level balcony of bookcases. I imagined I could probably spend days and days searching through so many books.

Vance stood from his seat, snagging my attention from above, making his way around the desk, keeping his devastatingly dark eyes directed on me, pillow and all.

I stood as well, gaining a sudden jolt of confidence, and placed the pillow on the chair behind me. Perhaps I could make him want me—make him want everything to be real.

"I'm surprised they don't think I might break down from my newly formed convictions and pressure you into making love to me, sending you in here wearing that."

I almost choked on the air in my throat from the shock of his words, and then thought it best just to ignore them. At least outwardly. I had a hard time catching my breath just thinking back to when he'd fingered the locks of my hair the night before. I took a deep breath. "What's the matter with it?"

"I like it on you a little too much, is all."

I laughed nervously.

"I'm sure they think more of me than that. And you," I ventured, referring to his previous comment.

"We can hope."

Not knowing how to continue, I said, "Thank you for the wedding trousseaux. I didn't expect that. But I guess I should have. It's not as if I could have worn my old clothes around this part of town and not stuck out like a sore thumb."

I wandered about the room a little, not really looking for anything, but wanting to seem busy for the mere fact Vance's intense gaze and magnetic charm, while simply conversing in the most general of manners drew me to him like nothing I'd ever experienced with anyone.

Strolling over to the fireplace, I examined a stuffed red fox displayed at the far end of the mantle above my head. But then I glanced over my shoulder and across the room, having decided to study my fiancé instead.

And he let me, openly, almost as if he enjoyed my perusal.

So this was what it was like to be on equal standing with a man, at least when it came to appreciation. That's what it was, I was slowly gathering. For as much as we'd been thrown into our situation against our wills, neither of us seemed to mind it all that much.

Vance slowly dodged the furniture between us as he made his way across the room.

Suddenly bashful again, I turned away, searching for anything to focus my attention on. There were only about a million books; the ones nearest me all about science. I reached up and stroked the fox's stuffed paw. "Why is it so important your family think we've made a love match? Does it really matter?"

"Since Estella already believes—I don't know, maybe it's a pride thing, but I'd like to not be seen as the brother who can't...." I could tell he had made it most of the way across the room already, nearer to where I stood. It sounded as if he was right behind me. "I don't even know what I'm trying to say."

I stopped examining the fox, but still didn't look at Vance. "I think I understand though."

"I'm glad you're up for the task."

"It will be quite a hardship, you know." I smiled down at the small blaze in the fireplace, unable to keep the mirth I felt hidden.

"I can already tell you'll probably hate every minute," he jested.

They seemed like such simple words, but they conveyed that he knew exactly what he was doing to me. It was a little of what had happened when he'd kissed my hand the day before, and when he'd touched my hair later that night, and then kissed my forehead. Although I had a hard time distinguishing exactly what my feelings were, I didn't want him to stop.

He would be my husband eventually, so it only made sense that we would establish this camaraderie. But was that all it was? It seemed like so much more.

When I could tell he stood beside me, I spun around nervously wringing my fingers together. I looked up and found that he indeed stood mere inches from me with an amused smirk on his lips.

"Did you happen to order a gown like this one?" he whispered, taking a bit of the lace ruffle near my waist between two fingers. He didn't hold on to the piece for long, but as soon as his hand dropped to his side, I wished it had stayed were it had been much longer, or even closer.

"I think so." I could hardly remember. He made my thoughts such a muddle. Had I really picked out my wardrobe only that afternoon? "I don't recall."

"Well, be sure to order one if you haven't already, and in your favorite color."

I smiled nervously and tried to imagine what he saw when he looked at me. Yes, I looked different, but yet very much the same because of my impossible hair. "Do you think this dress really makes such a difference in how I look?"

"That's a complicated question. As I've already told you a number of times, you are quite attractive, no matter the length of your hair. And you're delightful besides the fact. And refreshing. It's just that seeing you dressed like this finally convinced me how real all this is getting to be...and how much more difficult it will become."

I swallowed. "Difficult?"

Without warning, Vance's hand was at my waist where my newly fitted corset flared down slightly toward my hips. I couldn't resist leaning into him, causing his hand to circle around to my back. His other hand was suddenly at the back of my neck, gently caressing the edge of my hairline, tempting the pins loose.

"I hate my hair down..." I whispered.

"Your hair is gorgeous, even as short as it is." His fingers gently traveled to behind my ear.

"You probably shouldn't. The pins will come undone," I breathed, trying desperately to keep my senses. "Everyone would notice, and they'd think the worst."

"Perhaps not the *worst*, but at least they would know I couldn't keep my hands out of your hair."

"Is that what you want, for them to—?"

"My hands in your hair? Yes."

"I meant...you want them to think you want your hands—"

"I want a lot of different things right now, actually, Violet," he breathed.

I took his hand from my neck and held it at my lips. I didn't kiss his palm as he had mine the day before, but I simply let his knuckles rest there, savoring the touch as he allowed.

He leaned in again, and this time he brought his jaw to my cheekbone. He stayed like that for a long time, breathing unevenly. "It's odd, isn't it, how fast things can change from me finding you crying on the steps of Everston, to this."

"Yes. Very odd." My free hand came to his neck, where my fingers traveled to the same places he'd explored on me only minutes earlier. I could feel the blood rushing through his veins.

All I really wanted was for him to kiss me. He seemed on the verge, but so hesitant. And not what I expected from him at all. But why was this even happening? His plans had been to make his family think he wanted me...not to make *me* think he wanted me.

"What do you want?" I asked daringly, unsure of what I was really even asking.

"Too much." He didn't move; almost as if he was paralyzed. "What do you want, Violet?"

I lowered my hand from his neck to his chest. Pressing it against the lapel of his suit jacket, I pushed him away, but at the same time I still held his fingers entwined with mine between us. "I...don't know."

A lie, of course. For a split second, I was sure he'd been about to kiss me, but I'd been much too self-conscious to say that that was exactly what I wanted.

"You have no idea what the sight of you can induce a man to think, do you?" Vance grated out his words. He stepped away from me, backing into one of the chairs flanking the fireplace. "I've had plenty of practice in the past, allowing myself more than I ought... and I'd rather not let those kinds of things happen now, with you."

I let go of his hand, which he'd—for some reason—kept between us, wondering if I'd been completely delusional in letting myself get so carried away.

But I hadn't been the only one.

"Fair enough," I sighed, trying my best to seem as if I *did* know what kinds of things he referred to.

I had no idea what Vance's real motives had been getting me to such a state—to measure my reception of his advances? Or to make it simply look as if we'd spent the last half hour kissing instead of talking? Or had he wanted to kiss me at one point, and then changed his mind?

I turned to face the fire and thought about leaving the room. But my curiosity got the best of me, and instead, I asked, "Once we're married such thoughts and actions will be perfectly allowable, won't they?"

Vance groaned behind me. "Violet. It isn't proper to speak of such things right now, although yes, what you say is true. But for once in my life I'd like to do things in the proper order, the way God intended. A wedding first."

Goodness, so he did expect a real marriage.

The thought warmed me to my core, though I had little understanding of what it all meant besides how he'd made me want to melt just by touching me.

When had he decided upon the status of our upcoming marriage? Was it his intention from the beginning? Had he merely assumed I'd want the same things out of marriage that he did?

He would have been right. If I was to be married, I wanted a real husband.

I turned back to him. It fairly infuriated me that he would go so far as to almost kiss me, and then blame me for tempting him. But something nudged me to admit that, there in the library, his intentions appeared more admirable than mine. I was immensely thankful he was now the kind of man who cared about keeping the marriage bed pure, when he definitely hadn't been one to care before.

"Well, I guess I've been in here long enough to give your family time to talk about us and think us properly in love."

With no response to that, I knew when it was time for me to leave.

10

Wedding Plans

"How short a period often reverses the character of our sentiments, rendering that which yesterday we despised, today desirable."
—Ann Radcliffe, *A Sicilian Romance*

Friday, April 8th, 1892

The first few days at Everwood were quite an education. I received my first lady's maid—a girl of eighteen named Bessy—the same day my new wardrobe arrived, and I spent much of my time sightseeing in Boston with Natalia and Amaryllis.

Fortunately, I loved Vance's family. Although I'd never had any sisters of my own, or many close female friends over the years, Natalia and Amaryllis were just as pleasant, friendly, and accepting of me as Estella had been while we'd known each other at Everston. And Roxy, when I saw her, was slowly growing on me.

I didn't actually end up seeing Vance all that much. He didn't usually come home until late and spent most of his days at his family's offices somewhere in town called Everstone Square. For the most part, I was often left to spend my days—when not out and about town—with Natalia and Amaryllis and their babies, while

Estella spent much of her free time away from her family with Dexter, his sister, and Miss Claudine Abernathy.

Madame Boutilier lived in a leased townhouse a few blocks away on Beacon Street and seemed to have her own circle of friends she intended to spend her time with outside of her soon-to-be daughters-in-law. Which was fine with me.

I'd never been around babies much, and thought it interesting that Natalia and Amaryllis liked spending so much time with them. I'd always gathered—from working at Everston—that most of the mothers from their elite class depended on a nanny or an *au pair* to take care of their children.

A few days later when I strolled into the front parlor to spend the late morning hours with Natalia and Amaryllis, I found Madam Boutilier had joined them, and that Natalia's daughter, Julianna, and baby Rafe were not in their mothers' arms...or even in the room.

"Violet, do come in." Natalia stood and came across the huge space between us, her arms extended to me as if she thought I might run. It was true, I'd stalled in the doorway once I'd perceived something more than a morning visit with my new friends was planned. But really, I didn't know where she thought I would hide from them.

"We were just talking about your wedding and what will need to be done to plan—"

"I—I don't have much experience with such things, so I doubt I'll be of any help." The subject was still overwhelming to me; that I would actually have a wedding, and that I would marry Vance.

"Every decision will be passed through you, of course," Madame Boutilier added. "It is your wedding after all. We're only here to help."

I swallowed the lump in my throat. "I wouldn't know where to start."

"Have you and Vance decided on when or where?"

"I know your wedding to Mr. Everstone is planned for June," I said, speaking exclusively to Madame Boutilier. "And I think Vance has mentioned having ours sometime after that."

"Oh, I wonder if he means to get married at Rockwood? That's surprising." Natalia's hand was at her chest as she looked aghast at both Amaryllis and Madame Boutilier.

"I don't know. What is Rockwood?"

"It's our family's vacation home on Mount Desert Island, near Bar Harbor. My husband and I usually live there year-round, but we came to Boston to have Julianna, and haven't made our way back yet. It's not a place of happy memories lately."

"Vance hasn't told you about Rockwood?" Amaryllis asked.

"No, I suppose we've been occupied with other things."

"That's perfectly understandable. How long have you been courting?"

Oh what would Vance have me say? And why hadn't we come up with these answers already? I quickly decided that the truth would simply have to do. At least those days before the scandal would have to constitute as courting now. "A little over a week."

When I looked up, all three of them were staring at me, wide-eyed.

Natalia was the first to verbally respond. "Well. I guess Vance finally figured out what he wanted. I can't blame him though; you are everything everyone's hoped he'd find in a wife. And I suppose his hurry to marry you shouldn't surprise me. He never has been one to waste any time in getting something accomplished."

I desperately wished that what she said was true and not just their perception. If only Vance had truly wanted me from the beginning of our acquaintance, how differently I would feel about everything.

With a burst of conviction, I couldn't help but confess the actual situation. "There's another thing we haven't told you yet—though Estella and Dexter know all too well. There was bit of a compromising situation that escalated the timing of our engagement."

"We've heard about that," Amaryllis answered calmly. "And we understand that it was a trick done by your brother, rapidly taking the advancement of your relationship—?"

"It was an awful trick, but I suppose he thought he was helping."

After a considerable pause, Madame Boutilier genteelly steered the conversation back to the impersonal particulars. "So we need to ask Vance his preference about location. Rockwood or some location in town."

"And as for guests, do you have friends and family you'd like to invite?" Natalia asked kindly.

"No."

"No?"

"I don't have any family left to speak of; just my trouble-causing brother. And my friends, Estella and Roxy, will have been included already, of course."

"Well, I'm sure we'll be able to fill the church—or wherever it is you marry—for both of you," Natalia continued. "I suppose you probably haven't thought about what you'll do after the wedding?"

"After?" What on earth was I supposed to discuss with them about that?

"The dinner, the ball, the celebration?"

Oh that.

"I don't know. I've only been to something like that once—in November for Estella's wedding." I fingered the lace on the skirt of my new dress—one of the violet colored ones. "Do we need to have something so elaborate? I would so rather keep it small, maybe just a dinner afterwards? Would that be possible?"

"Anything is possible, Violet. But no matter what, we'll want to make it—whatever the size—simply outstanding." Madame Boutilier pulled a journal from a nearby table and opened it to the middle pages. "I'm certain we'll be able to pull something together to make everyone happy. I've already taken a few notes I'd like you to look over sometime—"

"Now, about the *real* 'after the wedding' plans," Natalia quickly interjected.

Even with that first false alarm, I still wasn't prepared for such a topic.

"Has Vance told you where he might take you after the wedding?" she continued.

To bed was all I could imagine after our last conversation.

"He hasn't mentioned where."

"Oh gracious, perhaps he's planning a surprise trip for you? Does he know where you would want to go?"

Home. It was the only place I could think I'd want to go after my wedding, and I didn't have one. What were Vance's plans for us? Would we live in Boston? Would he take me back to Bangor, where he'd been living for a few months until October? I was chagrined for not addressing these concerns earlier, instead of losing my head so spectacularly in his presence.

The door to the hall opened, and Vance walked into the room. His dark gaze found mine right away before it shifted hesitantly toward the folder held in his right hand.

I hadn't realized he was home. Despite the fact that he'd barely said anything substantial to me since Sunday in the library, I felt relief flood my features at the sight of him. Maybe he could better answer everyone's questions regarding the wedding.

Vance crossed the room quickly to sit next to me on the sofa, placing the folder on the empty seat beside him.

"We were discussing the wedding, Vance, but Violet doesn't seem to know what you'd want to do for the wedding or the honeymoon—"

"Doesn't she?"

Oh heavens, did he say such things just to embarrass me? Did they understand what he'd meant? What I'd heard?

"Do you have any thoughts as to where you'd like to have the wedding?" Madame Boutilier asked, obviously nonplussed.

"How about we have the wedding at Fairstone?"

"The wedding? At Fairstone? Whatever for?" Natalia asked.

"We can have everything there." Vance's attention was focused solely upon his sister, as if he felt he had to convince her that this was a good idea. "And Violet and I wouldn't have to worry about leaving afterwards. We'd simply stay home. You'd like that, wouldn't you?" He turned to me, his eyes smiling.

Could he really read my mind? How did he know I would value such things? I merely nodded my head, unable to collect my answer for the sheer shock I felt.

"Whatever do you mean?" Madame Boutilier sat rigidly in her seat, and for the first time I saw a bit of a disdain in her eyes toward Vance. "No honeymoon trip? Fairstone is a mess, and the house belongs to Nicholette—"

"Oh, we'd still have a honeymoon; perhaps we could leave the next day after the wedding brunch. And no, Fairstone does not belong to Nicholette. It belongs to me now."

Natalia's vivid smile virtually glowed at this news. "What? Did you purchase it from her? When?"

"I've been thinking about it and just finalized everything with her lawyer this week. I knew she likely wouldn't want the burden anymore, and I thought I'd take it off of her hands."

Vance had bought me a house? My own home?

I didn't care what he or his family thought of me or my actions in that instant, I clutched his arm with both hands, reached up and kissed his cheek. "Thank you, Vance." I didn't even care what was wrong with the house.

Vance put his arm around me, looked straight into my face—and I was sure he was about to kiss me back when Natalia cleared her throat loudly.

Goodness, was that all I needed to do to get a response from him—show some affection in front of his family? And had it merely been for the sake of making them believe he loved me? I couldn't tell.

"Vance, that was so sweet of you! For Nicholette and for Violet! Does this mean you're going to finally settle down, and in Boston?"

He sent a sideways glance my way, and almost smiled. "I suppose so. But like you said, the house is a mess and needs to be completely renovated."

"You will announce the engagement soon, won't you, Vance?" Natalia asked.

"I thought we'd put it off for a month or so; it will be better to wait until it's been past the official year mark of when Giselle passed away, you know, to be conventional, in case anyone notices."

"Good idea. I hadn't thought about it only being a year. So much has happened in that time!"

With a sudden lull in the conversation, I asked, "Where is this Fairstone house?"

"My brother Will and his wife had planned to move into a house just up Dartmouth Street once it was renovated, but he was killed shortly after their wedding. Nicholette left for Europe with her parents last June, leaving the house completely unfinished, except for Will's master's suite. That happened to be refinished first thing. But everything else is in shambles."

Vance took his arm from around me and turned to the other side of the sofa where he then opened the folder he'd brought in with him. He took out a number of photographs, shifting through them before handing one to me.

I held onto a corner, not daring to believe the massive stone structure in the photograph had anything to do with what we'd been discussing.

"This is Fairstone. I suppose we could call it an engagement present for you."

I stared down at the photograph, at a complete loss as to what to say. It *was* a mansion. What was I supposed to do with a house like that?

"You'll help me decide how to renovate it, won't you, Violet?"

I slowly looked from the photograph to Vance, still stunned, and almost in disbelief.

"Once it's fixed up, it will be a beautiful place to be married!" Natalia's smile was strictly for her brother at that moment—she did seem extremely happy that he was going to marry me. "And then to live, of course."

"You want my opinion on redecorating the interior of *this* mansion?" I held up the photograph.

"Who else would I have help me besides you?" he asked. The smile on his face suddenly seemed as though it were only there to cover up a disgruntled frown. He took the photograph from me and placed it back into the folder.

"You like it don't you, Violet?" Amaryllis asked. "To be sure, it will take a lot of time and money to get the task of restoring it to all its grandeur, but I'm certain it will be well worth it."

"I like it. It's just so big. And intimidating."

Just as I was about to reassure Vance that I did indeed love his gift—whether it was just for show or he genuinely wanted to give me my own home—the butler came into the room carrying a silver tray. "Excuse me, Mrs. Livingston, but there's a guest at the door." He walked across the room, but behind the furniture, to present a card to Natalia.

She took up the card. "Reverend Benjamin Whitespire? Who is—?"

"Goodness, Ben's made it to Boston sooner than I thought he would," Vance interrupted his sister. "He's a friend of mine—of ours." He sent a quick glance my way.

A friend of his? Was that true? I knew he and Ben had been acquaintances, but true friends?

"He's come to town to meet with The Boston Inland Mission Society in hopes of taking a mission," I added.

Natalia replaced the card and said, "Please do send him in."

I took Vance's hand quickly, sliding my fingers into this palm, purposefully catching his gaze and keeping it. I leaned in and whispered, "Vance, I love the house. I do. It's just so much more than I expected."

"I should have asked you first, what kind of house you would have wanted."

"I would have said any house you wanted to give me." I smiled, still holding his gaze. "And it is great what you've done for your sister-in-law while she's away and grieving. I was just wondering where we would live after the wedding before you came in—"

"And about the official honeymoon," he asked, behaving himself remarkably well, considering the subject matter. "Did you have any ideas about where you'd like to go?"

"I haven't thought about what we'd do at all. Have you?"

With the tilt of one side of his mouth and the telling sparks from his black eyes, he gave me my answer, and I gathered he wasn't thinking about the location at all.

I took my hand from his and realized that Natalia, Amaryllis and Madame Boutilier had been watching us quietly from their seats across the sitting area.

Amaryllis was the first to speak. "Nathan took me on a trip across America in one of the private rail cars. Where do you think you'll go?"

"I could take you to Europe," Vance cut in with a little more excitement than I ever recalled hearing in his voice. "On a leisurely, luxurious ship; what do you think about that?"

"I never would have thought of that, but I suppose it is an option." Just the thought of traveling to Europe, alone with Vance

Everstone; that was more "alone with a man" than I'd ever imagined before.

What would it be like to have *only him* for company for such a long trip?

I heard Ben talking to the butler in the hall, and before I knew it he was walking into the room. Vance stood to greet Ben, and then everyone else followed suit as he made the introductions. As I stood alongside Vance, I couldn't help but notice Ben's gaze travel over us; an almost embarrassed look fighting to transform his otherwise smiling face.

When he took my hand in greeting, I wanted to sink into the floor. Had he heard the rumors? I wasn't sure what exactly he knew about our engagement, but just the fact that Vance and I had gone from hardly knowing each other to becoming engaged and sitting there in Everwood together in such a short amount of time would have seemed a little risqué to someone like Ben. And if he *had* heard why…would he spread the rumors around Boston?

But no, he wouldn't ever do that; he wasn't that sort of person. That was why I'd always liked him so much. Because he was good. But the way he looked at me made me wonder if he had actually had some hidden feelings for me all that time? And if he had, why hadn't he done or said something about them? Even during our last dinner together at Everston he had acted as if I hadn't meant a thing to him, that he was perfectly all right with leaving Laurelton and never seeing me again.

He was exactly the kind of man I'd always thought I would marry, if I'd had the chance. And there he was, looking, suddenly, in all honesty as if I'd hurt his feelings by choosing to become involved with someone like Vance Everstone.

I'd never been in love with Ben, and the sudden thought of him attempting to kiss me as Vance almost had days ago, shifted through my thoughts, giving me pause: would Ben have ever been able to create such feelings in me?

I doubted it. Even now, as he stood facing us, I knew there wouldn't have been the same kind of barely controllable passion as I'd already experienced with Vance.

Although Vance and I had hardly seen or spoken to each other for days on end, just spending time and talking with him about our future as we had in the last twenty minutes had helped remind me how easy it was for him to draw me in. As much as I apparently tempted him beyond all reason, I couldn't deny that the struggle would likely be just as strong on my side, whenever it was he did get around to kissing me.

For some reason, although we'd come to where we were by accident, it was evident that it was an easy attraction between us. And over the five days since arriving to Everwood, I'd come to respect Vance's strict rein on the physical aspects of our relationship.

If it meant keeping those charged emotions from developing into an all-consuming fire, it would be well-worth it. I'd never in my life been tempted to think of letting go of my own foundational moral restraints, but that was also before someone as intriguing as Vance stood within my reach.

11

Deeper

*"He had been held to her by a beautiful thread which it pained him
to spoil by breaking...."*
—Thomas Hardy, *Far from the Maddening Crowd*

Later that evening, after an awkward dinner in the company
of the ever-watchful Ben Whitespire, Vance cornered me in
the hall as I made my way to the parlor where the women were
waiting for me. Vance and I hadn't been alone since we'd met in the
library on the day of our arrival, and I wasn't sure what he wanted.
He didn't usually *want* to be alone with me.

As I followed him down the hall, my hand on his arm, my
stomach twisted and turned.

He didn't want to spend time with me, did he? But there he
was, escorting me down the hall. It shocked me how comfortable
I felt with him. Who was this man? This Vance Everstone, who
seemed firing mad at me one day and calmly collected and atten-
tive the next time I saw him?

When we finally were shut inside a nearby room, his back to
the tall wood door, he unlinked our arms and sighed.

I didn't move far from him, situated at the frame of the door,
waiting for whatever was to come. I secretly hoped it would be the
culmination of what I'd seen in his eyes after I'd dared to kiss his
cheek in my overflowing gratitude regarding Fairstone.

When he didn't say anything—only stared at me—I said, "You bought me a house."

"I thought we might need somewhere to live."

"You've done so much for me, Vance. Given up so much. I can't help but think you would rather be back at Everston, in your solitary room, or roaming back and forth from Bangor, taking care of your lumber company, not settling down the street from your family."

"It's good to be back with them after all these years. I realize that now. I wouldn't have been able to come back without you."

"Surely, you would have been fine. They love you."

He smirked playfully. "They love that I brought you home with me." Vance still stood against the door, and I moved on into the room—which was merely another sitting room, but with a large piano and a golden harp situated at one end.

"So this Fairstone house needs to be renovated?" I asked. "And you want to get married there?"

"It's as good a place as any. None of the fashionable churches in town will have room in their calendars for at least a year and a half, possibly two."

"And you want to get married this year."

"Before the summer is through, in fact."

Didn't most engagements take some time, for whatever reason? Perhaps to let the bride get used to the changes happening in her life? Perhaps it wasn't that strange of an occurrence to get married so quickly when you matched well.

But did I match Vance? I felt like we did at times, but then there were always the times he shut me out on purpose. Would he be like that after we were married?

Vance didn't move too far from the closed entrance of the room, though I'd made my way to the beautiful harp and stopped to admire it. I'd heard of the instrument, but I'd never seen one in person. It was much taller than I'd ever imagined, and the sight was awe-inspiring.

"Won't remodeling Fairstone take time?" I eventually asked.

"The project will be finished in time, don't worry. I'm hoping to have it completed by the middle of May. But I'll need your help in selecting flooring and wallpapering and such. And furniture."

"Will we need to bring someone—?"

"Yes. And we'll begin with your rooms."

"My rooms? Won't the entire house be ours together?"

"The bedchamber and sitting area directly attached to the master's suite is reserved for his bride." Vance looked almost bashful for once.

"And I suppose you'll expect the door to be unlocked?" I asked.

His normal, self-assured grin crept over his lips. "The door?"

I blushed, embarrassed that he'd made me specify.

"Between our bedrooms." I didn't look at him now, but fingered the chords of the harp softly, apprehensively, for I didn't know what to expect if I actually strummed them with any force.

"My hope is that the door will always be unlocked."

Finally, still without looking at him, I glided my fingertips over the chords and the most marvelous sound filled the room with haunting echoes. And that was when I took the chance to say the words I feared asking, but desperately wanted the answer to. "Even though you don't love me?"

He took his time in answering, and I couldn't help but wonder what that meant.

"My time as Giselle's husband, although it didn't start out properly, and for as short as it was—and turbulent—we did have a consummated marriage." He circled the piano, keeping it between us as he spoke. "And it taught me that settling down, having an everyday, committed companion, and hopefully someday a family of my own, wasn't all that bad of an idea. I wasn't planning to jump back into making that happen any time soon, but here you are."

His every word had come out cautiously, as if he'd thought upon each one carefully before uttering it. "Don't you think we could make it work?"

"I think we can," I confessed, hoping I didn't seem too eager to comply. "I know this probably isn't proper to ask, but you will be faithful, won't you? I know there are all kinds of husbands—"

"In the past, it might not have meant anything to me to be trustworthy or faithful to anyone, but you will be married to a new creation—to the new man—who wants to be those things in all ways." Vance moved away from the piano, but stopped himself from coming too close. "Violet, I hope to have your forgiveness for getting you into this mess...for having to marry me against your wishes, but also for everything I've done before...."

"It is my goal, Vance. You already have my forgiveness concerning our situation, but really, none of it was actually your fault." I swallowed awkwardly, wishing to reassure him. "I have to admit, though, I might not fully realize what doing so about the latter concern will require of my heart until much later, when I better understand everything. But I will try."

This didn't require an answer, and he didn't give me one. But he did come around the piano just then, slowly, his eyes never leaving my face. It so often seemed as though there was a constant battle going on inside of him regarding me. He obviously found me attractive, but almost struggled with the fact. I suddenly recalled his arm coming around me earlier, and the flash of hunger in his eyes right after I'd kissed his cheek.

It didn't make sense to me why I enjoyed his attention so much, and why he created these tense feelings in me.

Would he ever love me? I knew many marriages were built on less than ours would be. And if the rumors about his past were even half true, making women fall for him seemed to be something he did quite naturally. It was certainly proving to be true for me. I had high hopes for our union, because if he remained as he'd been in the last two weeks, for the most part, I was quite sure I'd have little trouble falling in love with him, no matter his past. I hoped with all my heart that he would come to love me too, for all of his good intentions. But I also realized, at the same time, that it wasn't a guarantee.

Vance had made his way around the piano, slowly advancing toward me.

Backing up, I clumsily bumped into a chair, landed on the armrest and then immediately slid off to stand behind it. I really just wanted to avoid the same kind of terrible response he'd had the last time we'd come to be so close in an otherwise empty room.

Most likely because of my inelegant retreat, he'd seemed to come to his senses by the time he reached me. He no longer looked as if he wanted to devour me—which I found to be rather disappointing.

I was utterly pathetic.

"My family seems to like you, just as I knew they would." He was so vague sometimes; what did he mean by that? Could he tell I hadn't believed him on that score?

What else could he tell? That he had my heart wishing for things that I didn't understand? That because my future was now so intricately connected to his, I had no qualms about his desire to make our marriage real and not just contrived for the sake of my reputation?

And how would I ever come to say such things to him without sounding like a complete wanton?

"They are involved," I said half to myself, for I was definitely referring to more than just his relatives. "But they're kind. Which reminds me, I should go—"

"Wait just a minute, don't go yet. There's a reason I brought you in here, before I got distracted." Vance walked across the room to the table where he'd set his folder. He pulled a pamphlet out and handed it to me, turning it over.

"I wanted you to have this, so you'd be able to watch out for Steele, to let me know if you happen to see him lurking about." Vance pointed to a grainy image of a man at the bottom of the paper labeled ROWEN J. STEELE.

He didn't look like a rotten gambler who would trick Ezra into promising him his sister for the sake of covering a bet. He looked nothing like I'd imagined—and not scary at all, really. But I knew from briefly meeting too many of the men who'd pressured Ezra into transforming my mother's beloved ancestral home into a brothel that outer appearances oftentimes had nothing to do with the inner hearts of man. And if all Vance had told me was true, Rowen J. Steele seemed the perfect example of how deceptive appearances could be.

"He's not going to succeed, Violet. Not if I can help it." Vance stood around the edge of the small table, I assumed mostly to gauge my reaction to seeing Rowen Steele's photograph.

"Do you really think that Mrs. Ward finding us in my dorm room was my brother's doing?"

"I can think of no other explanation. I don't recall anything from between when we were attacked and when I groggily awoke to her shouting at you—for what definitely looked to be good reason."

"The most embarrassing moment of my life."

"For as much as Ezra's to blame, he seems to be trying to figure out how to keep you from Steele as much as I am. I'm not sure how cutting your hair off played into his scheme, and I'm not even certain this engagement to me will put a definitive hamper on his plans."

"What do you think Rowen Steele wants with me?"

"I'm sure everything you have to offer, Violet. And just because he can. I told you about the bet, but I didn't mention that I'd offered to buy the bet back from him."

"How much did you offer him?"

"Twenty thousand."

My safety was worth that much to Vance? But then his comment about comparing me to rubies came back to mind. I'd looked up the verse from Proverbs in the concordance Vance had made use of our first day at Everwood and thought of it quite often. It was a good reminder, after all: *"She is more precious than rubies: and all the things thou canst desire are not to be compared unto her."*

"And he refused?" I finally asked. "How would I have ever paid you back if he had agreed to take it?"

"You wouldn't have had to, because you never would have known a thing about it."

"And you would never have had taken a special interest in coming to Everston so much when you did, getting to know me for the sheer benefit of protecting me." I picked up Vance's folder from the table and placed the pamphlet back inside.

"Keep it."

"I'd rather not."

"If that's what you would prefer." His voice was gentle; he had such an air of protection about him…at least when it came to me. It was one of things I liked best about him. No one had ever made me feel as safe as he did.

What on earth had induced Vance to try to win me back from this Rowen Steele before he'd met me in the first place? Could it be that under everything he purposefully displayed to everyone, he had a good heart?

I could only hope.

I decided against moving away from him, although he was now only about a foot away, and I was certain I needed to join his sisters soon before one of them came looking for me. Still not moving my feet, I flipped through the papers in the folder and again caught a glimpse of the photograph of Fairstone.

"I really thought he'd take the money. And now I doubt he'll be surprised to find that we're engaged, for whatever the reason. At least not nearly as surprised as Ben was to see us together."

"You don't think Ben already knew? That no one had happened to tell him?"

"He isn't the biggest gatherer of gossip, as I'm sure you're well aware." Vance huffed, as if frustrated. The same kind of response he often had whenever the subject of Ben Whitespire came up. "I haven't spoken to him, well, since any of this happened." Vance indicated to the space between us, as if there was actually something there physically tying us together. "Dexter's been in contact, but I think it was a shock for Ben. What did you think of his response?"

I had every intention of pretending that I had noticed nothing untoward in Ben, but for some reason I couldn't allow myself to lie to Vance. "I think that he was sorry, that he regretted being too late."

"Are *you* sorry he was too late?"

I swallowed as Vance took a step closer, coming to stand mere inches from me. But he definitely wasn't interested in kissing me now. I didn't know what he was doing, or what he wanted.

Collecting my wits, I added, "He's a fine upstanding gentleman, whom any girl would be lucky to—"

"I know. You've said all that before. But how strong were your feelings regarding him two weeks ago?"

"I thought I liked him. But he never indicated that he…."

"That he what?"

"I don't know. I have no idea what he thinks, what he's ever thought about me."

"Oh, I can tell you right now what he's thinking. That man is sick with jealousy, because you're now mine and not his."

"It doesn't matter." I stood my ground, hoping to make a point that it didn't really concern me anymore what Ben thought.

"None of this makes you want to run into his arms?" Vance asked. "Because he is the better man; you've said as much before. He's a pastor intent on taking a mission; he wants to serve God with his every breath. And you're the kind of girl who would value such things."

"I could never do that, run into his arms. I'm engaged to you. I feel safe with you. And I hardly know him."

"You hardly know me."

"I know enough. I know you have a strong heart."

He huffed again. "Like I said, you hardly know me." Vance abruptly crossed the room toward the door to the hall, the frustratingly random wall going up without warning. I felt as if he was again suddenly closing himself off from me. I knew leaving just then would only make things worse, and so I followed him. Would I ever truly get through to him, even after our wedding?

Before reaching the door, he turned and I almost ran into him.

"I forgot to tell you. I found your Aunt Letty; she actually doesn't live too far away."

"In Westborough?" I asked, suddenly wishing I'd allowed myself to crash into him.

"South Boston. She has two adult children living with her, Cal and Mabel. Do those names sound familiar?"

"My cousins. It must be her." I stared up into his face, waiting for him to look down at me again, but he wouldn't. He faced the door, apparently ready for the conversation to be over. "How far away is South Boston from here?" I asked, more to continue the conversation than from a real desire for the information. "Is it a respectable part of town?"

"It is no great distance from Back Bay. The house is relatively new; they live in one side and rent the other. I gather that's where the majority of their income comes from, for I can't seem to find much out about your cousin Cal Hawthorne, or what exactly he does."

"You haven't met them yet?"

"I thought it best to take you with me to meet them."

"That's probably best. Should we tell them we're engaged to be married?"

"Yes, but I would definitely refrain from explaining exactly why. My goal is to keep the rumors from flying. Dexter's done his best in trying to contain them, but you never know." He finally glanced my way for the first time since running for the door. "Do you think your relatives know about how Ezra turned your mother's home into a brothel?"

"Heavens, I hope not. I doubt it, though."

"Good. We'll make our initial visit to them soon."

"Already?"

"There's nothing more to wait for, is there?"

"I'm unsure how receptive they'll be. I've never met them; they only know of me through my mother's correspondence with my aunt years ago, which I'll be sure to bring."

"Good idea." With that, he took my hand, opened the door and led me down the hall. And didn't say another blessed thing to me all night.

12

Recreations

"Who can map out the various forces at play in one soul?
Man is a great depth, O Lord.
The hairs of his head are easier by far to count than his feeling,
the movements of his heart."
—Saint Augustine

Saturday, April 16th, 1892

A few days later, upon coming from spending the morning in my room writing a new book and scribbling out a few practice drawings, I met Vance coming toward the head of the intricately carved staircase from the south wing.

He had been coming around a bit more than he had before, but I'd never known him to be home at such an odd time of the day. He still needed to be away at Everstone Square much of the time, organizing business concerning Greaghan Lumber. He would sometimes come home at midday for lunch, but then often not be home in time for dinner.

Without a word, Vance stopped me from continuing on down the stairs. First he did so with the uncommon look of delight in his eyes from spotting me, and then as he came up to me, a gentle caress just above my wrist, which then turned into him cupping my elbow, and then quickly sliding his hand about my waist.

Just as he had for Ava Cagney, but no one was there to see now. Which confused me.

"If you want to get your aunt's letters, I can take you to meet her this morning. I've already written to her, and she's expecting us any day now, and later I've arranged to have someone meet us at Fairstone to discuss what to do—"

"You want to go right now?"

"Did you have other plans?"

"Not exactly. I'm just not prepared. Can we go some other time instead?"

"Why? You're dressed, your hair has been properly taken care of—your maid has done a much better job than I did, wouldn't you agree?"

I fingered the messy strands escaping from behind my ear. "Bessy is quite talented, especially for having to deal with the shortness."

But oh, how I would have preferred to have his fingers in my hair instead of hers, every morning.

"I only have today, Violet. I'm sorry I didn't warn you before, but I'd figured you'd be happy to get out of the house with me." He brought his other hand around the back of my waist, bringing me face to face, tugging me closer. I wasn't exactly alarmed—only unsure of what to do in return. Would he turn on me again if I responded back?

"I am; I've been looking forward to it." I placed my hands gently on his forearms, taking in the rich texture of his suit and glanced down the stairs. And there I saw the reason for all the pomp and show. Natalia had come through the main hall below and had stopped to watch us.

"I'm busy the whole rest of the week. If we don't take advantage of today, we might have to wait another few weeks." He slid his fingers into the crook of my arm and guided me around the railing toward the north wing, where, as he obviously knew, my bedroom was located.

I didn't really know what to think of that.

Not that I hadn't also gathered exactly where Vance's room was. It was difficult to avoid the preoccupation I had with wanting to know what he was really like, deep down, apart from everyone else, and apart from all the things that any friend or acquaintance could tell made up the man he'd become. I wanted to know so much more. Having him lead me to my bedroom didn't help these overwhelming feelings.

He stopped guiding me some ways from my door, and still in plain view of Natalia through the ornate wood railing. "Bring your books too; I'd like to squeeze in an introduction to a friend of mine who happens to be an editor for a publisher based out of Philadelphia."

That made me want to run to the security of my room and not come out. "I can't show an editor my books. They aren't good enough."

"Isn't it your goal to have them published? How will that ever happen if you don't show someone who matters?"

"Can I at least show them to you first? You might change your mind after you see them."

"Very well; get them, along with your aunt's letters to your mother. I'll look at your books, and then we will leave."

I walked to my room, nervous because I knew Vance's eyes followed me all the way to my door. Inside, I gathered my gloves, reticule, a hat to quickly pin on, my aunt's letters and the one book I'd told Vance I'd show him when we were on the train. It was my favorite one—the one I figured anyone would like best.

When I returned to the hall, my arms laden with everything I needed to bring, Vance met me by the stairs. Natalia was no longer studying us from below, and he simply took my box of letters and headed down the steps, apparently expecting me to follow.

"Vance," I called after him softly as I followed, "Please take a look at my book before we leave. There's no sense in taking it if—"

He swiveled around to me at the bottom of the two flights of stairs. "Oh yes, let me see." He traded me the box of letters for the book and immediately opened it to flip through the pages. And then he stopped. "You painted these pictures, and came up with this story all on your own?"

"Yes."

"And you gave this same story about the fox to Wynn before she left?"

"Yes."

"It's touching, and perfect."

"Perfect?"

"For Wynn, and for my friend to see."

"What publisher does your friend work for?"

"Lippencott."

"No."

"No...what?"

"I'm not going to show someone from Lippencott my silly books."

"You'll never be published if you don't. And you said it's what you want more than anything." Vance reached up and tapped the edge of my book to my nose. "He's not scary."

"What's his name?"

"Quinn Culver."

I took the book from Vance and again handed him the letters.

"Violet, I promise he'll love this. I don't know much about children's books, but I bet Wynn loved it."

"She was thrilled. And Meredyth saw it too, and told me she liked it better than most of the books Wynn already had."

"Well then. You're ready. Let's go." He took my hand and walked me out the front door.

~

A while later Vance's carriage brought us to a quaint, double, side-by-side house in South Boston. Its wood siding was painted red, and it had six black-shuttered windows on the second level, four on the first, and two impressive dark wooden front doors situated at the center where the two living quarters met. There was a flat covered porch over them and a tall flight of steps with a decorative metal rail dividing them in half. It had taken quite a while to get there, and Vance had spent most of the time describing Fairstone to me and then asking my opinion about certain ideas regarding redecorating it.

Honestly, that was what I was most looking forward to all day—seeing Fairstone for the first time! I still wasn't especially excited to see my estranged aunt, nervous that she wouldn't care a fig about me. Not that I knew why it mattered. It didn't, really. And the editor, Mr. Culver…I was still quite anxious about that meeting. I wished I'd had more time to prepare!

Vance knocked on the door to the right side of the house. A housekeeper answered, and I immediately noticed that the inside was just as quaint as the outside. I hadn't known what to expect, but I'd been a little afraid I would be embarrassed for Vance to see how my relatives might live. I really didn't have a clue. What if they were more like Ezra than me?

We made our introductions to the housekeeper, handing her our calling cards. She then took our things and led us through the front hall past the tall straight staircase and stopped at the entrance of a front parlor. "A Mr. Everstone and a Miss Hawthorne to see you, ma'am."

When Vance and I walked into the room and I immediately saw that my aunt was much younger than my parents had been when they died.

She stood and took my hands. "Violet, dear! It must be you! I can see the resemblance right now! You look so like my own daughter, your cousin Mabel! And this must be your fiancé who was so good to write to me on your behalf. It's so nice to meet you, Mr. Everstone. I suppose you're somehow related to the Everstones who live in Back Bay, are you? It's not a common name—"

"In fact, Bram Everstone is my father, ma'am."

My aunt had stopped speaking mid-sentence at this information, her mouth still opened to form her next word, which seemed to be somewhat lost to her. Finally, after some seconds, she said, "Well! An *Everstone*! Congratulations! It's so good to meet both of you! I've always wanted to meet you, Violet, I just couldn't spare the trouble for a trip to Maine. It is so far away."

"It is far, isn't it?" I conceded. "This is actually the first time I've been away from the general area I grew up. I wasn't sure where you lived until lately."

She led us to a sofa where Vance and I both sat, while she took a seat on a chaise longue across from us, not hiding her admiration as she simply stared. "You are a handsome couple; you'll have beautiful children one day."

Vance cleared his throat, and I shifted beside him.

"Thank you. I hope so, Aunt Letty." And after a little pause, to collect myself further, I added, "I was unable to inform you last year, my mother seems to have lost track of your whereabouts over the years—"

"How is your mother? I have to admit, I never got back into my habit of writing when we moved here from Westborough. My joints have been giving me such pain, and Mabel won't sit still for half a minute to help me—"

"I'm sorry to have to tell you this...."

The Cautious Maiden 129

Vance stealthily took my now bare hand, stretching my fingers to entwine his in between them. I curled my fingers over his knuckles, the sensation effectively distracting me from what I needed to say. I swallowed before going on, "My mother and father both passed away last winter."

"You don't say." Letty's smile immediately vanished, and I could see tears glisten over her pretty green eyes. "I'm sorry." She dabbed at her eyelashes with her handkerchief. "I'm so sorry, Violet. And I'm sorry I didn't stay in touch. You've probably had an awful time of it; what have you been doing with yourself before your heroic fiancé came along to save you?"

Her words couldn't have been truer if she'd known the entire story of those last few weeks.

"I worked at a nearby hotel. And I was happy. It wasn't a bad year." I squeezed Vance's hand. "But I'm glad it's over."

"And your brother, Ezra? What's he up to? Married and living in your maternal grandparent's house, I suppose?"

"Um, I'm not sure exactly what Ezra's up to these days. I haven't seen him much lately." I didn't like lying, but there was absolutely no way to tell the truth. No respectable person would claim such a brother.

"But who has your mother's house then? She did love that place. I didn't imagine you'd ever want to move away, but I do see why you might for the sake of marrying your Mr. Everstone."

"The house has been lost to me." I nearly choked on my words, and quickly moved on to say, "I've had to part with it, but like you said, I've made a fair exchange. I have Vance now."

And how I wished it were really true.

"So you'll be staying in Boston?"

"I just bought Violet a house on Dartmouth. I'm going to take her there to see it today for the first time, in fact."

"Dartmouth! Heavens! I should say, Violet! A fair exchange, indeed!"

The front door opened before I could answer, and I heard someone hurry into the front hall with hard little steps, a woman's steps.

"Mother? Are you downstairs?"

Aunt Letty reached her arm along the back of the chaise longue, toward the entrance to the hall. "Do come in here, Mabel. I'd like you to meet your cousin Violet and her fiancé."

A second later, Mabel Hawthorne stood in the doorway, and I was presented with someone who looked more like me than I could have ever imagined. Except she was about four or five years younger than I and her gorgeous blonde locks were long and perfectly pinned and piled into the sort of style I wouldn't be able to wear for years. And I didn't know if it was just her hair, but I was sure anyone would say she was the prettier of the two of us. By far.

After we were all formally introduced, I could tell that Mabel couldn't help but sneak in a glance at Vance every so often. Not only because of who he was, but because he did look quite phenomenal.

I certainly couldn't blame her. I knew exactly how she felt. It always had been hard to keep my eyes off of him. I'd had months and months of practice while at Everston by then, and now it didn't even matter. I probably could have looked at him to my heart's content whenever I wanted and everyone would have simply thought I was quite besotted with my fiancé.

Because I basically was.

But I did strive to control it. I didn't need to act like a fool just because he was the most attractive man I'd ever seen.

And I was going to marry him.

Vance hadn't held my hand since Mabel had come into the room, but I gave him a quick look and found his eyes on me. He seemed genuinely happy that I'd found some of my own people, and that they were respectable. Well, at least Aunt Letty and Cousin Mabel were. I still had an inane fear that my cousin Cal would be just like Ezra.

We'd stayed at Aunt Letty's house much longer than either of us had expected, and ended up not having time to see his friend, Mr. Culver, before Vance's scheduled appointment with the interior decorator at Fairstone.

On the ride back to Dartmouth Street, I couldn't help but smile. Vance sat across from me—the seat he took every time he and I were in a carriage together, whether alone or with others—equally delighted, it seemed, for he too was smiling.

I was content just having a moment to recall the time I'd had with my aunt and cousin, and how it felt so good to be with people whom I actually belonged. While I did so, Vance took out my book about the fox and studied it quite extensively.

Eventually, after much quiet thought—and I could tell we were getting closer to Back Bay—I said, "And to think, if it weren't for Rowen Steele's bet and Ezra's meddling, I would never have had the chance to meet Aunt Letty or Mabel."

"Don't forget about my part in this happy occurrence. If it weren't for your engagement to me, and my thorough search for them in the first place—it really wasn't that difficult—but would you have ever dared come down to Massachusetts in order to start your search if it weren't for me?"

"No. And you're right. I owe everything to you, for first caring enough to keep me safe from Rowen Steele, and then for all this." I lifted my hands to indicate the carriage surrounding us and everything that meant besides.

"It's become much more involved than I ever thought it would." He sent me a clever grin from across the carriage, his eyes suddenly taking in everything about me from head to toe. "But it isn't bad, what's happened—what's happening between us."

"No. It's not bad," I added, shyly, my heart soaring at his half-amorous admission.

Just then the carriage stopped. The groom quickly stepped down from his seat and opened the door. "Fairstone, sir."

Oh, how I wished I'd begun that conversation sooner! Had he only said as much because he'd realized how close we were to being interrupted?

Vance stepped out of the carriage and then helped me down, not giving me any indication that he'd heard my last words. But then my eyes took in the amazing building in front of me.

Fairstone.

I didn't know how to describe the limestone mansion besides to say it was beautiful...perfection...everything I could have asked for and never dreamed of having.

And absolutely too big. At least for the likes of me.

It towered three stories above the street. I couldn't explain the tingling emotions running through me that made me want to dance, scream with excitement, and kiss Vance until he didn't know what to do, all at the same time.

When Vance suddenly took my hand and slid his fingers between mine for the second time that day, I realized I'd been staring up at the grand house ever since setting foot on the sidewalk.

"Do you like it?" He practically chuckled.

I fought back happy tears. "You can't be serious. This is mine?"

"Just wait until you see inside, you might change your mind about how great it is once you see—"

"Show me."

"Just a minute. I'd rather we waited until Mrs. Applegate and her assistant arrive to go inside."

"Oh, of course."

While we waited I couldn't take my eyes off of Fairstone, and Vance continued to hold my hand. The warmth of his skin through my glove was comforting, and yet also somewhat possessive. And I liked that. I wanted to possess him just as equally, but would I?

He'd only just opened up and given me a tiny taste of what it would be like to be his; telling me so candidly that he'd also become fully aware that something more than we'd either expected was happening between us.

We didn't have to wait long for Mrs. Applegate and her assistant to show up. They both seemed as equally excited to see the torn-up interior of Fairstone as I was.

Vance guided us to the main entrance, unlocked the door and led us into the empty mansion. And I quickly realized he hadn't been jesting about the mess. The walls were bare, the wood floor was covered with debris and there wasn't a stick of furniture. The large staircase went up the right side of the main hall and then turned to the left to meet the second level.

And there was so much to do.

How would it ever be finished by mid-May?

"It's quite a project, wouldn't you say?" Vance whispered in my ear. "It's been stripped of almost everything from before, and is ready to be recreated into something better. Will you help me, Violet? Are you up for the challenge?"

I had a feeling Vance wasn't actually talking about Fairstone at all, but himself.

Is that what he felt like inside? An empty shell of a glorious mansion? That when he'd become a Christian, everything he used to be had been cleansed and stripped away, leaving only the remnants of the true man God had in mind all along for me to discover?

I didn't know what had happened since earlier that week to make Vance behave so differently regarding me, but I wasn't about to complain either. If he wanted my help in any way, I would be at his service.

"I would be more than happy to, Vance." I took his hand in mine again. "Just lead the way."

13

The Tea Rooms

"Happiness is like a butterfly which, when pursued,
is always beyond our grasp,
but, if you will sit down quietly, may alight upon you."
—Nathaniel Hawthorne

Saturday, April 23rd, 1892

The Propylaeum, the tea room at which Vance had been so considerate to arrange for me to meet Aunt Letty and Mabel a week later, ended up being about halfway between Back Bay and South Boston. And I'd decided to invite Miss Claudine Abernathy and Roxy to join us since I had a feeling they would get along with my relatives.

Vance's carriage had dropped the three of us off at the tea rooms around four-thirty, and we sat there for about five minutes before Aunt Letty and Mabel came through the front door to join us.

"This is a lovely place; I've never been here before," Aunt Letty divulged once everyone was introduced and took their seats. "I *have* heard of it though. Your fiancé has excellent taste, Violet."

The waitress began to serve us our first tea with cucumber sandwiches.

After she'd gone, Miss Abernathy lifted her teacup; but before she took a sip, she said, "Vance had actually asked me to suggest a meeting place, Mrs. Hawthorne, but I'm glad you approve of my choice. It is a favorite of mine. And I'm so glad you asked us to join you, dear." She'd turned to me for this last part. "I had no idea you thought of inviting us along when I suggested it."

"I'd—well, I wasn't actually aware that Vance had made the inquiry of you, Miss Abernathy. But I'm glad you could come to enjoy one of your favorite places. It is wonderful."

It was actually more than wonderful. It was exquisite. For being simple tea rooms housed in a brick Queen Anne style mansion, it had all the dark elegance of Everwood inside.

"Roxy, how do you like The Propylaeum? Aren't you glad we came?" Miss Abernathy asked.

"It's beautiful," was all Roxy answered.

When it was clear that this conversation was going nowhere, I took a few cucumber sandwiches from the serving dish and collected them onto my plate. "Did you bring a cab, or do you have a carriage waiting, Aunt Letty?" I asked.

"My brother, Cal—whom Violet has yet to meet—dropped us off on his way out of town." Mabel answered for her mother. "He'll be back for us by six o'clock."

"What does Cal do for a living?" I asked, truly curious, since Vance had wondered. "We never discussed much about him last week."

"He does something with horse auctions here in Boston." Mabel clinked her teacup gently into its saucer. "I'm not really sure what, but it's the reason we moved here from Westborough four years ago."

Mabel didn't seem to be in near as delightful mood as she'd been while Vance and I had visited their home. It hadn't been too noticeable until this mention of her brother's job. Or maybe it had to do with their move to Boston? She had to have only been around thirteen or fourteen years old when they'd relocated.

Mabel's grayish-blue eyes nervously took in our surroundings, and then over and over I watched as they landed upon the open entrance to the next room, as if she were watching for something—or someone.

Roxy stuffed the last of a cucumber sandwich into her mouth, and when she was finished chewing, she said, "That sounds interesting. I mean about the horse auctions. I have a horse named Pip. My brother paid to have her brought down—along with his—on the train."

She was a rather shy young woman, and this was more than I'd ever expected her to say—but then I quickly wondered if that would be the extent of her contribution, so that outgoing Miss Abernathy wouldn't be able to criticize her about not participating.

"I've never been to a horse auction, have you, Violet?" she continued.

"Father and Ezra always took care of things like that. I've never had a horse for riding, but I've always wanted to try."

The conversation became awkward from there, as I couldn't help but be distracted by Mabel's gazing off toward the doorway. What was she looking for? I was beginning to regret combining my two worlds so soon. Perhaps I ought to have waited to get to know Mabel more on a private level before taking her out to place where she obviously didn't feel comfortable.

"I don't especially care for horses," Miss Abernathy said decidedly. "But dogs! Now that's another matter entirely!"

Aunt Letty gave a little coo of delight and launched into the virtues of her own dearly departed canine. As they discovered they were both seriously in the market for a puppy, the conversation effortlessly piled onto itself, and I breathed a sigh of relief.

With absolutely nothing to contribute on the subject, I glanced about the room. My gaze landed on Mabel's empty doorway, and I thought I saw Rowen Steele.

Or, at least half of Rowen Steele. Well, half of his face as he peaked around the doorframe and then disappeared.

Had it really been him, or was my imagination playing tricks on me because of Mabel's strange behavior? It seemed to have looked just like the same person in the lumber pamphlet Vance had shown me.

Suddenly I wished I'd kept the pamphlet; that I'd had it stuffed in my reticule so I could stealthily take it out and compare. It couldn't really be him, could it? How would he know I'd be at The Propylaeum Tea Rooms in Boston on a Saturday afternoon? And what did he plan to do, if it was him?

Just as I was about to suggest to everyone that we leave earlier than planned, a hand cradled the back of my left shoulder. I jumped in my seat so drastically I almost spilled my tea before practically dropping the cup to its saucer.

"Vance!" Miss Abernathy was the first to speak—and immediately put my mind at ease. "Here, pull up the seat next to Violet."

He had placed his hand on my shoulder for a brief moment—only long enough to unexpectedly terrify me—and then had gone in short search of an extra seat to add to the table. I was still visibly shaking when he brought his chair next to mine and sat down.

"I'm sorry; I didn't mean to scare you." He leaned slightly toward me, not trying to whisper at all.

"What are you doing here?"

"I was in the area, and I couldn't help but stop to see you."

"Of course you couldn't," Miss Abernathy said, obviously having heard our not-so-quiet discussion. She winked at me, smiling giddily. "I do love Violet *for* you, Vance. I'm so glad you love her too."

I nearly choked on the bite of a scone I'd taken to keep from having to acknowledge her wink. Once I was able to swallow, I said, "I was just thinking we were about finished."

Mabel pouted. "Are we? It's only a little after five o'clock, and Cal won't be back for us until six." She'd stopped looking at the doorway where I'd thought I'd seen Rowen Steele, but that, I had a strong suspicion, was because Vance was sitting beside me and had effectively caught her attention. Half the ladies in the room were looking at him, in fact.

"Let's not leave yet. We haven't even made it to the pastries and truffles." Aunt Letty looked at the slip of paper describing the courses. "The desserts are the best part of having tea out like this."

"Oh yes, the pastries and truffles! We must stay." Miss Abernathy slowly spread some jam over a scone. "We aren't in a hurry, are we? Just because Vance is here, and now all you want is to be with him." She smirked, knowingly. "I really cannot blame you though; he is quite the catch."

I suddenly felt as if I were suffocating between the five of them; all of them staring at me, thinking Vance and I were happily in love and engaged because of that. And it was all based on lies. Or mostly lies, at least.

"Perhaps I just need some air. If you'll excuse me, I'll be back in a minute." Leaving my gloves and reticule in my chair, I slipped from my seat and left the table.

Vance stood as I did, but he didn't follow me the short distance to the main entrance. I exited to the porch which extended around the front corner of the house with a wide circular area intended for a large gathering. There were a few tables and chairs there, but the outdoor seating had obviously not yet been open for service for the spring and summer months.

After taking a seat and relishing a few deep breaths, I tried to settle my nerves. I leisurely examined the intricate woodworking that made up the painted trim of the porch, but at a movement behind the curtains at a window along the side porch, I realized how foolish I'd been to go out there alone. What if it really had been Rowen—?

I stood and hurried back around the corner of the house to the front door—and found Vance coming outside. I refrained from propelling myself into his arms, but just barely.

What did it matter that he didn't love me yet? He was still my guardian and protector, and really, there wasn't anyone I felt safer with. I'd always been a cautious one with my feelings, and it still stunned me how he'd been able to—with his frankness and honesty—get me to a place where I trusted him so completely.

He closed the door behind him. "Did you like the tea room?"

"Yes, but I'm not very well-studied in the art of socializing." I reached up and grabbed hold of the nearest post, for lack of anything better to do. "It's been awkward at times."

"You'll get used to it before long, Violet." Vance took a few steps to close the distance between us and took a seat against the railing a few feet from me. "Claudine and your aunt seem to get along. Were they talking about puppies? And Roxy and Mabel both seem about your age, right?"

Well, at least one of them was, and I became suddenly curious about how old Vance thought I was. He couldn't have been much older than me, but his comment made me think he definitely thought me much younger.

"How old do you think that is?"

"I don't know; eighteen?"

"Really?" It was no wonder he'd treated me with so much precaution. He really thought I was as young as that? "Mabel might be eighteen, but I think Roxy's around the same age as Estella, and me. I'm twenty-three."

"Are you really?"

"I wouldn't say twenty-three is decrepit, but does it matter?"

"I'm actually relieved to hear you're not eighteen. At least, in a way." He crossed his arms over his mid-section and grimaced, and I wasn't sure how to take that.

"And how old are you?" I asked, moving a step closer, dragging my hand along the rail he sat upon.

"Twenty-eight, at the end of next September."

"You thought there was nearly a decade between us?" I stepped closer, testing his resolve. "Five years difference *is* better, isn't it? You must have thought me to be such a baby."

"Not exactly a *baby*, but it didn't really matter how old you were at first; you needed my help, and so I gave it. Your being years older than I thought does make me feel better about…our engagement."

I wondered if this revelation about my age would help loosen the rein he'd put on himself regarding our relationship. Now that he knew I was twenty-three and not eighteen, would it make a difference? I hoped so.

"Let's sit a while, away from the others. I don't think they'll mind." Vance stood, took my hand and guided me to where the tables and chairs were situated. He then helped me into a seat facing the side porch, took the seat across from me and didn't let go of my hand. Though I'd seen him smile before, none of the other times compared to how he virtually beamed now.

I willingly gave him my other hand, my heart soaring from this sudden attentiveness…and the fact that he'd stopped by in the first place, just to see me; that he hadn't been able to stay away. "I don't think they would mind at all."

Again, without asking anything in return, he gave so much. His warm blackish-brown eyes took their time as they seemingly burrowed into my soul, comforting me in ways no one had ever dared try before. Not even my parents who had always made me feel wanted and loved, had made me feel quite like this.

And it made me feel safe enough to confide in him: "Vance, I think I saw Rowen Steele in the tea room."

His dark eyes changed drastically at this. For once, he actually looked angry at me. "What are you still doing here, then? Why are you out here?" His grip on my hands grew stronger. "Is that really why you wanted to leave? What did he do?"

"If it was him at all, he merely looked at me from around the doorframe of the next room. But I'm not certain. It might even have been my imagination. Mabel kept acting strangely and looking that way, so I might have worked myself up into thinking someone was watching us."

"Violet, how long ago was this?"

"Right before you came up to the table."

"If it was him, he likely saw me come in and is long gone by now."

"Good," I sighed, relieved to hear such logic from him.

"I wish you'd told me sooner—"

"Would you have gone after him?"

"I would have; and I would have made sure he never wanted to see your face ever again. Or mine."

"How would you have done that?"

"Let's just say, he would have been thoroughly persuaded, and leave it at that, shall we?"

The main entrance to the tea rooms burst open and Mabel raced through, huffing for breath, "Violet, Mr. Everstone! Come quickly, Mother isn't feeling well at all."

Vance stood, bringing me to my feet as he did, and hurried us inside behind Mabel. Many of the people who had been sitting, having their tea, were now standing around, giving Roxy room to situate Aunt Letty onto the floor. Miss Abernathy—who was well over sixty years old—remained in her seat, a hand over her worried mouth.

Crouched beside Roxy, Vance asked, "What is it? What happened?"

"She started saying ridiculous things that didn't make sense, and then she grew faint, holding onto her shoulder as if it pained her. And now look at her, she's burning up."

"Mrs. Hawthorne?" Vance asked gently, "Can you hear me?"

"Yes, Mr. Everstone, but I'm feeling so weak. Do you think you can manage a way to get me home?"

"Of course, that was going to be my first suggestion. Do you have a carriage outside?" This was directed more to Mabel than my aunt, but they both answered in the negative.

"We'll take you in mine. Roxy, please alert my groom that we need the carriage. You'll see the Everstone crest on the side."

Roxy obeyed Vance without a word, running out the door.

For the first time since coming into the room, Vance took his eyes off of my aunt, his gaze searching the crowd until it landed on me. He reached up, took my hand and pulled me down to kneel beside him. "I'm not taking her all the way to South Boston like this. I hope you don't mind, but I'd like to have my family's personal physician examine her."

Aunt Letty heard this, and whimpered, "Oh no, I couldn't afford that—"

"I'll take care of it, Mrs. Hawthorne; you just focus on staying alert. We don't need you to faint on the way there."

Mabel reached for her mother's outstretched hand. "But Cal is supposed to collect us from The Propylaeum around six o'clock."

"We'll leave a message for him with the staff in hope that he'll join us at Dr. Meade's house, and then eventually be able to take his mother and sister home from there." Vance helped Mabel lift her mother to her feet. "Assuming she feels well enough to go home."

"Roxy and I will come along in the carriage to Dr. Meade's house. We wouldn't want there to be a chance that you and Violet would be left to travel across town in the dark, alone," Miss Abernathy stood with the help of her cane. "I know, I know, you're engaged already, but I would feel better if I could come."

"Come if you want," Vance spoke over his shoulder. "You know I have plenty of room."

14

Going Home

"Kiss me, so long but as a kiss may last!"
—Percy Bysshe Shelley

Vance's carriage did fit the six of us, fortunately. It was wide and spacious. Miss Abernathy insisted upon sitting next to my aunt, which meant Roxy sat with them in the frontward-facing seat, and I sat in the seat facing the back of the vehicle with Mabel and Vance on either side of me.

It was the first time Vance and I had been forced into such a position, squeezed up against each other as we were. I was pressed against his side as he sat with his legs sprawled out. I tried to breathe normally for those twenty minutes it took to get to the doctor's house; I tried to focus on my aunt and how she was feeling, but the intense warmth I felt from sitting so close to Vance was distracting, to say the least.

Upon arriving to Dr. Meade's fashionable residence in one of the row houses of Beacon Hill, the housekeeper met Vance and I at the door. After Vance had explained the situation—that he wanted the doctor to examine his fiancée's closest and dearest relative—Dr. Meade brought out two male servants equipped with a lightweight portable bed to help bring my aunt into the house. Dr. Meade's wife, who had remained inside with the housekeeper, greeted us amicably and led the entourage to a spare bedroom on the main floor, which was decorated just as finely as what I'd seen of the rest of her generously sized townhouse.

Upon arriving, Vance sent a missive to his family at Everwood explaining what had happened and that he and I were in the company of Miss Abernathy. All of this fuss wasn't what I'd expected from him at all, but I certainly couldn't complain. Surely, Aunt Letty would get the best care for whatever ailed her, and it was all because of Vance's thoughtfulness.

By the time Aunt Letty had been thoroughly examined, more than enough time had passed for my cousin Cal to have received the message regarding his mother at The Propylaeum. And yet, after we waited another hour for the doctor to decide whether he would have Aunt Letty stay close at hand in case the episode repeated itself, Cal *still* hadn't arrived.

Dr. and Mrs. Meade were more than happy to let Mabel stay the night with her mother; since it was determined it was most likely her heart which had been acting peculiar. And just as this had been decided, there came a knock to Dr. Meade's front door.

Vance and I had turned down the hall as the doctor's housekeeper opened the door, and I spotted someone who looked as if he could very well be my brother Ezra's twin enter through.

Since there really was no one to make introductions for us, Vance quickly walked me toward the front door and interrupted the housekeeper's questions, "I assume you're Violet's cousin, Mr. Cal Hawthorne? I'm her fiancé, Vance Everstone." He let go of my hand and offered it to my cousin, "And this is your cousin, Violet, of course."

"It's a pleasure to meet you both." Cal took Vance's hand and turned to me as he shook it. "Yes, I'm sorry I wasn't able to make it back at the time I'd indicated to my sister. I looked forward to meeting you at the tea rooms, under better circumstances than this."

I smiled in agreement and shook his hand as well. He didn't seem to be a no-gooder. Although he looked very much like Ezra, there was a difference in the upright way he carried himself. He was also dressed well and had impeccable manners.

He continued, "I had a bit of a run-in with some scoundrels along the road on my way back into town." At this, Cal's eyes shifted downwards, and I suddenly wasn't sure whether to believe him or not.

I spied Vance checking the time in a nearby grandfather clock, and decided it was probably too late in the evening to continue the visit. "We should probably go; Vance's family knows of the situation, but they are expecting us home soon."

"Don't let me hold you up; it was a pleasure to make your acquaintance. I've heard so much from mother and Mabel."

"We'll have to have the three of you to dinner at Everwood," Vance offered. "And my father's wedding is coming up. It's a private affair, but I think we can squeeze in a few more invitations. I'm sure the rest of my family would love to meet Violet's closest relatives."

At Vance's not-quite-true words, Cal's eyes again shifted downward, and I wondered just how much he knew about my rascal of a brother.

"That's a gracious offer," my cousin answered, "which I'm sure we wouldn't be able to refuse, Mr. Everstone."

⌒

It was already around nine o'clock—much later than I'd imagined it would be—when Miss Abernathy, Roxy and I set out for Back Bay with Vance in his carriage.

"To Hilldreth Manor," Vance directed to his groom.

Miss Abernathy had just seated herself next to Roxy inside and answered him through the open door. "Oh no, you ought to take Violet home to Everwood, and then drop us off—"

"It is fine; it will only be a few minutes from Hilldreth Manor to Everwood, and not worth the running about."

"Oh dear, I suppose, since you are engaged already, a few minutes' privacy in a carriage won't hurt anything."

"Thank you, Miss Abernathy. I know we're all exhausted, I'd just like to get everyone home as soon as possible."

"That does sound like a grand plan."

Not much was said on the ride to Hilldreth Manor. We were all tired after such an evening.

And then there was Vance—my ever-favorite subject to think and worry about...and daydream about.

He was seated across from Miss Abernathy, Roxy and I on the way from Dr. Meade's house to Hilldreth Manor. By the passing glow of a streetlight through the windows, I could tell that his eyes were fastened onto me for the entire ride. Was he thinking the same thing I had since he'd explained his plan to drop them off first—that it would leave us alone in the carriage?

Vance hadn't said much to me while at Dr. Meade's; he'd been too preoccupied with taking charge of the situation and making sure everything was as he wanted. Miss Abernathy, Roxy, and I had spent the majority of the time in Mrs. Meade's parlor, having more tea to make up for the fact that we'd missed half of what would have been served to us at The Propylaeum.

When Miss Abernathy and Roxy were both safely behind the doors of Hilldreth Manor, the carriage slowly lurched forward down Commonwealth Avenue toward Everwood. Without a second thought, I quickly took advantage of the steady lamplight, stumbled across the open space between our seats, and landed with an inelegant thud beside Vance.

"Oh, Vance," I almost sobbed as I cuddled my right shoulder in between his body and his left arm, burrowing as deep as I could, wrapping my left arm about him. "What a day."

He didn't answer, and I closed my eyes, my cheek rested against his chest. I could hear his heart beat wildly beneath my ear, but my comfort really came in having his left arm wrap around me, bringing me closer. Of all the times he'd made me feel like melting inside from heated glances and gentle caresses, this was such a different sensation—as if we were melding together, becoming one.

Despite how secure it felt to have him hold me like that, the troubles from the day would not leave me.

Rowen Steele was still a threat.

Why was Mabel suddenly so distant?

How ill was my aunt? Would I lose her so soon after finding her?

And what was my cousin Cal really like?

Once I'd settled my mind a bit, and my breathing calmed, I opened my eyes to the darkness and pulled away from our tight embrace. I felt foolish for throwing myself at him as I had, even if it had only been for a much-needed hug.

Vance was loathe to let me go; I could tell. His strong arm stayed in place, and I didn't try to escape again. He peeled the glove off of my left hand and held it with his right, slowly pressing each of my fingertips to his lips. He let out a long breath. "We really ought not to—"

"I know."

"We've already been thoroughly compromised as it is, and forced to marry."

I loosened my left hand from his grasp and reached for his face, blindly taking in every beautiful angle of his strong jaw, soft lips, and chiseled nose with my bare fingers. "I think *compelled* would be an appropriate word to use for us...for what's happened...and what's happening between us."

I felt his lips lift into a smile under my fingertips at my use of his own words.

He used to be such a different man, infamous for his scandalous exploits. It grieved my heart to think of all he'd been forgiven, but somehow by knowing the redeemed man, I couldn't help but feel for him, so deeply. More than I would have thought possible with any man only weeks ago. The unexplainable connection between us promised so much, if only he would let me in.

Vance brought his hand to hold mine against his warm cheek. He then kissed my palm. He had to feel it. It couldn't just be the fact that we were forced—or compelled—to marry.

"It's only appropriate that this all started with something as pure as my desire to help you out of the dire circumstances you weren't even aware were a threat." He pulled back the lacy cuff of my sleeve, his mouth creating a burning trail to my wrist, where he stopped, and simply held the evidence of my raging feelings to his lips.

I sucked in my breath, tried to breathe normally—but it was impossible.

"But in return for this gallant effort, Violet, you've stolen my peace."

And that's when the carriage stopped in front of Everwood.

I closed my eyes, wishing it didn't have to end. Vance let go of my wrist, then took his arm from about my shoulder. By the time I opened my eyes and tried to effectively gain some control over my emotions in hopes of seeming perfectly normal to anyone else I might come upon, Vance had exited the carriage and was holding the door for me.

I came down the metals steps, his bare hand holding mine as I did so. I tried to hurry away up the sidewalk, unsure of what to do, but he held me back, linking his hand to my elbow.

"Thank you, James," Vance called over his shoulder to his groom. "Go on ahead."

The carriage creaked down the street on its way around the block to the alleyway behind Everwood.

Vance walked me the short distance to the door close beside me, but there was a sudden urgency about the way he did so that I didn't understand. Was he trying to get me into the house, in the presence of anyone else so he wouldn't be forced to continue the conversation from the carriage?

But then he stopped me under the stone archway, basically an alcove far from the lamplight, right there along the street where no one would see us...unless someone from inside Everwood were to open the door.

Vance stood before me, but since we were enveloped in darkness, I couldn't tell exactly how close he'd come. "I want you to understand something, Violet."

"What is it?" I asked, sure that now I would be reprimanded for my emotionally overzealous behavior in the carriage, forcing him to admit things he apparently wasn't comfortable sharing.

"The slightest thought of you wreaks havoc within me."

That obviously wasn't what I expected to hear from him.

"I care for you, Violet," he continued. "More than I've cared for anyone else—"

"Anyone, ever?" I hardly knew how to believe him, but everything from the carriage moments before came crashing back. Yes, I could believe it. And I would.

"There's a closeness between us I've never experienced." Suddenly there was a new apprehensiveness to his words, as if admitting as much took some effort. "Have you?"

"Never."

"Not with Ben?"

"Why must you bring him up? There was nothing—" I reached into the darkness between us and quickly found the lapels of his jacket. He was actually already much closer than I'd imagined.

I wanted to shake Ben Whitespire from his head. But instead of shaking Vance—I would never have been able to anyway—I just brought him closer. He took a step, closing the distance between us. We were but an inch apart.

He let out a long breath. "I'm not sure if kissing you is a good idea."

"It is," I sighed, "most definitely. Let me assure you...."

"I've never held myself back from anyone so diligently, Violet."

I loosened my clutch upon his jacket.

"I don't think you realize," he leaned in over my shoulder, breathed the words against my ear, "just how difficult it is for me not to want to try everything I know. It's so easy...it would be so easy...."

"I don't want everything, Vance. I just want...something."

Without a word, Vance tipped my chin, and slightly tilted my head so I felt his breath against my jaw. And that was where he kissed me, at first.

My fingers again clawed into his lapels, bringing him crashing into me, pressed against me. He backed me against the stone wall bringing his face to mine. My eyes were shut against the darkness, but I felt how close he was to all of me. I couldn't resist him being so tantalizingly within reach, and I nudged his nose with mine, urging him to do what I couldn't do myself.

He lifted my jaw again, and this time, he finally brought his lips against mine, and I finally, truly knew what melting was like. All of those other times I'd felt like pooling to the floor were nothing to this. His smooth lips moved gently, effortlessly over mine, and I pressed in farther, shifting one hand to the back of his neck, wanting to convince him I was indeed kissing him back, in case he wasn't sure. At this, he tilted his head a bit more, deepened the kiss, and somehow managed to moan my name at the same time. His hands were at my waist, pulling me close.

I brought my palms to his face, my fingers rested against his cheekbones, trying to understand how I'd come to this; how I'd ever come to fall in love with Vance Everstone.

"Violet," he repeated quickly, between kisses and labored breaths, his hands still pressed against the small of my back. "Violet, you have no idea—"

I broke away just enough to speak, but quite breathlessly, "You're right, I really don't—"

With his lips still just barely against mine, and his hands not letting up, he whispered: "Ben wouldn't be doing this if he—"

"I don't want him the way I want you."

At this sudden turn, his hands eased off of my back, and his lips slid to my jaw, and then my ear, until he simply breathed into my hair.

I would never be able to walk from the sidewalk to the front door ever again—passing that exact spot—without blushing profusely. "We should go inside; your family is probably—"

"I'm not going in." His voice seemed heavier than before. "Not right now." He let go of me completely and backed a few steps away.

"But your family—"

"You can explain all that happened, and that I dropped you off. I need to go."

"I don't think they would mind that you—"

"Violet, trust me. It's best that I leave right now. Having more... of this...." He motioned to the space between us. "It's too tempting." Vance took a step for the door and pounded the knocker.

"What will I tell them?"

"Tell them I had things to do."

And before the Everstone's butler came to answer the door, Vance had disappeared out of the alcove and down the sidewalk, out of my sight.

15

The Walk

"*The heart has its reasons which reason knows not.*"
—Blaise Pascal

Sunday, April 24th, 1892

Has anyone seen Vance?" Nathan Everstone walked into the breakfast room, escorting his wife, Amaryllis.

"As far as anyone can tell, he never came home last night," Dexter answered. "Violet, did he explain where he was headed when he brought you home?"

I wanted to crawl back to my room at this abrupt news, and having to make Vance's vague excuses only made me feel all the worse. "He said he had things to do." I put my fork down, hardly able to think about taking another bite. I had so been looking forward to seeing him over breakfast. Where had he gone? And where was he now?

The general gist of our conversation before he'd left the night before raced through my mind, and a sudden vision of Vance's tousled hair and bare arm sprawled over my pillow in my dorm room came to me. Only now it wasn't my pillow, or my room, but someone else's....

Where could he be? Why hadn't he returned home?

Was it because he couldn't face me after that kiss? Had I done too much, pushed him too far? I'd unknowingly stayed up half the night deliriously and happily reliving every moment from the time we'd dropped Miss Abernathy and Roxy off at Hilldreth Manor to our time at the front door of Everwood. And now I wondered if I should have been crying instead, because I simply couldn't understand my fiancé.

"You could contact the office, perhaps he's spent the night there?" Natalia offered, trying to seem cheerful.

Dexter cleared his throat—not that it made a difference in how gruff his voice came out. "I've already sent someone to Everstone Square. He wasn't there."

"I'm sure he'll show up for church this morning," Natalia persisted. "He's probably...he's probably just—I bet he's at Fairstone. He did say the master suite was—"

"But why would he go there when he has a perfectly ready—and much warmer, I can imagine—room here?" Natalia's husband, George, reasoned. "It's not as if Fairstone is livable."

"Well, wherever he is, he'll show up soon enough. That's how Vance is, isn't it?" Estella sat down beside her husband. "Leave for Europe for years with nary a word to any of us, and then he just drops right back into everything like it was nothing."

Although there were some days I didn't see Vance at all, I'd at least known he'd be around, never far away. That seemed to have made all the difference between my feeling safe and secure in his protection—if not always in his regard—and not. For now, knowing that he'd purposefully left for the night with no real explanation to me or anyone, I felt like I hardly mattered to him. Despite the fact that he'd kissed me quite thoroughly right before he'd left.

I still could hardly believe he'd finally allowed himself to kiss me, yet his not joining the rest of his family inside the house and then never coming home for the night confused me. Was he mad at me because I'd wanted too much from him—more than he was apparently ready to give? Or was he angry with himself because his resolve had been broken? Perhaps he thought I would give in too easily before the wedding.

I wouldn't though. My resolve was strong.

Not wanting to burst into tears at the breakfast table, I excused myself and hurried up to my bedroom, my sanctuary. And that was where I nearly lost my composure. Was this what my life would consist of now and forever? A husband who disappeared to only God knew where with no word of explanation?

Being in love with Vance Everstone wasn't something I ever would have thought possible, but it was undeniable. And it hurt. Because although he wanted me, he still obviously didn't love me back.

⌒

Vance still hadn't come home by the time we were leaving for church. I'd calmed myself by then, and tried to convince myself that he simply already left Everstone Square by the time Dexter had sent someone there, because I really could not imagine him staying at Fairstone. It had been frigid inside the house even in mid-April, after having been shut up all winter long.

I'd walked the four blocks to Trinity Church with Amaryllis and Nathan, with little Rafe in his tram, while everyone else took the carriage. Vance still hadn't shown up by the time his entire family was congregated in their family's pew at the church. I sat at the end of the pew, between Estella and the aisle near the windows since I'd been at the end of the line as we'd filed in. I'd also been dragging my feet a little, looking around, hoping to see Vance arrive.

But he hadn't.

By the time the service had begun, I'd given up on him joining us. I didn't know what I would say to him when I saw him again.

I had too many feelings overwhelming me...between missing him, loving him, and wanting to strangle him.

As I stood with the rest of the congregation and flipped to the page indicated, the massive pipe organ began and Vance slipped into the pew to stand beside me.

And of course, the hymn we would be singing would be "Jesus Paid it All."

Of course, of course.

"I hear the Savior say / 'Thy strength indeed is small; / Child of weakness, watch and pray, / Find in Me thine all in all.'" Vance's deep voice resounded next to me, as I found myself whispering the words. My chest was too tight to sing.

By the time I regained my composure, everyone had sung a few verses, and I started in with the first words of the next line before I realized which verse it was; *"Lord, now indeed I find / Thy pow'r, and Thine alone, / Can change the leper's spots / And melt the heart of stone."*

I could feel Vance's gaze on me; and out of the corner of my eye—because I couldn't help but look—I saw him smile. I ignored him, turning slightly to the left, toward Estella, who grinned at the sight of her prodigal brother.

When the hymn was finished, and right before we were to sit, Vance muttered, "Beautiful, as always, Violet."

I still wouldn't look at him, though I could feel the air between us practically sizzle, charged with vivid memories from the night before. But so many thoughts and worries had bombarded me since then!

Fortunately the service began as we sat down and I could ignore him—and constantly think of him—in peace, without having to answer whatever he'd meant by what he'd said. Did he mean me? Or my singing? Or both?

As the preacher began his sermon, I found my eyes wandering until I spotted Ben Whitespire sitting at the other end of the long pew with Miss Abernathy and Roxy Blakeley. Recalling more of the night before than I should—especially during church—I tried to imagine Ben ever having such struggles regarding me. Although he'd never indicated any strong feelings for me, now I wondered if it was merely due to his mild personality. It wasn't as if he'd had any competition for me in Laurelton. I was sure he'd never counted Vance Everstone as such!

Ben and Vance really couldn't have been more opposite if they had tried. Meekness versus volatility. And yet, even as I respected Ben's mild manners, I was enigmatically pulled to Vance sitting beside me. And it wasn't just because we were now engaged, or that we were inexplicably attracted to each other. I'd felt it long before anything more than two words had been passed between us.

I didn't want to believe the worst, that Vance had turned from kissing me for the first time to...whatever it was he used to do before he'd become a Christian. But I was afraid. Mostly for the survival of my heart if it were true. Where had he been if not at home? He'd said he would be faithful...but what if that only meant *after* we were married?

I felt a tug at the skirt of my dress and tipped my head just enough to see that Vance had a hold of a small fold of the blue and white striped material. I shooed his hand and shifted over a little to the left, away from him.

"And now, I'd like everyone to stand for the reading of the Word," the preacher announced upon finishing the opening of his sermon. "Please turn to Romans chapter eight, verse one."

I stood, along with everyone else, and opened my Bible. Vance had his small, pocket-sized Bible open as he stood beside me.

"*There is therefore now no condemnation to them which are in Christ Jesus, who walk not after the flesh, but after the Spirit....*"

And there I was condemning Vance before giving him a chance to explain himself. I hoped he *would* explain, that there really was an amazingly believable reason he'd been missing for an entire night.

For the rest of the sermon, I had a hard time not condemning myself for passing judgment on Vance when I didn't know anything for sure. My fears were pretty convincing though, and by the end of the service, my heart was about as lost as ever. I didn't know what to think or believe.

As soon as the congregation was excused and started to disperse from their seats, Vance grabbed my hand and squeezed in between me and the pew to better speak with Estella and Dexter.

"I'm going to take Violet for a walk to the public gardens; but we'll be home in time for lunch." After telling them this, he then thought to turn to me, "Is that all right with you, Violet? There are things I'd like to—"

"Of course. I'd love a walk," I answered. Hopefully our time together would provide some much-needed answers.

Upon gaining everyone's approval, Vance led me to the back of the sanctuary and out the front doors of the church. Taking an immediate right, silently, arm in arm, we headed east back around Trinity Church—which was the largest, most elaborate church I'd ever seen. I couldn't pull my eyes from the stunning architecture as we passed.

"The park is about three or four blocks up Boylston from here; have you been there yet?" Vance caressed my arm through my dress as he guided me down the street. With each touch, every detail from the night before exploded into my memory, and I had to force myself from reciprocating his touch.

"I've gone a few times with Natalia and Amaryllis, walking the babies in their trams. We go straight down the boulevard down the middle of Commonwealth Avenue." When he didn't comment, I added, "Where did you go last night?"

"Well, first I came here." He motioned toward the church with his free hand. "You probably haven't met him, but my brother

Nathan was mentored by a man named Grig Wellesley when he lived in Boston last year. Dr. Wellesley works for the church, mostly in the way of organizing ministries."

"I've never heard of him."

"Well, he's my mentor now, and I needed a good dose of accountability last night, so he met with me."

"You spent the night at the church?"

"I spent a good part of the evening in the sanctuary. And then I went to Fairstone for the night."

"But it's been shut up, and it's freezing—"

"I started the process of having it reopened this week."

"Oh, I see." I hoped that didn't mean he'd be moving out permanently. I didn't like the idea of being at Everwood without him.

"Do you, Violet? Do you see how difficult it is for me to sleep, lying in a bed just down the hall and around two corners from where you're lying in yours, just waiting for me?"

"I've not been waiting for you to come to my—!"

"Not literally." He gave me a little smirk, obviously amused by my fierce response. "But it is about all I can think about when I'm in my room at Everwood. That's why I stay out past dinner most nights. I wait until everyone has retired, and there's no chance of seeing you as you head to your room. I can't trust myself to not eventually follow you."

"I wouldn't let you in."

"You say that, and you may believe that with your whole heart, but I know from experience how easy it would be to change your mind." Vance squeezed my hand as it rested upon his arm. "It's so much better if I simply don't see you in the evenings."

I really didn't have any way of responding. I remembered quite vividly how convincing just a kiss could be, and he was right. How could I trust myself to be strong when I didn't know if I could be?

"I need you to understand that I know what it's like. I'm ashamed of how I've lived, but I also remember. I don't know what

I was thinking before all of this happened. There's no way I would have lasted without marrying someone before long. And I'm glad it's you."

I was too, most of the time. When he was open and honest and not shutting me out.

We'd finally made it to the park, and Vance led me to a tree with wide, low branches reaching out along the ground; one at just the right level to sit upon. He helped me take a seat amidst the just-blooming branches, and then sat beside me.

"So what did you want to talk to me about?" I asked.

He swiveled slightly toward me on the branch, and took my hands in both of his. "I wanted to tell you that I'd compromised Meredyth. In actuality; it wasn't a trick. And it wasn't planned. It happened years ago, one of the summers while I was attending Harvard."

I let out a slow breath. That wasn't so bad. I'd already known he'd done such things, I'd just never known it had involved someone so close to the family. And I was glad Meredyth now lived in Washington state. It would be ultimately easier that way. I would likely never see her again.

"Natalia knew, but since there wasn't a *reason* to get married, we didn't at the time. But Mere and I both felt that we ought to, eventually. That was, until I found myself in France with a wife."

"And Meredyth fell in love with Lawry."

"Fortunately, yes."

Learning this about Meredyth was shocking, but it also seemed to lighten my perception of what the members of the Everstone family thought of me. If one of the their closest friends had been forgiven for such a thing happening in her youthful past, maybe they weren't as secretly judgmental as I constantly feared, about how Vance and I had been forced to become engaged.

"I forgive you, Vance."

"But that isn't the whole story; there's more."

That was when I suddenly recalled how he'd said he should have married someone, but hadn't. Wouldn't that have been Meredyth?

"What is the whole story?" I asked, hesitantly.

"My family is under the impression—because I allowed them to believe what they wanted last summer, that Wynn was Giselle's daughter from a previous marriage. Because of her close relationship with Lawry and Meredyth, my family never really associated with her much, so it never occurred to them that she didn't know a word of French."

"It never occurred to me either."

"I'm sorry that it seemed Estella lied to you at dinner about a month ago, right before all of this happened. But to her, it was what she'd been led to believe." He stopped, and I looked into his face, waiting for more. "What I'm trying to say is Wynn is *my* natural daughter."

Sweet little Wynn. It made sense now, her dark features and the way he'd specifically asked about Lawry and Meredyth traveling back to Washington; the way he'd insisted she was better off with them, and how happy he'd been that I'd given her one of my books.

"Where is her mother?"

"She died over a year ago while I was still in France. I should have married her a long time ago—she was completely ruined because of me. I sent her money to live comfortably, and I wrote her letters. But I wasn't paying close enough attention—since I was in Europe—and the attorney I had taking care of everything pocketed most of what I sent, leaving Olivia and Wynn destitute. I didn't know, or I would have come home earlier and taken better care of them."

With every sentence he uttered, my thoughts—about everything—compounded, until I couldn't keep anything straight, at least beyond the fact that hearing such sordid details straight from his lips was something I hadn't been prepared for.

"Olivia died of consumption and Wynn had been living on the streets when Lawry happened upon her." Vance wouldn't look at me now; instead, he stared off down Arlington Street toward Commonwealth Avenue. He did, however, keep ahold of my hands, which I was thankful for. I didn't want him to shut me out ever again.

"I should have married her," he continued. "She'd been much like Ava Cagney once; attractive, charming, the belle of every ball, dozens of men after her hand in marriage. It surprised me she didn't find someone to marry her, but now, I have a feeling she was holding out hope for me to change my mind, and then, eventually, it was too late."

Would I ever feel normal again? Instead of numb? I didn't know what to think. And he had to live with the knowledge that this was his past, every single day. It was no wonder he was finally driven to the arms of Christ.

"Do you still forgive me, Violet? Because I don't blame you if you don't. I'm hardly able to forgive myself most days."

I didn't want my answer to come too easily, but there was also something bursting within that begged for me to forgive him. And oddly enough, through all the muck and mire, I still found that I loved him. I couldn't help it, especially not after witnessing this bruised and broken side of Vance Everstone. And as I'd noticed before, his heart *was* indeed strong, to be able to become who God wanted after being who he'd once been took a strength of character that I couldn't help but admire.

"This is why you shut me out sometimes, isn't it? Because you figured I would ultimately come to hate you once I knew the truth of your past?"

He finally turned back to me and purposefully caught my gaze with his own. "Don't you? Don't you regret everything that's happened between us? Don't you regret that you're stuck having to marry me?"

"I don't hate you, I don't regret anything, and I still forgive you."

He stared at me, and I began to wonder if he'd heard me. But then he finally said, "And you still want to marry me?"

"Yes."

"You're not disgusted by the thought?"

"No."

"You told your aunt that you hoped we'd have beautiful children. Was that true? Is that still true?"

I blushed, thinking back to that comment. "I've always wanted a family, Vance, and, God willing, there will be children included in our future together. And I would be quite happy if they all turned out as splendid as Wynn Hampton."

"I'll never deserve you, Violet Hawthorne. I hope you know that." He didn't smile now, though that was what I expected. He actually looked as if he were fighting off tears. "I'm glad God wanted more between us than just me rescuing you from Rowen Steele."

"I am too, Vance. I really am." How I wanted to kiss him, to reassure him! But I knew better than to do such a thing, even if we were somewhat hidden from anyone wanting to spy on our little meeting. "Do you think it was really Rowen Steele at The Propylaeum last night?"

"I can't be sure. I hadn't heard he was in town, but he may be laying low." By the look in Vance's eyes, I could tell he'd been able to read my desires from a few moments before, but then he continued with, "I contacted Dr. Meade concerning your aunt this morning, and in his missive back, he stated that he thinks it was a solitary episode. She simply needs to rest now, and take better care of herself."

"I should visit again this week, to see that she has everything she needs."

"I want to come with you when you go. If it was Steele you saw, and he knows of your relatives, and that's how he knew where to find you yesterday; we need to be more careful. He may use that connection to get close to you again. He certainly isn't going to come near Everwood. He would know better than that."

"Maybe Ezra told Rowen about our relatives at some point. I never know what to believe regarding my brother."

"Perhaps Cal is connected to Rowen," Vance said, echoing my own suspicion. "I know it seems we're convicting him of more than is appropriate for our brief acquaintance, but he seems a likely culprit."

Vance pulled out his watch, took the time, and then placed it back into his pocket. "We should get going. It's almost time for lunch to be served." He stood and offered me his hand.

I took it, and he lifted me to my feet. I stood facing him, still holding his hand as we were half hidden under the new foliage of the low-branched tree. I reached up and kissed him on the cheek, lingering there for a moment, hoping he'd turn his lips to mine. I breathed out a sigh when he didn't, but I couldn't blame him considering where we were. And somehow, just knowing that he *wanted to* kiss me was enough.

When I stepped back, he had a silly grin on his face. "That was safe enough, wasn't it, Vance?"

"And more enjoyable than I would have ever imagined."

I played with his fingers between us, lacing and unlacing them, then moving my thumb over his palm and the back of his hand, examining it simply because I could. "I'm glad you told me everything you did today."

"I felt I needed to. After last night, you needed to know what you were getting yourself into."

From our private little tree, we walked a bit more through the park, and then crossed where Commonwealth Avenue's middle boulevard ended at Arlington Street.

"Christ has forgiven you for your past, Vance," I added as we walked. "And so have I. Judging someone for the things they'd done before they were a Christian doesn't seem right. You're a new creation now, remember?"

"Who still struggles."

"Well, fortunately, you'll be married soon."

"If it weren't for Father's wedding in June, I'd be tempted to make ours happen no more than a week from today. But I can't usurp their celebration."

"And what about Fairstone? Although you've had the house opened, the transformation is hardly underway. It wouldn't be finished nearly in time."

"It could be. Throw enough money someone's way, and they will make what you want happen."

A little later, after we'd walked a ways in silence, Vance asked, "When shall we marry anyway, Violet? We'll want to have a date set when we announce the engagement, which we should do soon."

"How soon can our wedding be after your father's and still be considered proper?"

"Proper? I don't care what's proper beyond not stealing their thunder. I care about having you all to myself, and that is all."

"Well then, let's make it a month after their wedding. That seems proper enough to me."

"A month exactly it is then, what does that come to?" Vance pulled a pocket calendar from inside his jacket with his free hand and checked the dates. "How about Sunday, July the third? Will you marry me after church in exactly..." he stopped to count, "ten weeks from today?"

"I'm fairly certain I'm free. And yes, I'd be happy to." I couldn't help but smile at him as we came closer to Everwood.

The walk down Commonwealth Avenue had always seemed to have a magical feel to it every time I'd been down it. I sighed contentedly as Vance and I strolled under the canopy of trees lining both sides of the path. How altered my day seemed now from this morning at breakfast! Not to mention from a month ago when I'd been working at Everston and hardly deeming any interest from one of the most stunningly attractive men I'd ever met.

And there he was on my arm, walking down the most fashionable street in Boston, picking out a day to marry me.

16

Everthorne

*"Therefore if any man be in Christ, he is a new creature:
old things are passed away; behold, all things are become new."*
—2 Corinthians 5:17

Friday, May 13th, 1892

It sounds as if Ben's meeting with The Boston Inland Mission Society went well." Estella sat across the sitting area of the spacious front parlor of Everwood; she'd been drawing in her sketchbook while I wrote out some ideas for a new story.

"They're fortunate to have him," she continued. "I wonder what Lanie Whitespire will do now that her sister is to marry and her brother plans to move to Tennessee?"

"I can imagine they're already prepared for his news— why would any mission not want to take on someone like Ben Whitespire?"

"So true. But he'll need to find a wife soon; they prefer to take on couples opposed to unmarried young men." She kept her gaze on her drawing, and then went on without looking up. "Perhaps he and Roxy will come to an understanding."

"I hope so. Ben deserves to be with a good girl like Roxy Blakeley. They already have an acquaintance, and they seemed to like each other well enough."

"But I'm not sure she thinks she's physically durable enough to handle the demands of being the wife of a missionary. She does tire so easily."

"So you think Ben wouldn't consider her?"

"Likely not. She'll need to marry someone who has time to care for her, and I can't imagine a missionary—or a man in any kind of ministry position—would. Ben will need a partner, a wife to work right along beside him."

"I suppose that would be best," I answered.

"What about your cousin Mabel? How does she feel about missions work? Have you thought about introducing her to Ben?"

"I know my relatives attend church in South Boston, but I'm not sure about Mabel's opinion on becoming a missionary. Honestly, she seems too preoccupied with society to have an interest in meeting a missionary looking for a wife."

"Speaking of marriages, the plans for your wedding are coming along nicely." Estella grinned down at her drawing. "I know what it's like to plan one with so little time before the big day. Just eight weeks from tomorrow!" She looked up at me at this point. "Goodness, long engagements must be dreadful, don't you think? You're excited to be married soon, aren't you?"

"I have to admit, I wasn't sure how to feel at first, but I am looking forward to it now."

"You know, Violet, I could tell you and Vance already liked each other before that dreadful thing happened at the dormitory." She stopped drawing again to look at me, and only continued when she could tell she held my attention. "And I think you would have eventually found yourself exactly where you are today—though, perhaps, not quite as quickly—even without your brother's shady interference."

Before I could answer her, one half of the pocket door opened, and Vance abruptly entered the room. "Well, it is official, Violet. Oh, good morning, Stella."

I quickly shifted my notebook to the floor, kicking it underneath my seat. I still wasn't quite ready for him to see the random thoughts and doodles scattered about the pages.

"Good morning, Vance; has it been announced?" Estella asked.

I looked up momentarily, but I didn't move from my seat. It took everything in me to refrain from dashing into his willing arms.

"It's in all the papers." He crossed into the room smiling, looking only to me, and plopped a newspaper folded open to an inner page on the table beside me. "We're to be married, and now everyone knows it."

I took the newspaper from where he'd set it on the table and scanned down the articles until I saw the "Hawthorne-Everstone Engagement" heading. I held my breath, taking in the moment. I'd looked forward to seeing the engagement announcement—my name in print—linking me with Vance for all to see.

HAWTHORNE-EVERSTONE ENGAGEMENT

The marriage of Miss Violet H. Hawthorne & Mr. V. X. Everstone will be an interesting event on Sunday, July 3, taking place at two o'clock in the afternoon at Mr. Everstone's home on the 300 block of Dartmouth Street. The attendants will be the groom's sister, Mrs. D. K. Blakeley of Laurelton, Maine and the groom's brother, Mr. N. L. Everstone of Greenbank, Washington. A small acquaintance will witness the ceremony. Mr. and Mrs. Everstone leave immediately afterward for a wedding trip to Europe.

"And to celebrate, I'd like to take you to see Fairstone today," Vance said.

"I get to see it?" I asked.

"Is it finished?" Estella asked at the same time.

"It is, in fact—"

"Can I see it too?" Estella interrupted.

"Of course; I'd actually prefer to not take Violet alone."

"As it should be." Estella smiled as she rose from her seat, holding her sketchbook and pencils. "I'll go tell Nathan and Amaryllis."

As she left the room, she closed the door behind her. Her tactic, quite obvious: to give Vance and me some unplanned, uninterrupted privacy. However, when Vance sat down beside me, I scooted over a few inches down the sofa. I wanted him to kiss me—oh so badly—but I also wanted to respect the distance he felt we needed to keep.

He'd kept up his habit of not seeing me in the evenings, and sometimes coming home for lunch.

"This is an odd time for you to be home." I handed the newspaper back to him.

He looked uncomfortable for a moment, and then said, "Violet, I'm going to stay at Fairstone from now on."

"You're going to move permanently?"

"It isn't a bad idea, considering I don't need much but a bed. Away from you."

"You want to get away from me that badly?"

"Not *want*, Violet. *Need*."

It was strange, the contentedness that had come over our previously unsettled relationship in the weeks since our discussion at the park. It was as if we'd known each other forever and had mutually decided that yes, we would marry. And that it was, indeed, a fabulous prospect.

"We should leave soon so we can visit your aunt this afternoon."

I kicked my heel into my notebook under the sofa to ascertain where it had landed. I slipped out of my seat and knelt down—in a rather unladylike manner—in order to collect it.

Vance quickly knelt beside me. He took my right hand for support as I reached under my seat. "What are you doing?"

"I don't want to leave my things lying around."

"What things?"

At this, I produced my notebook and pencil. "My writing."

I could tell by the sudden gleam in his eyes that the subject still piqued his interest.

"I haven't taken you to meet Culver. He's still around, you know."

I'd thought back about that missed opportunity over the weeks, and although Vance had given back my book about the fox, I figured he'd probably bring it up again. And I would be better prepared when he did.

"Perhaps you could meet with him about it, and I wouldn't have to go? I can't imagine sitting there while a stranger looks through my things."

"If that's what you want, then I can do that." Vance still held my hand, though he hadn't even attempted to lift us to our feet. Kneeling before each other as we were, felt oddly more intimate than standing or sitting, and I wanted to lean in to him so badly, just to put my arms around him. But I knew what that would lead to. He *was* mine now though—well, almost. Half-attempting to visualize what all that would eventually mean took my breath away.

I shook the memory of our first kiss from my mind. "I'll go retrieve them from my room."

"Them?"

"I looked through all of my books, and figured it would be best if he saw them all at once." I still held on to my notebook, clutching it close in case Vance tried to look inside. But he didn't. He simply smiled. And then he helped me to my feet.

"I'll make sure I have time to show them to him this week."

"Don't tell me when you go. I don't want to know."

He led me out to the hall where we found Estella returning from upstairs. "I was told we need to be back by four. Dinner will be served early tonight, and we have guests coming: Claudine and Roxy, and Reverend Whitespire before he heads back to Maine tonight."

I started up the stairs in order to retrieve my manuscripts, and called over the railing, "Sounds like an interesting time. I think Miss Abernathy is hoping to make a match between them."

I smiled, happy I wasn't the only one who saw the wisdom of such a pairing.

"I'm just glad I'm already adequately attached to you so she isn't doing the same for me; bringing all the Ava Cagneys around, trying to capture my attention." His lack of sudden sourness at the mention of Ben surprised me, but perhaps he'd finally come to realize that our friend held absolutely no threat to my affections.

"It is quite apparent that your attention has already been snagged, Vance," Estella added. "You're not very good at hiding the fact."

"And why should I?" Vance laughed. "It's too fun to see all of you simper and smile sheepishly because of what's going on, wouldn't you agree, Violet?"

"Oh yes, I quite agree." And with that, I ascended the staircase, turning only slightly to see Vance's dark eyes follow my every step.

I had a total of seven stories I'd written and illustrated, the pages all bound together with grommets. I loved each and every one of them, but carrying the pile of them down the street a little later to take to Fairstone seemed dangerous. What if they were misplaced? I always knew where they were; they were that important to me. But as Vance had said, I needed to show someone who

mattered if I would ever have the chance of having them published. For some crazy reason he believed in me. And that gave me
confidence.

After a short walk down Dartmouth, we arrived to Fairstone,
but before Vance took out his key, he said, "I think you'll be pleased
with the outcome of the renovations, Violet, but if there's anything
you don't like, I am more than willing to change it."

"Oh, Vance, do open the door," Estella insisted, her hands
clasped together before her chest.

"I've hired a cook so far, and a housekeeper and butler," Vance's
continued to stall us at the steps. "But not too many of the other
positions yet. I know it's a larger house, but I wasn't certain how
many servants you would feel comfortable with, and I didn't want
to overwhelm you."

"I'm sure whatever you think is fine."

"Well, we'll have those three to begin with when we marry,
and I have my valet, and you have your maid. That should do for
a while." With that, he unlocked and opened the arched double
door. He let his sister in, but then purposefully stood before me,
keeping me from entering behind her. "And there's another thing I
wanted to tell you. I thought we'd call the house Everthorne from
now on. What do you think?"

"As in, Everstone plus Hawthorne?" I asked, completely
shocked by how much happiness one made-up compound word
could produce in me.

"Exactly."

"I do love it—the name Everthorne. It's perfect for us."

He finally opened the door for me to go inside, but I stopped
with only one foot on the threshold. What I saw took my breath
away.

Where before the debris from the destruction had littered
the dirty floor from corner to corner, now the polished wood
floors shone. Gleaming, dark wainscoting reached five feet up the

walls where it met the beautiful blue-and-aqua-striped wallpaper I'd picked out for the grand front hall. The rails of the massive wood staircase had been replaced with a different style, intricately carved, and the two new glittering chandeliers overhead sparkled when Vance pushed the button for the power.

I could hardly believe that this house *and Vance* would both soon be mine.

He came up behind me and took me by the hand and showed us to the front parlor where the walls had been papered with the same wallpaper as the front hall. The mantle of the fireplace had been replaced and Vance had the room furnished with the loveliest tufted beige furniture set I'd ever seen. In the next room, through double pocket doors, was a room with more seating, but also a piano. Did Vance play? I did—just a little—but nothing to warrant an entire room dedicated to music. But perhaps we would entertain in that room.

Across the hall abutting the back wall to the staircase, there was a dining room with a built-in sideboard along one wall with a number of leaded glass window cabinets and another fireplace at the end of the room. The dining table seated twelve, and I still could not imagine myself being hostess to so many guests for dinner!

Down the hall, toward the front of the house and across from the parlor, was a large library. After we'd gone through the main rooms, we headed to the back of the house where there was a small office, which I assumed was for the servants. And around the far corner from there was the kitchen and the back staircases—one going up to the next floor and another down to the basement.

Vance introduced us to his cook, Mrs. Paltrow, and then guided us toward the front of the house again, to the foot of the main staircase. "I think you'll be able to handle the rest on your own while I'm in the study."

As Estella and I ascended the richly carpeted stairs, she said, "It's a shame the ballroom is on the third floor. You will likely host at least one ball, eventually, I assume."

"Oh, the dreaded day."

"Balls aren't my favorite either, but I do look forward to the one after father's wedding in a few weeks."

"I've never actually been to a ball before, besides the small celebration at Everston for your wedding," I admitted.

"You know how to dance, don't you?"

"I was taught to dance. My mother knew how and although we didn't have balls and parties to go to in Westward, we had fun together." The thought that my mother and father would miss my wedding reached my heart for the first time, and I was suddenly overwhelmed with sadness.

"Fortunately, the ball won't be too elaborate. It will be private, with only the family and our closest friends."

Truly, the only thing that mattered to me about the ball was that I would be allowed to dance with Vance all I wanted. I'd have so much face-to-face time with him, while holding on to him and twirling around the room. With that perspective, I could hardly wait.

"Let's go on up to see the ballroom first." Estella took my hand and guided me to the smaller open staircase nearby that led to the next floor. "I have an idea something else might be up there too."

"What else would there be besides attic space, and possibly bats?" I cringed. "I truly hate bats. I was attacked by one once. You don't think…?"

"I doubt there will be bats in the rooms we'll look at. And we'll avoid the unfinished sections, just for your sake." Estella went ahead of me on the wooden stairs. "Not that bats are a special favorite of mine either."

My eyes lingered down the wide hall before following Estella up the steps. I remembered where Vance's room was from when

I'd been given my initial tour a few weeks ago, and where mine was attached. I couldn't wait to see it, but maybe Estella knew it would be more special if I saw it later with only Vance, once we were married.

At the top of the stairs there was a large landing with two sets of double doors on either side. The entrance to the ballroom was already wide open and Estella glided into the room, with me at her heels. I'd never actually been inside a real ballroom—Estella's wedding ball had been in the hotel's elaborate dining room.

But this...was amazing. It had to be the biggest room I'd ever seen. And surely, there couldn't have been much more on that level, seeing that the ballroom was about as large as all the space on the first floor put together. There were wall-hung electric lights situated every few feet and six chandeliers hanging from the ceiling.

Before I knew it, Estella had left the room, so I followed her out to the landing where she lingered outside the other double doors, which were closed.

"You should peak in. I think you'll be surprised."

"I assume that means you've already looked and haven't seen any bats?"

"No, I didn't see any bats."

I stepped toward the door, turned the knob, opened it a crack, and looked in. There weren't any curtains on the many windows in the large room, and the sun shown in, illuminating a black wrought iron crib, as well as a white bassinet.

Opening the door a bit farther, I took in more of the details. There was a fireplace situated in the corner with matching gray velvet chairs flanking it, a wooden rocking horse painted white, a tall wooden doll house, a few built-in dressers, a miniature piano and a wall of shelves filled with books and all kinds of toys.

Had this all been there before? Vance hadn't taken me to see the attic when he'd first shown me the house, so I didn't know what to make of it. Could it be that he was really that interested in starting a family?

I walked into the room, taking everything in. I wasn't sure how to feel about it, actually.

"It isn't uncommon to be prepared, but I must say, he's even more ready than I am, and I'm the one who's going to have a baby by Christmas."

"Oh, Estella! That's wonderful news!" I said, almost a little jealous. But how ridiculous; there I was standing in my own nursery. Surely my time would come soon enough. I pushed away the thoughts of how my mother was only able to have two children. "When do you think you'll have the baby?"

"November, most likely."

"Have you told anyone else?"

"Amaryllis and Natalia both already guessed, and I'll tell Father and Madame Boutilier right before the wedding. I don't want to distract them from the preparations."

It would be a joyous time for everyone. I still had a hard time believing this was my family now; that they had all welcomed me so entirely just because they thought Vance was in love with me.

"Do you really think Vance did this? What about Nicholette? Could it have been left—?"

"Vance said the only room finished when Will died was the master suite."

Oh yes. He had indeed said that.

Going over to the rocking horse, I tipped it forward, setting it in motion.

"Vance told me lately that Wynn was his natural daughter." Estella was across the room near what looked to be a closet. "And since Giselle was expecting when she died, perhaps he's already reconciled to becoming a father."

I'd never taken his feelings regarding Giselle's baby into consideration before; that Vance would have been preparing to be the baby's father—even if it hadn't been his—for the months they'd been married. He had said it was difficult to witness what had happened to Giselle, but he'd never mentioned why. Was it because of the loss of the baby?

"He also told me that he's told you everything concerning his past, and that you don't hold it against him."

"How could I? He was an entirely different person back then."

"Indeed, he was."

I turned to cross the room, intent on heading back downstairs in hopes of finding Vance. As I did, Estella opened the closet and ducked her head inside the dark compartment.

She immediately backed across the room. "Oh, it's an unfinished—ew, now I know what you meant."

Before she could reach over to shut the door, about a dozen screeching black winged creatures flew out of the closet, their rat-like bodies darting about the room haphazardly, the sound of their wings distinctly bringing back the vivid memory of the only other time I'd ever witnessed a bat—and how it had landed on my head with its claws entangled in my hair.

I ran out of the room, and heard Estella slam the door behind us and follow me down the steps.

Upon making it down to the second floor, I heard Estella start for the back stairs as I headed toward the main staircase. I wanted to get out the front door; I could just imagine a whole colony of bats coming after me.

But upon turning the corner of the hall, I collided with Vance outside his room.

He clamped his hands around my arms, bracing me before him, concern etched across his face. "Are you all right? I heard a scream."

Had I screamed? I didn't know. "There are bats in the attic—"

"So you made it to the—?"

"There were bats."

Vance chuckled; he wrapped his arms around me, drawing me closer. "I'm sorry, but did you happen to notice anything else besides the bats?"

His nearness and his laughter—although it was at my expense—somehow calmed me. The bats hadn't followed me down the stairs, after all, and suddenly I was in Vance's arms, which made everything else hardly matter. Yes, he could laugh at me all he wanted, as long as he would hold me while he did so.

"Yes, I noticed the nursery. Did you do that?"

He loosened his arms from around me, but then drew my hand to his chest. "Do you like it?"

"I loved it until the bats were introduced. We really need to finish off that section of the attic."

He laughed at me again, and this time, I was the one to grab him by the arms. I took a step nearer and lifted to my toes—just enough to catch his smiling lips with mine. He didn't fight me off as I was afraid he would, but sighed and immediately bent forward to finish the kiss…except it wasn't exactly finished. It had only just begun, and then kept going.

It wasn't a feverishly passionate kiss like the first one, either. Vance had again wrapped his arms around me, but his hands had stayed at my back, lightly pressing me to him. I put my arms around his neck, not about to let him go. After a few minutes, he uttered between our lips.

"So you liked the nursery." He leaned back, breaking the intense connection. He propped a finger under my chin, still tilting my face to his.

I opened my eyes slowly, and sighed. "It was thoughtful. I know you've mentioned it, but I didn't know you were so ready to have a family." I lifted to my toes to quickly kiss him again. It was much too heavenly to be that close; I was unable to stay away.

His mouth tipped into a small roguish smile as he allowed another small kiss. "I didn't know I wanted a lot of things until recently."

Vance gently took me by the elbow and guided me to the head of the stairs. "I'm not sure you've realized just how close to being a father I've already been with Giselle's unborn child. Her baby would have been my son or daughter, had it lived."

"I thought of that while upstairs." My heart hurt just thinking about the pain he must have gone through. I couldn't imagine losing a child, no matter what age. Was that part of the reason he'd decided to marry Meredyth right away upon returning from France: to create the family he'd already decided he wanted?

"I'd grown attached to the idea of being a father, and had been prepared, but now, it's not just about that. I want a life with you in this house, with our children."

"I still can't believe you want me—"

He stopped our progression, leaned in and added quietly, "It wasn't a chore meeting you back in October, Violet. Or getting to know you now. It's true, I cared very much about helping you, but I also had to be particularly careful since...since I wasn't accustomed to finding someone so attractive and then not also permitting myself to...." He stopped for a moment, and I could only stare at him in wonder. Was he serious?

"It was a constant struggle, Violet, to not revert to my old ways, to at least try and engage your interest in an indisc—"

"An indiscretion? With me? You thought I was attractive, in *that* way?"

"Can you not tell? It was awfully tempting to try..."

"I wouldn't have."

"I know." He took a step closer. "You were what saved me from even trying, Violet. You were a constant reminder of what I wanted to be like; strong in your faith and stubbornly obedient."

"I don't know how you could tell that—"

"Anyone could see as much if they only looked. And I'd been looking far too much for my own good...."

My emotions were in an uproar at these confessions from him. He'd wanted me from the very beginning of our acquaintance... and not just because he was stuck with me?

"Vance! There you are!" Estella started up the stairs toward us, Mrs. Paltrow lagging behind her. "Did Violet tell you about the bats? They're trapped in the nursery, everything will need to be cleaned, and I have no idea how you'll ever get rid of them."

"I'll hire someone to deal with it, Stella, don't worry."

"But your beautiful nursery! I'm so sorry to have opened that door—I thought it was merely a closet, and Violet warned me about bats."

"Did she now?" He slanted a grin my way. "But it can all be cleaned, dear sister, quite easily, in fact."

"We should probably be on our way to visit Aunt Letty," I said to change the subject as we all descended the stairs together.

"Have you had enough of Everthorne, already, Violet?" Vance asked.

"Everthorne? Have you renamed the house?" Estella asked. "How wonderful!"

"It is perfect, isn't it?" I said clutching my reticule with one hand and my fiancé with the other. Everything seemed perfect, actually.

17

Midnight

*"...And yet I have had the weakness, and have still the weakness,
to wish you to know with what a sudden mastery you kindled me,
heap of ashes that I am, into fire."*
—Charles Dickens, *A Tale of Two Cities*

A few weeks later, I trekked down to the dark basement-floor
kitchen of Everwood to eat my "real" dinner by lamplight,
as I usually did every evening once everyone else had retired to
their rooms. I would have been horrified if anyone in the family
ever found out, but I was desperate. After living in Boston for
close to two months, I still wasn't used to the richness of the food
served to the Everstone family. At times, dinner was downright
awful, and I choked down as much as I could of what I could stand,
while hoping not to insult anyone with how much of other dishes
I hardly touched.

From my first days at Everwood, I knew there were other
things to eat than what we were served at dinner every night.
Lunch wasn't usually too bad, and the servants obviously weren't
served the same things as the family. I would often be starving for
something tolerable to eat by the time I went to sleep at night.

After the first week of going to bed hungry, I'd taken up the
habit of making my way down to the kitchen at night to find something to tide me over until breakfast. I never saw anyone, but it

was obvious that the cook had noticed and taken pity on me. Now when I went down, I would find a simple plate made up of a combination of meat, bread, fruit, and cheese with a note labeled: *for Violet*.

Hopefully, Mrs. Paltrow would prove to be a simple cook. I hadn't met the two newest hired servants, but I'd heard all about the butler, Brubaker, and Mrs. Jefferies from Vance over lunch one day. I was extremely happy that I would be allowed to take my maid, Bessy, with me. Not that I felt I especially needed a maid, but I had grown fond of her.

As I finished up and placed my plate on the sideboard next to the large porcelain sink, I wondered for about the thousandth time how exactly Ezra had lost me in a bet playing poker. I didn't know the first thing about the game; how could a mere laying of cards have so much power over men and their decisions? And how was it that he'd actually "lost" me?

Looking through the books in the library didn't seem a likely way of finding out—there were too many to search through. I would simply have to ask Vance when I had the chance. Other than our carriage rides to go visit Aunt Letty and Mabel once a week, I'd really only seen him in the company of others since he'd taken me to see Everthorne. And we had behaved so well that day!

I didn't see him nearly as much as I would have liked since he insisted on staying at Everthorne. I really didn't think he needed to take quite so many precautions. It couldn't be *that* difficult. We'd kissed outside his rooms, even, and nothing had happened.

When I made it back to my room, I took my writing box out and looked my newly created books over again. In reading the ones I'd already created, I would often be inspired to write something new, sometimes keeping my light burning much longer into the night than I should. But there were usually no plans set for the morning hours, a luxury I found myself quickly adapting to. Having so much time did wonders for my writing too. I'd thought up a few more books since coming to Boston, had rewritten them to where I adored them, and had a number of illustrations for both.

I could still hardly believe how entirely Vance supported me in my dream of becoming published, although I knew it was impossible. Even if he had a friend who was an editor, that didn't mean a thing. It was simply too difficult. But just the fact that it meant so much to him to try to do all he could for me to achieve my dreams made my love for him grow.

It had been over two weeks since I'd given Vance my collection of finished books to show to Mr. Culver. But I wouldn't usually let myself think about that. I'd been nervous to show them to Vance in the first place, but now I was nervous to hear what his editor friend thought of them.

Just as I was about to turn out my lamp, I heard a clink against one of my windows. I stood, nearing them cautiously, listening. Again, the clinking sound—it came from my window facing the back courtyard and stables.

Pulling back the rose-colored jacquard velvet curtains from where they met at the middle of the window, I peered out while trying to stay hidden. There was a lamppost, fortunately, and I was able to make out Vance's form in the courtyard, staring at my window and holding a handful of pebbles. I immediately reached for the latch and swung both window panes out just as he was about to throw another pebble.

As I leaned out the window, I could tell he saw me just in time to avoid pelting me with stones.

"Violet, can you come down?" he whispered as loudly as he dared. "I have something I need to tell you."

"What is it? Can you not tell me from down there?"

"I need to see you. Meet me at the back door." And before I could answer, he'd moved closer to the house and under the roof of the back porch where I couldn't see him.

I quickly pulled my dressing gown on over my nightgown and pushed my bare feet into my slippers. My hair was down, but I didn't mind Vance seeing it. He'd said on a number occasions that he loved it that way, even if it was shorter than I liked.

I took the back stairs, thinking it would be faster, and unlocked the door—only then realizing that it could very well have been a trick. What if Rowen Steele had somehow forced Vance to ask me to come down, and I would be walking right into his grasp?

But the door opened, and only Vance stood there, looking so amazing I wanted to cry with joy over the fact that he was all mine. I almost launched myself into his arms. And although I'd contained my urge, I found myself there regardless.

He held me, his arms wrapped around me, without a word, for the longest time.

"Violet, I...I missed you."

"I've missed you too, Vance. So much. I wish we didn't have to spend so much time apart."

"I shouldn't even be here now, but I had to come right away to tell you we need to be careful associating with your cousins." I tried to stay close as he said these things, but Vance forced me to lean back, so he could look me in the eyes. "I just came from following your cousin Cal, and found him in the company of Rowen Steele."

"Oh no! Really? Why would he?"

"I'm not sure." Vance brought a hand to my neck, and then slowly cupped my jaw. "I'm not going to take you to see your aunt again, and I don't want you to go there on your own either."

"But they're my—"

"Your safety means too much to me," he whispered.

I responded just as quietly, "They might not know who Rowen Steele is, or what he's—"

"We're not going to take that chance. They might not know what he's up to, but it doesn't matter. Whatever is going on, he is using them to get close to you."

"You're right. It's better that way; I even wondered if he had brought you here and threatened you in some way to get you to throw the pebbles at my window."

"And yet you opened the door for me."

"I hadn't thought of it until I'd unlocked it, and then there you were. All alone."

"Which reminds me, I've delivered my message... now I need to go."

"Since you're here, couldn't you just stay in your old room for the night and have breakfast with us in the morning like you used to?"

"Most definitely not. Not with you standing in the doorway, in only your nightclothes and dressing gown, I assume, blocking my way to my room with every breathtaking curve."

"I'll move out of your way."

"I'll only follow."

For once, the threat of something happening seemed so much more tangible. How would I separate myself from him for the night when I wished never to leave his presence again? "Yes, perhaps, it is best you not come inside."

He took a few steps back, keeping his hand where it was at my jaw, yet effectively pulling me out the door to the covered stone porch.

Vance gently closed the door behind me. He then took my hand, but quickly pressed it to my side—keeping it between me and his palm; his other hand was still at my jawline. "You have no idea how easy it is to get carried away."

"Talk to me about something then. I was just wondering about the game of poker earlier tonight. How is poker played that men can lose so much in so little time?"

Vance chuckled in the shadows created from the pillars of the porch.

"Poker. Gambling. Bets. How does it all work?" I persisted. "How is it that a bet can create such a stronghold, to keep men to something they've promised as if it were the law?"

"Well, there's a certain code to poker. It—like many other forms of gambling—is a game of chance and pride. The gamble is, will the chance of your hand beating all others pull through for you?"

"How did Ezra lose me exactly?"

"I remember quite clearly, actually. I was at The Hawthorne Inn, and I'd already gone out—"

"Were you really gambling with them, then?"

"I was actually there for Dexter's benefit, spying on your brother. He's been trying to shut down The Hawthorne Inn for about as long as it's been a brothel. I'd only just begun helping Dexter when Stella found herself stranded at Everstone there last summer."

"You are such a sneak; you're so much better of a man than you want to lead anyone to believe."

"I just don't usually care what anyone thinks of me. Good or bad. Now let me get back to what I was saying." He tweaked my nose, but then with his other hand at my waist, he glided our fingers together until they were linked behind me, against the small of my back. He pulled at me, quickly closing the distance between us and let out a long breath.

I laughed quietly. "You were saying?"

"I'd laid my hand down, going out for the round. It never mattered what I had in my hands, I almost always went out. I was simply there for show. And I'd almost walked away from the table until I heard your name uttered, but even then I wasn't too concerned. Your brother mentioned you quite a bit in the company of Rowen Steele, almost like he was baiting him. And that was when I saw the gleam in Steele's eyes as Ezra slid your photograph across the table. There was something that grabbed my attention at that point—likely God's guidance—because I'd never felt anything like it before. At least concerning a woman."

Vance shook his head, laughing quietly to himself. I could just barely see his cheeks bunched up into a smile. "I couldn't get you out of my mind, and I hadn't even seen the darned photograph to know what you looked like. Steele had quickly won the game and greedily took it and shoved it into his vest pocket. And then I saw you. I wanted to pursue you almost from the beginning of our acquaintance, but I didn't know how to take my desire for getting to know you better as something good—something that would end respectably. So I avoided you as best I could; while also wanting to keep a close eye on you. It was quite the juggle."

"I remember when we met. I felt like you recognized my name."

He leaned in, combing a hand through the hair from behind my ear to the back of my head. "Your name...that reminds me! Your name in print!—I forgot to tell you!"

"What is it? Is it something about my books?"

He laughed. "I took your books to Culver over a week ago. He asked me to simply drop them off and that he'd take a look at them when he had time. I saw him earlier today before everything concerning Cal and Rowen Steele distracted me. He was just on his way to catch the train back to Philadelphia." Vance had both hands at my arms now, almost shaking me excitedly. "Violet, he loves them. He wants to publish them, just as I knew he would."

"Who? What? Lippencott? No."

"Yes, Lippencott." Vance slipped an envelope out of his jacket pocket. "This is the contract you need to sign and mail back to him."

I grabbed it from his hand and hurriedly ripped it open. Turning around so that the lamplight was now behind me and shining on the cream-colored papers, I read the name of the publisher at the top of the page, and then my name, and my book's names all listed together, because they wanted to buy every single one.

In my excitement, I crumpled it with one hand, spun back around and grasped Vance around the neck, vaulting myself against him. I clutched him to me with both arms. "All because you believed in me more than I ever would have believed in myself. This is all happening because of you."

And then I kissed him.

He kissed me back, of course, his arms coming around me hungrily. His lips didn't stray from mine, but stayed steady and strong with just the perfect amount of pressure. He could have kissed me like that forever, and I would have been just fine.

But then something in me changed, and it didn't seem we could possibly be close enough. I wanted, more than anything, for him to follow me inside the house, to never leave me again. Was it the air around us that had become electrified, or was it me? Or him? Or everything?

And how would we ever stop?

Vance lifted me from my feet and caught my legs at my knees over his arm, and then opened the door, all while still kissing me.

He carried me inside, leaving the door wide open behind us. I didn't care, and I guess neither did he. I just wanted to stay close, to keep kissing him, and go wherever he wanted to take me. We made it to the back stairwell, where he was forced to put me down. But I didn't let go of him, or stop kissing him. I stood a step above him, pressed against him, still longing for more.

Until he stepped back, and in so doing, broke the connection between us. I fell back from the shock, landing with a thud upon the wooden stairs, the crumpled contract still in my hand.

"I'm sorry," he said, though I wasn't quite sure what he was referring to...kissing me, inadvertently making me lose my balance...or so much more.

I looked up at him. He was just barely visible in the shadows created by the light down the hall. He braced the doorframe with both arms rigid, looking in all honesty as if he were fighting the urge to rejoin me on the steps. And I think I would have even welcomed him if he had indeed lost the battle.

But he didn't. He stayed where he was, breathing heavily, staring at me. "I don't blame you, Violet. But *this* is how easy it is."

With the help of the stair rail, I stood, understanding fully for the first time just what he'd meant all those times he'd insisted that we should proceed with the utmost caution. He'd been right. It was easy to get carried away, to forget everything, to forget what was right, what was best, and to just want what was within our grasp. He'd been right there in mine and proven it to me.

"I understand now," I admitted. "It is easy. I'm sorry I kissed you." I felt incredibly foolish. How many times had he warned me that I wasn't as strong as I thought, no matter my beliefs and convictions?

"I'm glad you kissed me, Violet. I'm just glad that we were able to stop before getting upstairs, or down the hall, or anywhere comfortable, really."

I took a backwards step up the stairs. "You make me incredibly happy, Vance. That's why I kissed you."

"It's an honor that you can still say that after what we almost just let happen. You do realize what almost happened, don't you?"

"Yes," I could feel the heat flush my cheeks. "You should probably go to Everthorne now."

"Dearest fiancée, I do believe that would be smart." He didn't move from the doorway though. "I think its best that I see myself out though; no need to...." He turned his attention to the knob on the door to the stairway. "Is there a lock on this thing? I don't believe I ever noticed before; ah yes, there is." He stood in the dim light of the hall and shot those devastatingly dark eyes my way one more time. "I'm going to lock this, and you're going to go to bed. And if by chance I am tempted to throw pebbles at your window ever again, you might want to consider not coming down, no matter what I say to persuade you."

"Good night, Vance."

He paused in the doorway for a moment, and smiled. "Violet, you're the sweetest, most forgiving person I've ever met. You should hate me right now."

"I could never hate you." I wanted to expound, to tell him that indeed, I loved him more than I ever imagined I could. But what would his answer to such a blatant proclamation be? I hoped that he'd return the sentiment, but I couldn't be sure.

"I hope that's true, Violet. With everything in me." He then closed the door, leaving the stairwell pitch black. I heard him go on out the back door, and I sat down on the wood steps again.

I was still shocked at how quickly I'd gone from happy elation from Vance's news to throwing myself at him. I put my head in my hands at the memory.

He'd been so right. Staying pure had nothing to do with good intentions. It took so much self-control and accountability and precaution. It had taken everything in Vance, I could tell, to tear himself away from me. And if he hadn't, oh, I couldn't fathom how I would have lived with myself afterwards. To think that if we had allowed things to get out of hand, all I had been accused of in my dorm room scandal and all I had denied in confident, self-righteous indignation—would have become entirely true!

18

A Riding Lesson

*"That he thought me worthy to be spoken to—
capable of understanding and duly appreciating
such discourse—was enough."*
—Anne Brontë, *Agnes Grey*

Friday, June 3rd, 1892

The week after Vance told me about my book contract from Lippencott was the last week before his father's wedding. And as usual, I rarely saw him besides when he came home for lunch. An almost ecstatic atmosphere pervaded Everwood as the wedding preparations at Trinity Church were set and the plans for the ball were completed. Bram and Evangeline—which I'd been instructed to call them from that week on—would have Everwood to themselves for the few days after the wedding before leaving for Prince Edward Island in Canada.

After that, the house would stand empty as his children and their families stayed at Everthorne with Vance for a few days, and I stayed with Miss Abernathy and Roxy at Hilldreth Manor for the month until my own wedding. Although I didn't like the idea of being separated from everyone, I knew it would be best that way; Vance and I not staying in the same house together.

And it would just be the beginning, for Nathan, Natalia, Estella, and their spouses and children, would be traveling up to Rockwood on Mount Desert Island for the summer, only returning to Boston for my wedding in early July.

Then at the end of the summer, Nathan and Amaryllis would travel back to Washington, and Dexter and Estella would return to Everston.

The day before the wedding, as everyone packed and got their things ready for the two-day-move to Everthorne, I found Vance leading a horse I didn't recognize out of the stable...a horse with a sidesaddle.

I immediately went down the steps to greet him.

I hoped, with this wonderful surprise of a morning in his company, I would be able to tell him what was on my heart lately; that I'd fallen in love with him. It was undeniable, and also fortunate, since the engagement had come first.

How was I supposed to get my feelings—the deeper ones, past all of the emotions I felt when he kissed me—out into words? And did he feel the same way? Or was he simply drawn to me enough physically to want to marry me solely based on that?

He'd mentioned on the way to Boston that he'd never been in love before, but there were so many times since then that he'd insinuated that he felt more for me than he'd ever allowed of himself. Everything was so difficult to figure out.

I'd started to count the days to the wedding, until we could be together, alone, as much as we wanted and never had to be so careful with our emotions and what they led to. And surely by then we'd be able to confess how we felt openly and with our words.

"Are you going to teach me to ride today? Whose horse is this?" I asked, almost shouting; my excitement obvious as I crossed the brick drive.

"A little bird told me you were finished packing for your temporary move to Hilldreth today. And I thought we could use this afternoon to steal away. Being in the public's eye, it should be safe enough."

"And the horse?"

"This is Lancelot, *your* horse."

I jumped a bit in my excitement, hugging Vance unabashedly. When I let go of him, he quipped a smile and full out laughed at me. I turned back to my horse, who let me stroke his nose. "Oh, Lancelot, I'm so happy you're mine."

"I'm glad you like him, I wasn't sure about his color, being so dark and so unlike my Bristol...."

Really, Lancelot's coloring was the most gorgeous dark sable brown I'd ever remembered seeing on a horse. And he was perfection, even if he didn't match Vance's dapple gray Morgan horse.

"He's a stout little horse, and he just seemed to fit you."

I stroked Lancelot's ears, taking in everything about him. He was such a gentle boy, it was no wonder Vance had chosen him for me. "Will I need my new riding habit, or will this dress do?" I was uncertain, as always, of what propriety demanded.

"I don't care what you wear," he answered easily, barely able to hide the fire behind his eyes. "We won't be doing much today, just an introductory lesson." Before I could answer, he continued, "Have you mailed the book contract yet?" He pulled Lancelot's reins to guide the horse to stand between us.

"I haven't signed it yet," I admitted over the top of the sidesaddle, hoping he wouldn't be mad.

"Do you want me to look at it?" Vance offered hesitantly.

"I'd like that; but whenever you have time will be fine," I stated shyly. I wasn't sure if he had something planned already for after my riding lesson, but I didn't want to assume he meant to spend the rest of his day with me.

He'd hardly seen me since the night he'd given me the contract, but I knew it was because he thought it safest to stay away. It meant so much to me that he wanted to be careful.

It had bothered me, on occasion, that he already knew quite well what marriage was like. What had Giselle been like? What about Olivia Rosselet? Were there others besides Meredyth? I didn't really want to know. I really just wanted to forgive him, but those unanswered questions were always in the back of my mind.

"What do I need to do first, to begin riding?"

"I'll help you mount. Fortunately, Lancelot's small." I looked up, just in time to see the uncertainty in his voice reach his eyes. And then he offered, "Perhaps I should have had Amaryllis teach you."

My gaze met his. It was the first time his wall had even slightly made an appearance in a number of weeks, and I wasn't about to let him go hiding behind it—for whatever reason. "I want to learn from you."

"She would be a better teacher."

"But I want to spend my time with you, and she's still busy packing right now."

"All right then." Vance turned me by the waist so I stood next to Lancelot's shoulder. "I'm going to lift you up and you're going to put your right knee around the upper pommel at the side of the saddle, and your left foot in this stirrup. I'll help position everything once you're in place." Only, he didn't lift me up, he just stared down at me for a moment. "You are beautiful, Violet. I don't think I tell you that enough."

I smiled at him. "And I don't think I've ever told you, Vance, that I think you're wonderful." *And that I love you.* I closed my eyes, feeling completely foolish for chickening out at the last moment.

He laughed, and then before I was prepared, he gripped me at my waist and hoisted me into the air toward Lancelot. I landed a little sideways from how I imagined I should have been on the saddle, but I quickly corrected my balance and got my right leg into place around the upper pommel. Once I made myself as comfortable as I could, loosening my skirts from around my legs, I positioned my left thigh under the bottom pommel.

Vance took his time in adjusting some straps on the saddle and turned his dark eyes to me, silently handed me the reins.

"Have you ridden him for yourself yet?" I asked.

"I wouldn't just throw you upon an untested horse. He's a good rider, and I think you'll do just fine on him. Amaryllis tried him out with the sidesaddle, as riding with one is a bit different when it comes to control." He took a long slender stick from the groom standing nearby and handed it to me. "You'll use this whip for control. Are you ready to learn how?"

Holding the whip like a sword, I said, "I guess so." But then I thought differently. "Actually, I don't know." I examined the extravagant leather handle of the whip he'd given me, not wanting him to realize how apprehensive I felt suddenly.

"Like I said, this is just an introductory lesson, Violet. We likely won't even leave the driveway today. I'll lead you about a little and let you get used to him. We need to let him gain your trust, and you'll need to learn to trust him at the same time."

"The connection is rather similar to courtship, isn't it?"

Vance's eyes flew to mine. "It is, though I have a feeling you liked Lancelot a bit more upon first acquaintance than you did me."

"That isn't true. I liked you more than I should have, more than was sensible. I tried to make myself not think of you when you came around. It wasn't exactly the easiest thing to do." Well, that was a start at least, to so much more I wanted to say. "Even before I knew how much you'd changed from the rumors I'd heard, I was entirely too intrigued by you."

"You could have surprised me. I've already told you how I struggled while getting to know you at Everston. If I'd had any indication you felt that way, it wouldn't have been good."

"I've always been cautious concerning men. That's probably why Ben never made a move either."

"Perhaps," he answered tersely.

"I suppose I've been considered somewhat unapproachable in the past."

"Now, I wouldn't say that." He put his hand on mine for a moment. "At least, not anymore. Not when it comes to me."

"No, I suppose not. And I have learned to trust you, Vance. You've proven to me that you care; that my purity is as important to you as it is to me."

He didn't answer except for the lingering look he gave me.

How did a girl ever find the right way to say such meaningful words as "I love you" when she wasn't positive of the reception? And why wasn't I positive? What I'd just alluded about him proved that he loved me, at some level, at least.

But what if it wasn't the same level? That was what I was most afraid of—that his love wasn't as all-consuming as mine. Yes, he'd admittedly wanted me months ago, but what if he felt the exact same way now as he did back then?

Lancelot sidestepped, throwing me off-balance.

"Keep your posture straight, aligned with his." He immediately took my horse's reins and steadied him with a few calming gestures, all the while keeping a hand securely at my back. "You don't want to put too much weight on the left side. Although it seems you're well-secured, you can still fall off."

"I will be careful." His thoughtfulness brought up a new bravery I hardly recognized, boosting my resolve to somehow tell him how I felt. He would be pleased I was in love with him, wouldn't he? "You were the one to insist that I stay at Hilldreth Manor for the next few nights, weren't you?"

"And thank goodness that was an option, or I didn't know what I was going to do."

"I would have locked my door."

"That reminds me, you never did see the second level rooms of Everthorne, did you? You haven't seen your rooms yet—"

"I'm sure they are lovely, Vance. I really don't mind waiting to see them."

"If that's what you want, that would be easiest. It is best that you not come back there until after we're wed. It's only a month, after all."

"And two since we'd become engaged," I added.

"I would have married you a month ago if it were possible."

I shifted in the saddle. I still couldn't admit the words to my feelings. "I feel as though we've never really been strangers, that we somehow recognized something important in each other right away."

Vance's gaze held mine for a long time, and he smiled, but he didn't answer. Could he tell what I wanted to confess?

Finally, he said, "I suppose I should actually try to give you some useful instruction instead of just stand here and stare at you all afternoon." He handed me the reins. "Here, hold them evenly, don't allow one rein to be longer than the other. When turning right, you'll pull right, and left to go left. It's actually very easy."

I did as he told me, still keeping the whip in my hand, crossed before me. And although Lancelot didn't move from his place, I could tell he was ready to go left or right when I indicated.

"Now hold the reins one handedly, and here, hold the whip like this." He took my right hand and lowered it to the back right side of the saddle. "As I ride, I use my legs to tell Bristol how fast I want him to go. But since yours are both draped over to the left side, you'll need to use the gentle pressure of the whip to help tell him."

He let go of my hand and allowed me to hold the whip in place, hardly touching Lancelot's hindquarters.

"When walking at a slow pace, I simply sit, my legs relaxed. But the faster I want to go, the more I'll press into his sides."

I sat still, silently listening to his every word, staring down at him as he spoke. He really was the most amazingly handsome man, even while merely instructing in a horse-riding lesson.

"With your whip, you'll apply pressure here." Vance positioned the whip into the correct place for me. "Telling him exactly what you need to get him to do what you want."

"He'll really know what I want with so little direction?"

"He's been well-trained, Violet," Vance assured me.

One of the Everstone carriages rolled out of the stable, down the drive, coming quite near us before turning to park near the back door. A number of servants immediately started to bring out trunks and small boxes, loading them onto the wagon hitched to the back.

Everyone was moving out, and I had a strange, sad feeling something wonderful was about to end. It had been remarkable to be a part of such a family for the last two months, and now they would all be going back to their own homes, so far apart, and Vance and I would stay right there, down the street. It was an odd sensation to realize I could miss something so drastically after only knowing it for two months. But the love and acceptance from Vance's family had seeped into my very being, and the thought of not having it nearby hurt far more than I'd anticipated.

Vance paused our lesson as the busyness of the servants loading the trunks and boxes took over the courtyard. Vance stood by Lancelot's head, caressing the white blaze down the horse's nose and watched his siblings' things be loaded onto the wagon.

I studied him for a long while. Always the confident one, he seemed now to be uncertain, even upset. Wasn't he used to living so far apart from his siblings? Especially since he'd been the one to be the farthest away for the longest amount of time over the years, traveling about Europe.

He eventually turned to me and asked, "Are you ready for me to lead you around the drive, or have you had enough of a lesson for today?"

"I suppose we should be finished, it looks like it's about time to leave." The wagon, having been loaded—even with my trunk included to take to Hilldreth Manor—was pulled down the drive by the carriage, around the corner of the mansion, and onto the street to stop outside the front door.

"I'll walk you down the street to Hilldreth Manor. Let them take care of your trunk. I'm sure they won't mind just dropping it off. I want to spend more time with you, just because, and doing so with Claudine and Roxy seems just the perfect thing."

"You'll stay and visit with us? Perhaps have tea? And join us in playing some cards?" The thought of Vance having a part in the sedate atmosphere at Hilldreth Manor was amusing. He would do those things to have the chance to spend time with me?

"As long as you're there, I might even have the time of my life," he said dryly, but he also gave me the most amazing crooked lift of his lips. Oh my, he was much too irresistible, and he hardly had to try. Vance reached for my waist, and kept his hands there for a moment. "Is your contract still in the house, or has it been packed away already?"

"It's in my reticule. Inside the house."

"I'm already looking forward to our next lesson together."

"You should probably actually help me down from my horse now that this one's finished, shouldn't you, instead of simply looking as if you might."

He let out a long breath, "I suppose I should." He lifted me off the sidesaddle, placed my feet gently on the brick drive, and grabbed Lancelot's reins to guide him back toward the stable.

I walked to the house alone and went in the side door, immediately heading to the front of the house where I'd left my reticule. Bram Everstone stood near the front door as each of his children and their families said their temporary goodbyes. The last of the group had just finished, and left out the front door to gather into the awaiting carriage.

"Where have you been this afternoon?" my future father-in-law asked.

Bram Everstone had a similar smile to Vance's, and the same dark black eyes. Vance would probably look very much like his father in coming years, and it made my heart jolt—as if I were looking into my future. Bram, however, was as intimidating as the day was long, and I still couldn't exchange words with him without feeling nervous.

"Vance gave me my first lesson in horse riding. We didn't get far though, only a general explanation as I sat upon my horse for the first time."

"It's good that he's taking things slow. It's better that way."

I couldn't help but think of our engagement and how *not slow* that had come about. "I hope you don't mind that we'd decided to get married so soon after your own wedding—"

"Of course not. I'm just happy Vance is marrying you. You're the best thing that's happened to him in a long time."

Just then, Vance met us at the door, coming into the house from outside. "Ready for the walk to Hilldreth, Violet?"

"All ready." I held up my reticule and turned to Vance's father. "Thank you; I guess I'll see you at your wedding. Goodbye."

"Goodbye, Father. See you tomorrow." Vance offered me his arm as we went out the door and through the front corridor.

I opened my reticule, immediately produced the folded up envelope with the contract inside and handed it to him. He unfolded it and read it over while we walked.

After a little while, he said, "This is a good contract. Culver obviously didn't want you thinking of going elsewhere with your manuscripts." He handed it back to me as we reached the front door of Hilldreth Manor.

I refolded the paper as it had been when mailed to me, but the creases from when I'd clutched it in my hand as he'd kissed me and carried me to the stairwell the other night were still visible, and I felt my cheeks flush at the sudden memory.

"We'll have you sign it at Hilldreth, and I'll put it in the mail for you."

"You really think Mr. Culver values me so entirely?"

"Publishers don't give book contracts out lightly. You know that. They must really love your work."

I so wanted to respond with, "And I love you," but it wouldn't come out. I wished he would tell me first. It would make everything so much easier.

He had to love me, right? He showed me in so many ways, he just never said the words. Had he ever said the words to anyone?

I doubted it, and it made me wonder if he ever would.

19

The Wedding Ball

"The realities of life do not allow themselves to be forgotten."
—Victor Hugo, *Les Miserables*

Saturday, June 4th, 1892

Y ou look stunning, my dear." Vance's gaze lingered upon the details of the yellow creation I'd decided upon wearing to his father's wedding ball the following evening. We again stood together in the corridor from the sidewalk to the front door of Everwood, only now, instead of being blessedly alone, we were surrounded by people.

"So do you," I answered. *As always.* It felt odd to find myself standing opposite him, to take his hand and force niceties in the exact place he'd first kissed me. And I knew he knew it was the same spot; I could see it in his eyes.

"Look for me once the ball begins; I want to show you off during the first dance. After that it doesn't matter what we do, but I plan to have you by my side. It's the best chance we'll have to spend time together, since we'll be in the safety of the crowd."

"I look forward to it," was all I was able to get out as I was shuffled through the line, away from him.

Vance had been near me at random intervals earlier that day, while we waited for the private ceremony to take place, and then afterwards when everyone gathered around to congratulate the newlywed couple at Trinity Church. And he'd held my hand quite often during those times. He'd even kissed me on the cheek when he'd escorted me to Miss Abernathy's carriage to proceed to the ball.

I went through the remainder of the receiving line, which consisted of Vance's family, and at length approached the newlywed couple just inside their grand home. It felt strange to greet each of them as if I had not just spent two months living in that very house, seeing most of them nearly every day. And despite the mass of strangers all around me, for the first time, I felt I half-belonged in the fine world Vance had made a place for me in.

Miss Abernathy and Roxy Blakeley were in front of me in the line, and were to be my companions that night whenever I wasn't with Vance. I didn't really know many people there—and it didn't shock me that I wasn't the most popular addition to their society. I didn't know how far the rumors had come, but I was certain there were some who had met me and thought the worst of me. I was banking, however, on the repeated assurance from Vance's family that it only mattered that we would be married soon.

When the crowds were gathered inside the hall and ballroom of Everwood, the newlywed couple was again announced and the ball officially began. I stood along a wall with Roxy, waiting to catch a glimpse of Vance, when I noticed Ben Whitespire threading through the crowd.

"I didn't realize Ben Whitespire was back in town." I pushed off the wall and turned to Roxy. "Did you know he was invited?"

"He'd told me once that he'd be back to Boston soon, for the wedding. I've heard he's in town searching for a devout young lady willing to marry him so he can then go on to the mission in Tennessee."

"Has he never mentioned perhaps taking you—"

She shook her head slowly, letting her eyelids fall close for a moment before opening them again, and staring at me. "He won't ask me."

"I don't see why not. I'm surprised the thought hasn't occurred to him, since you know each other already. You seem to get along well enough."

"I'm sure I'm too sickly to be a missionary."

"Did he tell you that?"

"It's what I know."

"Would you go if he asked you to?"

"I don't know." Roxy's gaze scanned over the crowd. "He won't ask, anyway."

With every word, she seemed to shrink away from me. Perhaps she felt that my questions had been too invasive. "I can't imagine anyone wants a sickly wife—no matter if they're a missionary or not."

"You have more a chance of meeting someone here in Boston though, don't you think?"

"That is true."

"So will you stay? Or will you travel back with Dexter and Estella to Everston later this summer?"

"For now, the plan is for me to stay with Miss Abernathy."

"I'm so pleased to hear that," I said, trying to coax her into friendliness again after perhaps over-stepping my bounds. "Everyone else will be leaving soon, and I haven't made any friends besides my new-found relatives." I refrained from mentioning that I wasn't even sure these relatives were, indeed, friends.

Suddenly, with a new wind, Roxy said, "Mabel is wonderfully entertaining. She always brings up the most interesting things, and seems so set on including me."

"I'm glad you think so." I couldn't say I had quite the same opinion of my cousin, but that was likely because I hadn't made up my mind about whether I could trust her or not.

As I was just about to continue on about both of us staying in Boston, Vance appeared through the crowd and joined us.

He bowed ever so slightly, taking my hand. "Violet, may I have the honor of the first dance?"

"Of course, you may." I felt a twinge guilty for leaving Roxy along the wall alone, as Miss Abernathy sat in the nearest chair about ten feet away, but how could I refuse? With a simple smile, and a wink, Vance had my hand in his and my feet willingly walking across the room.

It had been years since I'd danced, but I didn't think about that. I only cared that I'd have Vance all to myself for those wonderful minutes we'd be face to face, uninterrupted.

"Have you seen my aunt and cousins? They were invited to attend, weren't they?"

"And as far as I know, they responded in the affirmative. But no, I haven't seen them." He looked around distractedly, as if looking now might prove that they'd indeed come. "I figured I'd merely missed them while keeping busy, but if you haven't seen them either—"

"I was under the impression that they were looking forward to coming, but perhaps—perhaps the grandeur of the event kept them away?"

Vance led me to the middle of the room, and as he did, the orchestra started into a beautiful piece I didn't recognize. His left hand took my right, his right hand came around my waist, and I sucked in my breath.

"It is quite an undertaking—" I said, trying to breathe normally, "—attending a ball like this, but then, since the wedding was so much less formal, you'd think they would—"

Vance leaned in, bringing his mouth nearer to the left side of my face. He whispered, "Let's not worry about them for now."

But even as Vance held me and waltzed me about the ballroom, I couldn't stop thinking about them. I didn't understand their absence, and it worried me that maybe my aunt had taken ill again. But then, wouldn't my cousin have sent me word? Wouldn't Miss Abernathy and Roxy had known of it and told me? My relatives hadn't come up between us at all in the last day of my staying at Hilldreth Manor; there had been so much going on.

For a moment, the thought of returning to Roxy, to ask her what she knew of them came to my mind, but then Vance's hand grasped my waist a little closer. As if he could tell.

"I'm sure they're fine," he said, proving that he could read me quite well. "Since witnessing the connection between Cal and Rowen, I wasn't all that desirous of their company, anyway."

"I wasn't thinking about Cal, but Mabel and Aunt Letty. Do you think they took offense to my not coming by to see them lately? Maybe I should have told them of my reasons."

"I've sent someone by to check on them, letting them know that you'd become busy with your own wedding preparations."

It wasn't a complete lie—for I had been called upon a lot more in those last weeks. Natalia and Estella wanted to make sure everything was just as I wanted, now that Madame—or rather, *Evangeline Everstone*—had ceased being involved.

"Do you know who *has* come to the wedding?" he asked.

"Ben."

Vance's entire demeanor changed, his dark brows came down lower than I'd ever witnessed. He couldn't have hidden his frown if he tried. "That's not who I meant, but is he here? He must not have come through the receiving line."

I immediately regretted bringing up Ben, for I could tell that just his name still sent Vance's imagination into wrong directions. I didn't know how he'd ever become so preoccupied with the thought that I'd once been attached to his friend, but it was immediately obvious that it was still something that bothered him. Hadn't I proven to him, on more than one occasion, that *he* was the one that I wanted to be with?

"Who did you mean if you didn't mean Ben?" I asked.

"Ava Cagney."

"Oh, is she such a family friend that she was invited?"

"Her family has long been associated with my mother's family in Bangor—as far as I know, her entire family came."

"Do I have to see her again? I'm not sure what I should say to her."

"You really ought to; it would be the polite thing to do."

"You care so much about being polite now?" My own streak of jealousy came roaring back. What if Ava had been one of the women he'd spent time with before he'd decided to become a Christian? He had mentioned once that a woman like her would be perfect for him, hadn't he?

"For the benefit of my father's wedding, yes."

"I'll endeavor to speak with her then."

"Thank you, Violet," Vance whispered, evidently pleased with my willingness. "I know society life isn't something you especially enjoy, but thank you for trying. You've done well in the last few months; better than I expected. And once we're married, you won't have to do anything you don't want to. No hosting balls or dinners, if you don't want to."

"You won't mind?"

"I know it wasn't what you were raised to do. Though it's obvious to everyone you were raised to be a lady, there can be made allowances when it simply isn't in one's nature to entertain."

"But should I? As your wife, will it be expected of me?"

"I don't care what anyone expects of you, Violet. You can do whatever you like. What matters is that we match better than I ever—"

The end of the waltz cut Vance's sentence off when everyone in the room stopped to clap for the orchestra. But he didn't seem intent on finishing what he'd been meaning to say once we moved off the floor.

Did he really trust me so entirely? That he thought we matched the same way I thought we did? I hoped so, and at times, I genuinely felt it was true. But not at that moment, particularly. Did it have to do with us bringing up Ben and Ava; two people who seemed much better socially suited for either of us than we were for each other?

Before I had the nerve to bring up my concerns—if I ever would have been brave enough, that is—Ben Whitespire stood before us.

"May I have the next dance, Miss Hawthorne?"

Vance scowled noticeably, and dropped his arm from mine. "Of course you can," he answered for me, and stepped away.

Taken aback by Vance's abrupt manners, I could only look around nervously, wondering if anyone else besides Ben had noticed how my fiancé had just treated me—as if I didn't mean a thing to him. Suddenly, it didn't seem like there was much holding us together, and it scared me that he might feel it, too.

This wasn't at all what I expected from the ball. Why had I let my expectations take flight? How could I have been so sure of Vance's feelings only yesterday, and now wonder if he cared anything at all for me?

It felt awkward to dance with Ben when I knew Vance watched. He remained silent, and I found myself at a loss for how to begin a conversation. I'd thought I had known him satisfactorily while I'd worked at Everston and attended his church in Laurelton. But now that I knew Vance so much more intimately, it felt like Ben and I were merely acquaintances who had lived in the same area for a time.

Everything between Vance and me was so much more. Always, so much more.

Not long after the dance had begun, Ben finally spoke up. "Ezra told me what he did."

"You mean to my hair?" I feigned innocence.

"I mean," he lowered his voice considerably, his dark blue eyes revealing so much; too much of what I hadn't known was there months ago—"concerning the bet and the compromising situation with Vance."

My heart thudded nervously; I couldn't believe he knew, that he'd resisted placing judgement, that he'd believed in me enough to talk to Ezra, to still be there dancing with me. "You've spoken to Ezra, and he admitted he'd—?"

"I had to know what happened, so I tracked him down. I found him at The Hawthorne Inn, of course, and I made him tell me everything. He was more than willing when he realized I would do all I could for your safety."

"How was he?" I asked, still always worried about my brother despite the awful decisions he'd made for his life.

"Honestly, he wasn't nearly as cocksure as he usually comes across. He seemed in a panic, like he didn't know what to do next. When he found out I was coming to Boston, he actually begged me to make sure you were safe, so afraid that putting you in Vance's grasp wasn't exactly the best thing to do, once it was done. And he told me things about Rowen Steele, Violet...."

"What kind of things?" I asked, almost afraid to hear the answer.

"Things a lady's ears should never hear." Ben lowered his voice to a whisper. "Rowen's a dangerous man. He's not someone to mess around with. I think your brother realizes this now, but it's too late. If Rowen is as determined to have you as it seems, you're not safe...."

I swallowed; my throat suddenly dry. I'd thought I'd been safe...but perhaps the feelings of safety and protection that Vance produced in me were only a delusion.

"I wish he'd chosen *me* to save you, rather than Vance. I would have gladly married you. Did you not know how I felt?"

"You would?" I asked, utterly shocked at this admission. "I mean, I wasn't aware that you would—I wasn't aware that you felt that way. You never said anything to...."

"I was going to ask you to marry me once I got back from my meeting with the mission society. But things happened so quickly, and then there you were at Everwood, engaged to Vance."

I couldn't answer. What was there to say?

"I know I shouldn't mention these things, considering you're engaged to him now," he went on, his gaze focused on mine, keeping me from glancing away.

I studied him with a new perspective. What if Ben had tried to capture my heart before everything with Vance had happened? With his serious eyes, and always barely-there-grin, he was attractive...and confident, and godly. He would have been an excellent husband.

I desperately wanted to look around to see if Vance was indeed watching our conversation. And if he was, could he tell what we were discussing? What I was thinking?

"But if you wanted to reconsider your decision; if you think perhaps you would rather come with me to Tennessee, I'm sure I could convince the board at the mission society that the rumors were based on slanderous intent, and that what was seen to have happened was actually orchestrated by your brother, who was simply trying to protect you from a situation he'd helped create."

"I've been engaged to Vance for months now—"

"It's always a lady's prerogative to break an engagement, and I'm sure everyone would understand—"

"My reputation would be ruined, for I would never be able to convince everyone of what *didn't* happen—"

"If you married me you wouldn't be ruined. We'd move far, far from here, where no one would ever know anything about your brother or the last few months. And I love you, Violet. I have for quite some time."

I could tell he spoke in earnest; that his feelings were true. And I was at a complete and utter loss as to how to respond to such words, so evenly spoken yet indicative of such depth. The very words I had yet to hear from my betrothed.

His hand at my waist now felt to linger there differently, as if I could feel his desire for me seeping through the yellow material of my dress. And his eyes...I found myself hoping that Vance wasn't paying close attention. I didn't think there were any clues regarding the conversation from my own expressions, but oh, I'd never known that simply being loved by someone could create such a powerful, confusing reaction in my heart.

Ben had been my longed-for suitor *once*. Just not now.

"I'm sorry I kept my feelings mostly hidden from you for so long, but I had a lot to deal with concerning my choices for the future, and I thought you had an idea."

"I didn't," I was finally able to say. "And it's too late—"

"You can't mean you actually want to marry Vance, do you? It isn't because he's—he hasn't made real what everyone believes to have happened at the employee dormitory at Everston—?" he whispered urgently, as if that was any of his business.

"I wish you'd not said that." I tried my best to keep my voice down, but it was difficult when the anger I felt at his insinuations bubbled forth. "You know Vance now, and his convictions. He considers you a friend; you have to know he would not allow such a thing—"

"I must apologize; I'm sorry—I'm distraught and I cannot account for what was just said." As those words left his mouth, the music stopped and I took a step back from him. He took his hands from me, but then offered me his arm. I took it, and he silently led me off to some potted trees blocking off the corner of the large room. Once we were alone, he continued, "I can only think of you, Violet. Why do you feel you must marry him, when I'm here offering you my heart, and a way to be freed from—"

"As I already said, it's too late—"

"You cannot *want* to marry Vance."

"I *do* want to marry him." I let go of him and took a step toward the edge of the trees.

He didn't follow, but only stared at me as if seeing someone he didn't recognize. And perhaps he didn't recognize me. Did he really think I would consider breaking my engagement a month from my wedding?

"Does he feel the same way?" Ben called after me.

"I think so."

At least, I hoped so with everything in me.

"Ah, I see then, how it's been all along."

Did he? What exactly did he see? What did that mean?

When I didn't answer, Ben silently escorted me to where Roxy now stood next to Miss Abernathy's seat. He let go of me and immediately turned to Roxy, "Miss Blakeley, may I have the next dance?"

Roxy's eyes lit up. I could hardly believe the ignorance of my earlier questions to her—after what had just transpired between Ben and me. I'd completely misjudged his feelings and intentions, and I hoped I hadn't given her the impression that he would consider marrying her.

Ben had just walked off with Roxy when I noticed Vance escort Ava Cagney onto the ballroom floor. She was gazing up at him, laughing at something he had just said. His hand seemed to be the same length as her small waist, and it rested there so easily.

I tried not to let my jealousy get out of hand; after all, I'd just finished a dance with Ben. It wasn't as if we weren't allowed to dance with others at a ball. It was just, well, from what Vance had said in the receiving line, and at the beginning of the first dance, I thought that we'd spend much more time together than we had already.

"I'm looking forward to your wedding in another month, Violet." Miss Abernathy interrupted my thoughts.

"Thank you; I am too," I replied awkwardly, wishing to skirt the topic. "Do you happen to know if my Aunt Letty and cousin Mabel were planning to come tonight? I didn't see them at the wedding."

"It was their plan to come. But I, too, noticed their absence. I was hoping they'd made it to the ball, and that it was only that I hadn't seen them yet."

"I don't believe they are here."

"How strange. I knew they were excited to be invited, and had each purchased a new gown, but I suppose they can still plan to wear the new gowns for your after-wedding celebration in a few weeks."

"Vance and I aren't having a ball, only a dinner."

"Oh, well, that's too bad."

"Had Cal been planning to come with them?"

"As far as I know," she answered, her light brown eyes meeting mine.

I wasn't sure I wished to ever see him again if he was connected to Rowen Steele in any way, but I couldn't very well let Miss Abernathy know about my apprehension.

A few moments later I realized that the third dance had ended and that Vance and Ava came through the crowd together, toward where I stood.

Upon reaching us, Ava didn't wait for a reintroduction to me— or even an introduction to Miss Abernathy—but launched into sharing her breathless excitement, as if we were long-lost friends.

"Miss Hawthorne, it's so good to see you again. I saw the write-up in the paper about the wedding, that is to happen so soon, and Vance was just telling me all about your plans. What an exciting time."

I hardly knew how to respond.

"You are too kind, I am sure, Mrs. Cagney. I didn't realize you'd be here."

"I wouldn't have missed it! I do hope you didn't mind that I stole your fiancé for one little dance. But you did seem engrossed in whatever it was you were speaking of with Miss Abernathy."

So she already knew Miss Claudine Abernathy too. It shouldn't have surprised me.

"You hardly noticed us, I wager." With this, her eyes gleamed and I wondered at her choice of words.

"We too were speaking of the wedding in July. I suppose your family will attend it, as well?" Miss Abernathy asked, saving me from responding.

"That's the plan at the moment, yes," Ava answered. "We try not to miss any Everstone wedding, though it seems everyone missed Nathan's, since he so scandalously eloped with his fiancée without a word to anyone!"

"Eloping with one's fiancée isn't considered scandalous, Mrs. Cagney," Vance interjected. "Just unconventional."

"You would know about scandal, wouldn't you, Vance?" Ava teased.

What was she insinuating? Did she mean about his scandalous past, or the way we'd scandalously been forced to become engaged?

"Speaking of Nathan, I need to find him before too long, if you'll pardon me, ladies." Vance excused himself with a bow and left our little circle.

Miss Abernathy stood with the use of her cane for the first time since the ball had begun. "It seems I've lost track of Roxy. If you'll excuse me, I want to find her now that she's had her dance with Reverend Whitespire."

She hobbled away, leaving me with Ava Cagney. I searched the crowd for anyone else who could help me, but I didn't see a single familiar face. I really didn't want to speak with Ava alone, but I also didn't want to wander around the place like a lost kitten.

"Come, take a walk with me," Ava suggested.

We strolled through the crowd until we came to the front parlor, which served as the refreshment room. There weren't nearly as many people there as were in the ballroom, but neither was it anywhere close to being empty. Ava suddenly stopped next to the table of refreshments and grabbed a plate.

"You know, Violet Hawthorne, I know how it is you came to be engaged to Vance; that he'd been found in your bed—"

Horrified that she'd speak of such a thing so plainly, and within earshot of so many people, I grabbed her arm and whispered, "It wasn't what it seemed—"

"Oh yes, I've heard." She wrenched her arm from my grasp and continued speaking loudly. "It's endearing that your brothel-owning brother tries to convince everyone that it was his doing, that nothing really happened, and that you would never choose to do such a terrible thing, even with the likes of Vance Everstone." She delicately lifted a strawberry and popped it in her mouth.

Several heads turned our way, and the hum of conversation quieted.

"I wouldn't," I said nervously.

"But what does it say that you're now engaged to him? It must be true. That he'd so carelessly seduce you like that surprises me though, in such a way that all of Everston would find out about it."

"He didn't—"

She lowered her tone, and almost hissed the next words. "And now, thanks to my invitation to this wedding, everyone here knows it too. And your pitiful brother's plan to redeem you—it only makes you look all the worse, making everyone talk all the more, wondering if Vance had indeed seduced you, or if you perhaps solicited your brother's help to make everything happen as it did, to be so conveniently discovered as you were."

"Why are you doing this?" I pleaded. Women were tittering over their teacups and several men began looking at me appraisingly. I could feel the wall of their judgment and amusement closing me in.

"I was this close—" Ava held her thumb and finger less than an inch apart, "—to having him for myself. And you could tell, couldn't you? Is that why you took your chance the very night I arrived? So I would never—"

"You never had a chance with him," I uttered below my breath, and then I turned to leave the room. I didn't know where I would go, or what I would do, but I had to get away from her.

As I reached the secluded hall near the stairwell at the back of the house—to lock myself into and hide away—I felt a hand grip my elbow. I turned to find Ava once again clutching onto me, her face distorted into an ugly frown, as if I were the one trying to destroy her life. "You didn't know, did you? I've already had plenty of chances with him, just not drastic enough for him to offer me a proposal."

"I don't want to hear anything more from you," I said quietly but emphatically. I pulled away from her, finally reaching the open door to the stairs. I grabbed the doorknob and turned around. "You're despicable, and nothing you say means anything—it is all lies and trouble, and you just want to destroy what you don't—"

"And you, you're not better than me, Violet Hawthorne. I simply cannot understand how you attracted Vance Everstone in the first place. You're so...unsophisticated. How did you ever accomplish such a thing?"

"What's the meaning of this?" I heard Vance's voice behind me and turned to find both he and Ben standing side by side, looking as if they'd just run from wherever they'd come. "Violet—"

Before anyone could say anything more, I stepped over the threshold of the stairwell, pulled the door shut and locked it behind me, shutting myself in darkness. I sat down on the wood steps—just as I had the last time I'd been there—and waited. There was nowhere else to go.

I heard shuffling feet, a long silence, and then a light knock upon the wooden door. "Violet, are you still in there? Are you all right?" Vance asked through the crack.

"Yes." It was all I could make myself say.

"Will you let me in?"

"No." And before I knew what was happening, tears were running down my cheeks.

"Violet, are you crying?" he asked gently. I could tell where he stood as he blocked the light from coming in through the crack of the door.

It didn't escape my notice that the situation was very much like the first time Vance had ever spoken to me—me in tears, sitting on some steps, with my hands covering my wet, tear-covered face.

But this time there was a barrier between us, and I didn't answer.

Ava's last question repeated over and over in my mind, an echo of my own recurring doubt. How had I ever accomplished snagging Vance Everstone's attention? And had I, really?

Having her put it to me so bluntly made me wonder if Vance would have ever truly wanted me if it hadn't been for the scandalous circumstances surrounding that morning at the dormitory.

Quite suddenly, I knew the answer.

No, he wouldn't have. He would have eventually become engaged to someone more fitting than me. For as Ava had said; I was, indeed, completely unsophisticated. I'd tried to fit in, with finery and horse-riding and tea-sipping, and I had lulled myself into believing that Vance's world could be mine. That *he* could be mine.

But I was still just Violet Hawthorne, a girl from nowhere, with nothing but a string of scandalous rumors and a few passionate kisses attaching me to him.

And suddenly, I feared it wasn't nearly enough.

20

A New Mission

"...it strikes me with anguish to be torn from you."
—Charlotte Brontë, *Jane Eyre*

Saturday, June 11th, 1892

I spent the week after the wedding at Hilldreth Manor, seques-
tered from everyone, claiming a headache, not wanting to deal
with the rumors that Ava Cagney had so efficiently and effortlessly spread about Vance and me. When I thought about Vance's
family and closest friends having to confront the rumors, deny
them, or explain them away on my behalf regardless of whether
they believed they were true, I really did feel the blood pounding
in my temples. I no longer expected anyone to truly think we were
innocent.

Vance's siblings had presumably left town; I'd already said my
goodbyes the night of the wedding. Instead of the incessant visiting and chatting that had been my life for months, my time was
now consumed with my books, the ones Mr. Culver hadn't seen
and contracted yet.

I hoped and prayed that the rumors wouldn't change
Lippencott's decision to publish my books.

There were mere days left until my wedding, and yet my fiancé hadn't felt the need to speak to me beyond sending written messages that were far from lover-like. Each time I opened one of the rather distant, factual missives, it only had something to do with cancelling the plans we'd had for that week.

I was mulling over this when a knock sounded on the door of my temporary bedroom. After some minutes debating whether to answer or not, I asked, "Yes? Who is it?"

"Vance is here to see you," Roxy replied through the closed door.

"Is he?" I sat up from the edge of my bed, scattering my books on the floor.

He'd come, finally, after all? How was I supposed to act?

He wouldn't be happy with me since I'd hidden myself away in the stairwell at Everwood during the ball, and shut him out. I hadn't known what to do, how to deal with the situation, so I'd hid. When I'd finally felt composed enough to rejoin the party, I'd gone up the stairs and then come back down the main staircase.

And to my surprise, everything had seemed as normal as ever. But Vance had been nowhere in sight, and Miss Abernathy and Roxy had both tired of the festivities by then and wanted to go home. I hadn't been able to tell if they'd heard about Ava's tactics or how she'd aimed her attack to drag my name through the mud. They hadn't said much on the way home from the ball, and hadn't endeavored to really try to speak to me at all during that week.

After examining myself in the mirror, I opened the door. I was afraid to see Vance again, but still a little hopeful that he'd forgiven me for shutting him out, since he'd come.

"He's waiting for you downstairs in the back parlor." Roxy moved out of my way. Her solemnity didn't bode well for what I expected to find in the back parlor. With every step as I went down the stairs and through the dark-wood-paneled back hall, my courage wavered. The pocket doors to the room were open just wide enough for me to sneak through.

Vance stood right away, but didn't come to greet me. "Please shut the door behind you; I've asked them not to disturb us."

"Oh, all right." I swiveled on my feet to close the doors. It was far from an amorous request, more like a command, and my heart sunk a little lower, which surprised me was even possible.

I'd had a feeling ever since the ball that things between us had changed; that they'd been irreparably damaged by the scene Ava Cagney had created and my cowardly response to it.

"I've come to make a serious request of you," Vance began. "It's something I've thought long and hard about all week, and I think it's for the best."

For the longest time neither of us said anything, both of us not moving from what seemed to be our designated spots on the floor.

"I know Ben's in love with you."

My gaze suddenly locked with his. "What does that have to do with anything?"

"You should marry him, not me." Vance took a few steps, but in the opposite direction, toward the far end of the room. "Ava has been spreading all kinds of rumors all over town since the ball, and I think it is best that—"

"But I don't want to marry Ben," I replied impulsively.

"You didn't want to marry me two months ago either, and yet you eventually warmed to the idea. And Ben is the better choice, by far. He can take you to Tennessee, away from Ezra, away from Rowen Steele, away from everything for a new start." He still spoke facing the other side of the room, and I hadn't moved from my place by the doors. I was too stunned by his suggestions, practically numb with the pain spreading through me from my bruised and broken heart.

"You don't really want to marry someone like me, Violet. Believe me. I have too many skeletons in my closet for a good girl like you to have to deal with. Everything they're saying about us is believable because of who I used to be. You shouldn't have to go through such degradation—"

His humility shamed me. "It's not your fault, and I don't care. I thought because we would marry, everything would be fine, that no one would care about the rumors—"

"That was before Ava brought everything front and center at a ball given in celebration of my father's wedding...my father, one of the most influential men in all of New England. People are still talking about it." Vance raked his fingers through his thick, cropped hair, evidently exasperated by the turn of events. "The brunt of the drama happened while you were hiding, and then no one knew what to think because you'd disappeared."

I made my first move to cross the room, hardly able to stand by the door any longer. What could I do or say to change his mind back to wanting me? "I'm sorry; I should have opened the door for you—"

"It doesn't matter now. It helped me to see how useless it was for me to pretend I could come to Boston and fit in to the society my family's been a part of for generations. No one will ever believe I'm a gentleman, and no one will respect you as they should." He paused, and took a deep breath. "However, if you marry Ben and move to Tennessee, you would be the respected wife of an esteemed missionary."

Vance walked over to the game table we'd played at with Miss Abernathy and Roxy the day before the ball. How could so much change in such a short time? He leaned back against the edge of the table, bringing his arms across his mid-section. He looked like a guard dog, and I had a feeling it was his heart that he was again barricading from me.

"But we've announced the wedding. It's in less than a month. Surely it would be more dishonorable to break it off now; what would people think?"

"That you've come to your senses."

"I don't want Ben, I want you." I wrung my fingers, nervously. Was he really so ready to foist me off onto someone else? "I'm grateful that it was you Ezra shackled me to, and not a hundred other different men."

Vance shook his head slightly, his eyes closed for a moment before darting open. They were leveled straight at me. "Grateful... to be stuck with me?"

"Despite your past, you're becoming a better man, I can tell. I don't know what else I could think to ask for in an intended husband. If you are willing to fight these rumors—if you truly don't care what society thinks, then why should I? I have lived without Boston's approval my whole life! Why should I begin to care now?" When he didn't reply, I added, "I don't care what anyone else thinks—only you."

He looked noticeably agitated for a moment, as if I'd penetrated the barrier, and he didn't know what to think about it. But then he said, "Ben has everything you really need. I should have told you before now... that he told me he was in love with you long before I ever found you on the steps of Everston sobbing about your hair. I should have stayed out of it. I should have pretended I didn't see you there and simply gone into the hotel a different way. Go with Ben; he and the distance he provides will safeguard you."

I could only stare at him, stunned; the tears behind my eyes burning to let loose. "But I didn't love him. I still don't love him now, I—"

"You would have, if not for me. If I hadn't become involved and tempted Ezra to reinforce the connection we'd made, what happened in your dorm room wouldn't have happened, you would have continued working at Everston until Ben came back from his meeting with the mission society, you would have said yes to his proposal, and you would have loved him."

Yes, what he said made sense. Those things very well could have happened. But they hadn't. And instead, there I was in love with someone who didn't seem to want me in the least, though he'd done a pretty good job convincing me he did for those last two months.

"And he would still marry you now."

"I know."

"He would take you to Tennessee in a heartbeat." Vance uncrossed his arms and edged off the game table. "Did he mention anything to you at the ball—?"

"He asked me to marry him," I stated, much more calmly than I felt. "He asked me to reconsider my engagement to you, but I told him I wouldn't. I told him I wanted to marry you, and that you wanted to marry me."

"Well, he'll be happy to find that you were mistaken."

I couldn't have formed an answer if I tried, and I struggled to keep my tears hidden as I crossed the room toward the door.

Had I been mistaken? Everything about those last two months in Boston flitted through my mind, reminding me of a way of life I'd only dreamt about, and it wasn't because of the mansions and fancy dresses—it was because of how I'd felt with him.

Vance, although I'd only really known him since the end of March, was the one person I felt safest with. He'd done so much for me; made me care for him, made me fall in love with him, made me want him, only to now throw it all back in my face. What was wrong with him, that he would be so cruel?

And what was wrong with me that I didn't want to let him go? He was right. He didn't deserve me. He deserved to be alone, and he knew it. I'd been foolish to think that his good intentions could someday come to mean more. He'd never loved me. He would have told me if he had.

I had been deluding myself that a happy marriage would be possible. And now...now I really didn't know what to think. Or do.

As I came to the double pocket doors, I forced myself to breathe, to catch just enough breath to say, "So, I would—you would have me break our engagement in order to marry Ben, and you don't think I would run the risk of permanently ruining my reputation doing so?"

"You'll be unknown to anyone in Tennessee. Your reputation will be based on your character, not your past circumstances. And, most importantly, Rowen Steele will never find you."

"How does one go about breaking an engagement?" I could hear the tears in my voice, and was certain he could too, but there was nothing I could do about it.

"I'll tell my family you had a change of heart, after realizing you could have someone like Ben Whitespire instead of me."

It wasn't true, but it sounded believable, at least.

I tried to think beyond the fog in my head, but the only thing that seemed right to do was to turn around, throw myself into his arms, and force him to hold me—to love me.

But I couldn't. He would just stand there, stoically, keeping his hands to himself and his heart shut away from me.

There was nothing I could do. Nothing but keep my chin up high, show him a strength I didn't feel and walk away. He hadn't even given me a ring to return, only two sweet months that had permanently changed my heart forever.

21

The Train Station

"I have no thought, no view, no hope, in life beyond her; and if you oppose me in this great stake, you take my peace and happiness in your hands, and cast them to the wind."
—Charles Dickens, *Oliver Twist*

It didn't take long to break my engagement to Vance.

No longer than it had taken to create it out of practically nothing in Dexter's office at Everston.

I didn't see him again after leaving the back parlor that awful Saturday afternoon when my world had come tumbling down around me.

Again.

Miss Abernathy and Roxy said little when I told them I'd decided to marry Ben instead of Vance. A silence seemed to descend over Hilldreth Manor for the next weeks. Roxy shut herself away in her room most of the time, and when she did emerge, she barely had two words to put together. Miss Abernathy only chatted with her new Pomeranian puppy, Winston, who accompanied her everywhere.

Perhaps they thought me foolish, indecisive, even cruel—breaking Vance's heart.

I wanted to scream that it was really quite the opposite.

Vance had, for whatever reason, changed his mind about marrying me, but he wasn't about to go around telling everyone that it was his doing. If it were known by the public that he'd found some fault with me, it would have truly ruined my reputation more than ever.

It hurt deeply that he had stood by me, protected me, told me he would do anything for me and acted as if he were in love with me. And that he then did *this*.

I was now more lost than ever—more than when Ezra had forced me out of my parents' home and turned it into a brothel. Even more than when he chopped off my beautiful locks and then drugged me in order to be sure I was placed under the powerful protection of Vance Everstone.

Soon after I told Miss Abernathy and Roxy my news, I wrote a letter to Mr. Culver at Lippencott about my changed circumstances. I also sent a message to my aunt and cousins regarding my plans to move to Tennessee, but each day brought no news. It seemed they had disappeared—even Miss Abernathy hadn't seen or heard from her new friend since they'd missed the wedding at the beginning of the month.

I did count it fortunate that Vance's family was safely in Bar Harbor, where they could receive his news however they chose.

Because of the implications concerning Rowen Steele and the integrity of the mission society, the plan was for me to quietly make the move cross-country. Everyone thought it would be best not to bring undo attention to myself before taking the train down to meet Ben at Roan Mountain Station, the town where the mission would be settled. He'd already started on his way down to Tennessee in hopes of finding someone to marry when the mission society contacted him by telegram that I'd changed my mind about his proposal, and that I would be down to meet him—to marry him soon.

The Boston Inland Mission Society had recently acquired another young couple headed to the same mission, a Dr. and Mrs. Hatfield, who were to be my escorts. Sending me to the mountains of Tennessee seemed fitting; it was over a thousand miles away from both Rowen Steele and Ezra, and from what I'd heard, it was similar to the terrain of north-central Maine. It really did seem to benefit everyone, having Ben marry me, especially since I was the one he'd wanted all along.

My heart was broken, but there was a numbness that had taken over since my last glimpse of Vance.

I'd come to realize I'd put too much trust in him and his protection; too much faith in his feelings for me. Somehow I'd lost sight of my true Savior, Protector and Lover of my soul, the Lord Jesus Christ.

And somehow, through it all, Vance had kept his sights straight with what little practice he had, and I had failed miserably. His rejection of me even came from him trying to be more conscientious, and more Christ-like. I wanted to hate him for it too, but I couldn't. He had done what he thought was best for me.

～

Monday, June 27th, 1892

The morning of the day I was to meet the Hatfields at the train station for our trip to Tennessee, Miss Abernathy suddenly took an interest in speaking to me again. "Violet, you haven't packed half of your gowns. You'll want them; there's nothing wrong with taking them. They're yours." She pointed her cane to the giant pile of dresses on the chaise longue in my room.

I eyed the chiffon-layered, gauzy heap. "But they were part of my wedding trousseau, but for when I'd planned to marry someone else; someone very different than a missionary. Is it proper for me to keep them?"

"You have all these trunks to pack them into, so why not?" she asked, plopping her little dog onto my bed to open one of the many empty trunks the servants had brought up for me. "If you truly don't want them, perhaps you can give them to some of your new friends?"

"I hadn't thought of that. Perhaps I will take them all." I studied the massive pile silently; there were so many! I had no idea what it would be like in Tennessee, but every girl loved pretty dresses—surely I could find good homes for most of them. I glanced up quickly to ask, "Will you come to the train station with me when I leave tonight?"

"Of course we will." Miss Abernathy soon fell silent as she walked about my room examining my things as I packed the rest of the gowns. "Vance probably never told you he's in love with you, did he? He is, though, I promise you. I've never seen him as he is with you; so gallant and chivalrous."

I kept myself turned away from her, staying busy, and refused to answer.

There was no answer. Because she was wrong. He didn't love me. He'd thought he wanted me for a spell, and obviously had got over it.

"I'm not sure who you're in love with, Violet, or what you mean by breaking off things with Vance to run off with Reverend Whitespire. I thought you loved Vance, but now...now, I just don't understand."

Neither did I, actually.

"I'm not in love with anyone," I lied. "My reputation has been ruined by the shady actions of my brother. I have to marry someone, and Ben is the best choice."

Miss Abernathy harrumphed loudly.

"Vance and I agreed a long time ago—well, months ago—that marrying was our only option, but considering the opportunity with Ben, we thought it best that I—"

"Are you telling me the break was mutual? That Vance wants you to marry Ben?"

"It is best."

"Violet, you shock me." And she walked out of the room without another word.

I finished packing, hurriedly throwing the rest of my belongings into the now-opened trunks scattered about my room.

My maid Bessy had come with me to Hilldreth Manor, but had been let go when I'd announced I was leaving to become a missionary. As I flung dresses into the trunks, folded up ribbons, and balled stockings, I was relieved that no one witnessed either my haphazard packing or my sour mood.

The trunks were filled in no time, but what Miss Abernathy had said about Vance being in love with me ricocheted through my heart. I wished it were true. But I knew better. It had been clear to me that she'd always believed Vance loved me; ever since meeting me for the first time.

And she'd obviously been wrong.

⌒

My horse, Lancelot, was tied to the back of the carriage as Miss Abernathy, Roxy and I rode to the train station later that evening. I'd met the Hatfields once at the mission society, and I didn't look forward to having to pretend I was happy to be going with them. I couldn't very well let on that going to the mission at Roan Mountain Station to marry their colleague was actually the last thing I really wanted to do. I'd have to live with or near them, and they needed to believe this was my choice. They already knew that Ben was in love with me—they'd been led to believe that we'd had a lover's quarrel at some point in the past but that I couldn't stand living without him now that he was moving so far away.

Yes, it all sounded quite believable.

I was so tired of living a lie, and this was just the beginning. My whole life would be a lie from then on. Forever and ever.

As I sat across from Miss Abernathy and Roxy, I tried not to look at them. Miss Abernathy seemed to be quite put out with me, while Roxy looked pale and acted as if she were going to be sick.

Fortunately, it wasn't a long drive, and once we'd arrived, the busyness of getting my horse untethered from the back of the carriage and my trunks brought down and loaded onto a cart was distraction enough. I held onto a large bag with my most precious possessions in it—my books.

I really wasn't sure what to do or where to go—did Miss Abernathy know?

Before I could ask, I noticed Miss Abernathy's face transform from a disapproving frown to a gleeful smile.

I turned around to find Vance—of all people—stalking up to the three of us. He looked about as unhappy as Miss Abernathy had been a moment before, his dark even brows low over his eyes, and his steps decidedly determined. He was aimed straight for me.

Why had he come? To make my going away worse?

"What are you doing here?" I asked when he stood before me, not caring how rude I sounded.

"I've come to apologize." His dark eyes stayed steadily on me, so focused, not noticing a thing of everything going on around us on that busy sidewalk. He acknowledged neither Roxy nor Miss Abernathy who both now stood behind me.

"For?"

"For breaking our engagement; please forgive me." He took my hand in his, stretching his fingers into my sleeve, caressing the tender skin there.

"What is that supposed to mean?" I pulled away halfheartedly, which achieved nothing.

"It means, I'll marry you, if you'll only stay. Don't go. I need—I need to marry you. I *want* to marry you."

I was stunned into silence.

Before I could gain my composure, he continued, "If you'll excuse us, Claudine, Miss Blakeley, I'd like to speak with Violet in private." He managed to link my arm around his and led me away without waiting for their response. He looked at me intently as we walked around the corner of the building to a vacant area everyone passed by without a glance.

When we came to a stop, I let go of him and backed against the brick wall. "What are you saying?"

"I thought I was doing what was best, but as it turns out, I've had a difficult time deciding exactly what that is. I've been miserable without you. You're all I can think about." He shook his head, took off his hat and let it drop to the ground. "How would I know you're safe? How would I live knowing you were his, and not mine?"

I could tell he wasn't speaking about Rowen Steele, but Ben.

"But you gave me up. You wanted me to marry Ben. You told me—"

"I never *wanted* that, believe me." He grabbed my hand, but this time he simply held it tight. "I was trying to do what was right. But it wasn't."

"It wasn't?" I repeated.

Vance's gaze left mine for the first time. He seemed so different, so unsure of himself. As if he were truly afraid I wouldn't take him back.

"Would it help to know that Ben has decided to marry a young woman he met on the train down to Tennessee?"

"Instead of me?"

"I was just given his telegram from the mission society. They contacted me. They aren't sure what to do with you now. Which is why you should marry me."

"Surely, you're mistaken!" I exclaimed. "He knew how desperate of a situation I was in…why I needed to marry him."

"But it's not too desperate anymore, Violet. There's my offer, after all." Vance smiled rakishly, suddenly with much more confidence. "Perhaps he wasn't sure enough of your affections. And can you blame him, when you'd refused him and told him you wanted to marry me, only weeks ago? And now you can."

I didn't answer. I wasn't sure how to yet.

He was who I wanted to marry, the only man I'd ever been in love with, and although he'd hurt me dreadfully…there he was now, asking me to forgive him and to reconsider; asking me to take him back.

And of course I would.

But I was still as confused as ever in regards to what he felt for me. He hadn't mentioned love, only that marrying him was what he wanted me to do.

"Will you marry me, Violet? Tonight? So we can forget this nonsense of going back and forth and just be done with it?" He produced a diamond ring from his breast pocket and held it before me. It sparkled radiantly in the lamplight. "I've waited too long already; these last two weeks being the worst of it, thinking I'd lost you."

He'd never given me a ring in all those months we'd been engaged the first time. Did it mean this was a genuine proposal because of his genuine desire to marry me?

I couldn't help but love him all the more for this thoughtful touch. I knew he had a good heart, although sometimes terribly misguided.

"You never lost my heart, Vance." I brought my hand up to the ring and slipped it snugly onto my finger. "It's been yours—"

He took two steps forward, and reached up, slid his right hand behind my neck, bringing me swiftly to him, and pressed his lips to mine—right there, not too far from the crowded sidewalk, as people walked by and went on with their business! My hands rested at his shoulders, savoring the solidity there, and the glorious fact that he was indeed *mine*, once again.

He kissed me much longer than I'd ever dreamed anyone would dare kiss on a public sidewalk. He kept his one hand at the back of my neck and the other at my elbow, maintaining a respectable distance between us. But oh, the blazing fire just his lips on mine could create!

He wanted to marry me *now*? As in leave the station, be married, and finally go home?

It was everything I wanted, suddenly within my reach.

After a few minutes I broke away, breathless, recalling where we were, my luggage, my horse, and oh gracious—Miss Abernathy and Roxy!

"Can we? Can we really?"

"Can we...what?" he asked; I could feel his heart pounding underneath my hand.

"Marry tonight? Your family won't mind? I would go home with you to Everthorne?"

"Yes, and no." Fire blazed from his eyes as he purposefully, and slowly, contemplated his last answer. "And yes."

I knew exactly what that last "yes" entailed, and why he'd answered me so deliberately.

"We need to tell Miss Abernathy and stop my things from being loaded onto the train, to have them and my horse delivered to Everthorne instead." I could tell my cheeks were flushed, but I kept talking regardless, hoping he wouldn't detect my bashfulness. "Where will we marry on such short notice?"

"Trinity Church."

"The fashionable church your father was just married in? I thought it took years—"

"Not when all you need is an officiant and two witnesses. And that's what we'll have. Dr. Grig Wellesley can officiate, and Claudine and Roxy Blakeley can witness. And we can go home to Everthorne afterwards, together."

I grinned giddily, unable to contain my joy. Fifteen minutes before, I'd been terrified of my future, broken-hearted and afraid I'd never be happy again—and now I had everything I'd ever wanted restored to me, tenfold.

22

Trinity Church

"Simplicity is the ultimate sophistication."
—Leonardo da Vinci

Hello Vance. Miss Hawthorne," Dr. Wellesley greeted me with a quick handshake as he held open the door, ushering us into a semi-darkened back corridor of Trinity Church.

That he already knew who I was didn't shock me. Not with how much time Vance had been spending with him over the last few months.

I could hardly tell a thing about the elderly gentleman's appearance, as not many of the wall lamps in the hall were lit.

"It's nice to meet you, Dr. Wellesley. I know Vance values your friendship, and that your mentorship means a great deal to him."

"Our two witnesses are close behind us, in another carriage."

Dr. Wellesley didn't seem surprised by Vance's remark; he only smiled. Did he already know why we'd come? In the dimly lit corridor, I found Vance's hand and took it in mine. He squeezed his fingers between my own, holding my hand tight.

A few moments later Dr. Wellesley asked, "Would you like to marry in the garden you just walked in through? With the moon shining overhead, it would be fitting for a clandestine elopement."

"That sounds quite lovely, but how did you know the purpose for our visit?" I asked, my curiosity getting the best of me.

"I sent a message before meeting you at the station, that he might expect us," Vance quickly said.

"Might?" I whispered with a hidden smile.

"I hoped." He leaned in and breathed the words into my ear. "But I couldn't be absolutely certain."

I flushed remembering the last kiss. Yes, he would have known what my response would be. Even if I'd never told him I was in love with him, he had to know. I covered my confusion by addressing Dr. Wellesley.

"Do you live in adjoining quarters?"

"I have a room close by, but I basically live here at the church. I had a nice little room at an inn a while back, but the building was burned to the ground last summer, so now I spend most of my time here."

"I'm sorry for your misfortune. I hope you didn't lose much in the fire."

"Just a few earthly possessions, but nothing of consequence. And through the process of going through my misfortune, as you called it, I was able to meet the gentleman you've come here to marry tonight and to witness the transformation in his life. That has been worth it to me."

I turned to Vance, drawing nearer to his side. That he had Dr. Wellesley's high regard meant so much. I had a feeling that he knew Vance better than anyone did.

A knock sounded upon the door we'd just come through. Dr. Wellesley reached to open it and Miss Abernathy and Roxy entered the church, the few dim lights illuminating the hall casting shadows over them. Miss Abernathy handed me something, and as I took it, I realized it was a fragrant, white peony from along the walk outside the church.

"You'll need to have a flower for your wedding, Violet."

"Thank you," I said simply, and took it from her, bringing the fragrant bloom to my nose. I'd always loved the sweet scent of peonies.

"Dr. Wellesley, this is Miss Claudine Abernathy, a dear friend of my family's, and my youngest sister's sister-in-law, Miss Roxanna Blakeley, who is currently visiting from Maine." Vance turned his attention to everyone else, but still held my hand close between us. "Claudine, Roxy, this is my friend, Dr. Grig Wellesley, who will be marrying us tonight."

"This is a splendid thing you're doing for Vance and Violet, Dr. Wellesley. You would never imagine how many prayers I've sent up on behalf of this young man throughout the years, hoping for the Lord to bring him to Himself, and then that He'd have someone like our dear Violet for him." Claudine nudged Vance with her cane as Roxy stood silently beside her. "Though there were times my heart hurt for him over the years, thinking all was lost, here we are, ready to celebrate with them. I'm happy for you, Vance, for so many reasons."

"Thank you for doing this for us," Vance said, though I wasn't sure who he was exactly speaking to—all three of them? They were all doing us a favor, after all. "With our wedding plans cancelled and Rowen Steele still a threat, it is best to—"

"You don't have to convince me of why you wish to marry this young lady," Dr. Wellesley uttered. "You've already said plenty in the last months to vouch for this hurried wedding—" he scratched the scruffy whiskers at his chin, "Well, I suppose not exactly *hurried* since it was already planned once."

"There's absolutely nothing wrong with getting married when in love and equally yoked," Miss Abernathy responded.

Vance didn't say anything in response to this—but then again, neither did I.

"I'm just so happy the two of you were able to resolve whatever misunderstanding you'd had, Vance, that would make your fiancée practically move across the country to marry someone else. And well, I don't even know what to think about Reverend Whitespire now!"

Roxy sighed beside Miss Abernathy. Yes, I couldn't imagine what she must have felt after hearing about Ben's thoughtless and uncharacteristic actions, but still, I couldn't help but be thankful for his rash decision to marry another. Now that I wasn't on my way to Tennessee with the Hatfields, I felt such an immense relief.

"You ready?" Vance asked.

Dr. Wellesley took a slow step down the hall. "I'll be right back with the papers you'll need to sign."

Vance took my hand and guided me outside, and then along a brick path that led to an arched entryway through a stone wall. The pathway winded through the walled-in garden area toward another row of peony bushes. I heard Dr. Wellesley guiding Miss Abernathy and Roxy behind us. We stopped at a small wooden table nestled against a gazebo covered with fragrant wisteria blossoms. Dr. Wellesley set the certificate upon it, along with a basket containing a bottle of wine, a stemmed glass, and a folded white cloth. He then gestured to Vance and me to stand before him.

Vance lifted my left hand to his lips, slipping the diamond ring he'd just given me at the train station off my finger with a sly smile. "I promise I'll give it back."

Still in my stylish gray traveling suit, I felt far from the society bride Vance's family had turned me into over the months. What would the newspapers say now? They'd never caught wind of our broken engagement, quite purposefully, or my plans to marry Ben Whitespire and were, I suppose, still looking forward to reporting on the elaborate details of the ceremony at Everthorne…which wasn't to be. But wouldn't they be surprised to find that we were already married—and living serenely at Everthorne. Or would we be in Europe? My mind whirled with the details of what I was about to do as Miss Abernathy and Roxy took their places as witnesses to our right and left.

Before I knew it, Dr. Wellesley had started the ceremony with the simple words, "Let us begin."

I stood before Vance, holding the peony Miss Abernathy had picked, completely undeterred by how thrown-together everything seemed. I didn't care. It was much more like I'd envisioned my wedding compared to what Vance's family had been planning at Everthorne. With the fragrance of the nearby row of peony bushes, and the moon and stars shining over us, the setting was more beautiful than I could have ever asked for.

"Vance and Violet have come to witness before us, telling of their commitment to belong to one another in holy matrimony. This wedding, an act of complete faith, each in the other, is the heart of the faithful relationship created between them." Dr. Wellesley held his Bible open, but didn't look at it as he spoke. "Vance, if you would take your bride's hand and give her the ring symbolizing your faith and commitment."

Dr. Wellesley set his Bible down, took the bottle of wine and poured a small amount into the glass. Vance slowly placed the diamond ring to my left hand, as I held my flower in my right. "My faith and commitment, to you *only*, Violet. Behold, you are consecrated to me with this ring."

"But what about mine?" I asked, hardly audibly.

"Your what?" Vance answered with a whisper.

"I have no ring for you. What about the symbolism of my faith and commitment—your consecration to me?"

"That's what this is for—" and Vance took the glass of wine from Dr. Wellesley, took a small sip and then handed it to me. "If you'll drink from the glass."

I tipped the glass and drank what was left inside, which wasn't much. Dr. Wellesley immediately took it from me and wrapped it snugly within the white cloth.

"This glass represents you, Vance and Violet, as a couple. Just as the glass, when it is broken, will enter a state from which it will never emerge." He placed it upon the tiled floor between us, and with a nod of his head, "Vance, you may now—"

Vance stomped upon the sheathed glass, crushing it against the brick pathway.

"You will also now enter this new life together as permanently as this glass is now shattered," Dr. Wellesley explained. "You will be one, committed and bound together forever by your vows." He then handed each of us a piece of paper. "For the benefit of the shortened ceremony, you merely need to read them—"

Without being asked twice, I held up mine and started reading aloud by the light of the torches along the path. "I, Violet, take thee, Vance, to be my wedded husband, to have and to hold, from this day forward." My left hand was still clutched by Vance's right. "To cherish, till death do us part, according to God's holy ordinance; and thereto I pledge myself to you."

"And now, Vance."

After a split second, in which he seemed only able to stare down at me, he looked down to his paper and read, "I, Vance, take thee, to be my wedded wife, to have and to hold, from this day forward, to cherish, till death do us part, according to God's holy ordinance;" until, for the last, most wonderful sentence, he looked me in the eyes, "And thereto I pledge myself to you, Violet."

"Inasmuch as Vance and Violet have declared their devotion to each other before you, their witnesses, by the authority vested in me, I pronounce them to be husband and wife."

Miss Abernathy clapped excitedly as soon as the words were said, and Roxy followed her example after a short delay. We then all signed the marriage contract, and Miss Abernathy gave me a hug. "I have been praying for you, Violet. For a long time."

I smiled at her, at her joy in seeing me wedded to Vance, whom she'd known since he was born.

So that was it? I was really Mrs. Vance Everstone so quickly?

"Well, I'll say. Thank you for the unexpectedly romantic evening!" Miss Abernathy hobbled back through the arch we'd entered the garden by. "But it's getting to be late, and I think Roxy and I will be headed home now."

Roxy followed her quietly, and I realized she'd not said a single word since we'd left Hilldreth Manor earlier that evening in heading to the train station.

"Thank you for being a witness for my wedding, Roxy," I said as she walked away.

She turned, and at least attempted a smile. "I am happy for you, Violet. More than I can say."

"Come along Roxy, dear, let's leave them be. They'll want to be alone now, now that they can."

Vance and I followed them to the outer garden area. Dr. Wellesley walked behind us, and after a final blessing-filled goodbye, went back into the church.

Miss Abernathy and Roxy went on to their carriage without another word.

When Vance helped me into his carriage, I took my normal seat, facing front. And then as he entered after me, he came to sit next to me. Our arms were immediately around each other as the carriage started down the street. I held him, my cheek pressed to his thudding chest, and he simply held me back. I hadn't known such contentedness was even possible; how two people could be joined and become one so effortlessly.

The only thing either of us said the short distance home to Everthorne was Vance's secret whisper in my ear: "I am my beloved's, and my beloved is finally mine."

23

Home

"On the secretly blushing cheek is reflected the glow of the heart."
—Søren Kierkegaard

When we arrived at Everthorne, we were greeted at the door by Brubaker, the butler.

"Welcome home, Mr. Everstone. I trust the wedding went well?" He took our hats, as well as the bag with my current manuscripts, which I'd left in the carriage during the wedding.

"Very well, indeed," Vance answered as he slipped out of his jacket and handed it to the butler.

Seeing him in just his dark gray waistcoat and shirtsleeves did something funny to my heart. It began beating erratically, and I had to literally force my lingering gaze from him.

"I'm glad to hear it, sir."

Vance looped his arm about my waist. "And since you haven't officially met yet, this is my wife, Mrs. Violet Everstone. Violet, this is Brubaker, our butler."

Brubaker turned specifically to me and added, "It's nice to finally meet you, Mrs. Everstone."

"Thank you, Brubaker. It's wonderful to finally be home."

He bowed a few inches. "I'm sure you'll do a splendid job of making Everthorne a home, indeed, ma'am. Your luggage was delivered to your rooms earlier, and your horse is situated in the stable." Before I could answer, he again faced Vance. "I trust you'd rather not be disturbed for the remainder of the evening?"

Vance cleared his throat gruffly. "Quite right—"

"Oh, do wait just a minute before sending them up!" An older lady stepped out of the dining room down the hall with a tray balanced in her hands. "I've made up a little something for the two of you. I hope you don't mind, Mr. Everstone."

"Not at all, Mrs. Jeffries." Vance grinned, obviously not surprised by his housekeeper's foresight.

The woman stopped in front of us, and while still holding the tray, slightly bowed her head, "Mrs. Everstone. It's a pleasure to meet you."

Vance's hand slid up my back as we both studied the tray she presented to us. It was filled with chocolate-covered fruit of all kinds. "Violet, this is our housekeeper, Mrs. Jeffries."

"I'll take this up to your rooms, then." She was headed up the stairs with the tray before either of us could respond.

I was a little bemused at her industry. She couldn't have known about there being a *Mrs. Everstone* for more than a few hours. Once Brubaker had excused himself and headed down the hall and Mrs. Jeffries had made it to the landing at the top of the stairs, Vance wrapped his other arm around me, bringing us face-to-face. From the adoring look he gave me, I could almost believe he loved me.

"You're finally mine," he uttered.

I nodded my head, blushing shyly, but it was enough of an answer, for his arms tightened around my waist. He bent his face closer to mine, but he didn't touch my lips with his. Instead, he pressed his cheek to mine and whispered in my ear, "Remind me to thank your brother the next time I see him."

"You really don't think we would have eventually come to this if not for his meddling?"

"I doubt it. I wouldn't have allowed it of myself."

"Why not?"

"Because I could never deserve you, Violet."

I reached to touch his shoulder, then ran my hand down his arm and heard his quick intake of breath. "So you think, husband. Yet here I am, willingly."

Even if Ben hadn't decided to marry someone else, giving me hardly any other option, I still would have chosen Vance once he was there at the station asking me to. There was no contest. I loved him. And being married to Ben—no matter how formidable of a gentleman he was—while being in love with Vance would have been, I was certain, veritable torture every day for the rest of my life. Would I really have gone through with it once I'd made it to Tennessee?

"I'm sorry about the last three weeks. If it helps to make you feel better, I was absolutely miserable, first as I tried to convince myself to break our engagement, and then as it was broken. I thought I was doing what was best for you."

"That you were equally as miserable does make me feel a little better." I smiled nervously.

When we'd met at the train station, it had already been past dinnertime, and now what were we to do? It seemed so strange to be alone, and be expected to retire for the evening together.

"I was a coward, Vance. I should have let you in at the ball. I ran away in fear from you, when I should have run to you—"

"I never imagined that Ava could be so vicious, that she would risk her own good name to slander yours. She doesn't know how much I've changed in the last year. And I have to admit, the side she revealed at the ball would have matched me quite well before. I was just as cruel once—"

"But you're not now." I placed my right hand over his heart.

He leaned over me, bringing his face close to mine. He whispered, "You're too good to forgive me so easily. You've forgiven so much."

He was so close to saying what I wanted to hear, perhaps all he needed was solid confirmation from me.

"That's because I love you," I whispered back.

He didn't answer audibly, but brought one hand from my back to my elbow, then to my shoulder, and finally my neck. He raked his fingers through my short hair; easily loosening the strands from their pins. I heard a few of them fall to the polished wood floor, but I didn't care.

The hand still at my back pressed in, bringing me flush against him, and I reached up and kissed him, much like the time a month before, right after he'd given me my Lippencott book contract. But this time, it didn't matter what the consequences of my daring actions would be, because we were married.

As he kissed me back, and kept kissing me, I gripped the back of his arms with both hands, and I could feel the contours of his muscles through the material of his shirt. I remembered the vision of him in my bed at the dormitory...his bare arm, his shoulders, his tussled hair. I couldn't help but press farther. I wanted all that; I just had to get past my nerves.

Vance broke away, but stayed ever so close, his breath mingled with mine. "You took my name today, Violet. You're Violet Everstone now. You're mine, and I'm yours. Will you take me, all of me?" He paused for just a second, but before I could think of anything coherent to say, he hurried on, "I don't want to push you. I know you never expected to see me again mere hours ago, but here you are, now my wife, and I hope—"

"I do," I breathed my answer. "I will." I still stayed so close, but took a step back, bringing him with me. "I don't know about you, but I'm famished for one of those chocolate covered strawberries Mrs. Jeffries had on the tray she took up to my room."

"Well then, by all means, let's go find that tray. I wouldn't want you to starve."

I smiled, took his hand, and led him to the stairs. We went up the steps slowly and awkwardly. I still wasn't certain I was ready, but I would be. I would be eventually. I'd been halfway there once before, hadn't I? Why did I feel so nervous?

Because this was planned. Purposeful. This was what we were supposed to do now. And it seemed more staged than exhilarating as I took those long, arduous steps up to the bedroom which would now be mine, next to his.

As we made it to the head of the staircase, I heard Mrs. Jeffries whistling toward the back of the house, likely taking the back stairs down to the kitchen.

"They'll leave us be, as promised," Vance assured. "Would you like to see your room? I hope you like it."

"I'm sure I will. How many bedrooms are there?" I asked, hating how forced I sounded.

"Six, plus the nursery on the attic level."

"Could we perhaps make one of these bedrooms," I motioned down the hall, "the nursery instead of having it in the attic? I like how involved Natalia and Amaryllis were with their babies, and there would be less chance of, you know, bats."

"We can do anything you'd like, dear wife."

Vance guided me to the second door to our left and opened it for me, allowing me to enter first into the dimly lit rooms. And "rooms" really was what it consisted of—the main bedroom, an attached bathroom and another space that opened up to the bedroom that was set up as more of a sitting area.

And fortunately, it wasn't all too big, which was a fear I'd had upon first setting foot in the house. The only time I'd actually seen the rooms, they had been bare of any wallpapering, flooring or drapes—and now, it was the picture of perfection in shades of pink, beige, and white. The colors complimented the dark wood trim of the doors, windows, and crown molding. The bed was white with beige and light pink pillows and coverings. It was something of a sleigh bed, but without a footboard, and if I recalled correctly, was considered French Provincial, and matched all of the other pieces of furniture in the room. The tray of chocolate covered fruit from Mrs. Jeffries was situated on one of the night stands next to the bed.

There were two floor-to-ceiling windows facing the doorway we stood in, covered in lace and pink brocade. Between them was a mirror almost as tall, situated in front of a vanity table. There was a sofa in the corner, and a fireplace with a wardrobe next to that which was opened to display all of the dresses from my wedding trousseau. And hanging on a hook, seemingly set aside, a fine, velvety blue-and-lace dressing gown and matching slippers I'd never seen before. Next to that, was the door to Vance's bedroom.

I swallowed, unable to take a step farther into the room with Vance standing beside me. Suddenly, my thumbnail was between my teeth, and I chewed it nervously. "Um, may I have a few minutes, in my room, alone?"

"Of course, I need to go downstairs for something anyway."

I really doubted he had anything to actually take care of downstairs, but I welcomed the distance his errand afforded. I needed some time to myself, some time to gather my nerves and to prepare.

The truth was, I had no idea what to expect, except that the times in which Vance had kissed me up to that point had basically turned me into a pile of mush. As I slipped off my gray dress suit I'd donned that morning, expecting two days of travel, I decided to keep my chemise and corset on, foregoing completely changing for bed. I pulled on the brand new dressing gown and slippers and looked in the mirror above the vanity.

My hair had basically come undone downstairs when Vance had tunneled his fingers through it, which seemed appropriate, since I knew he loved it that way.

As I stood there, staring at the mirror, I heard the door from the hall to the next room—Vance's room—open and then close.

I sat upon my new bed, running my hand over the fine material of the coverlet. Was I supposed to sit there and wait for him?

After a few moments, I stood again.

I couldn't.

Quickly stalking over to the door to his room, I stood there silently. It would mean so much more to him if I came to him; a proof of my love and my willingness.

That was when I realized he'd never said he loved me after I'd admitted as much to him. He'd only kissed me. But that wasn't exactly reciprocation; that only meant he still *wanted* me as much as he ever had...which meant I needed to reach deeper into his heart.

I wanted it to beat for me. I wanted to make him respond to me in ways I'd only had glimpses of in the last few months. Maybe once the flames were fanned, he would tell me. Maybe once everything he wanted was within his grasp, he would realize what I wanted to hear from him?

With a slow breath out, I knocked on the door.

When he answered, I had a quick look at his bedroom, but I could barely focus on the darkened interior. I could only see the man standing before me. He was still dressed in the clothes he'd met me at the station in, minus his jacket of course, which was downstairs. And now he was missing his cravat, his shirt collar opened exposing his neck.

I stepped over the threshold and closed the door behind me. His eyes hadn't left the securely tied bodice of my dressing gown since he'd opened the door, and his breathing had become noticeably uneven. But then he smiled, shaking his head slowly. "I'm sorry, I just didn't expect you would—"

"I can go back to waiting in my room, if you'd like." I crossed my arms snugly around my upper waist, nervously snagging the lace with my fingertips.

"No." He swallowed loudly, which made me smile. "No more waiting." He unbuttoned the top button of his waistcoat.

Suddenly, I felt brave, so fiercely courageous. I took a step forward and helped him with the next button down.

Cautious little me, who'd never touched a man, let alone kissed one until I'd been forced into this arrangement with Vance, and now all I wanted was to show him how much I loved him, how much I belonged with him, no matter what he thought he did or didn't deserve.

He stopped and stared down at my fingers working at the next button. "You don't know what you're doing, Violet."

Was it that obvious? I stopped, burying my face into his chest, completely embarrassed; my fingers still lingering around the third button down I'd just freed.

His arm slid across my shoulders. "I meant you don't know what you're doing *to me*," he chuckled, his voice low. And then with one long dark look, he silently asked my permission again. There were no words to convey what exactly the look meant, only that it was a strange mix of respect, anxiety, and desire.

And it had such an effect on me that I couldn't help but take a small step closer, pressing my hands to his chest. In no time at all, he had me against the door, his lips on mine, his hands—still hesitantly—at my shoulders.

"Violet, it's been such a long wait."

A long wait, as in, since the last time? With Giselle? With Ava? Or who else? Those sudden, awful thoughts made my breath hitch in my chest, and I had to stop the kiss just to help collect my bearings. I locked my hands around the back of his neck, and kept my forehead bowed against his collarbone.

I hated that he had such a past, but how could I judge him when he'd turned to Christ and at the same time so willingly turned from those old ways?

I knew it would take so much more than I had in me to constantly forgive him when these thoughts would creep up. Who had they been? How many times? How many women? And would I be enough to keep him satisfied?

God would have to help my heart, and I would have to consistently ask for His help. It was the only way. I needed to somehow forgive, but then *forget* as well.

Slipping my hands down the front of his waistcoat, I caught the corner of a piece of paper sticking out of his pocket. "What's this?"

He pressed his hand against mine over his heart, forcefully. "Just Ben's telegram."

"What exactly did it say?" I grabbed for it.

Vance stopped me by holding his hand over his pocket. His other hand held me back from reaching for it again.

I drew back, wondering at his defensiveness. "How did he explain—?"

"You don't want to see it."

"Yes, I do. I don't care about him. I only want to know what he said."

"No."

"What could he have possibly said that would—?" I darted my hand around his blockade and was just able to snag the paper and slip it from Vance's pocket.

"He didn't say anything worth—"

I unfolded the paper and read:

CONFIRMED [STOP] WILL MEET VH AT RMS WEDNESDAY PM PREPARED TO MARRY [STOP]

Confused, I looked at the date. It couldn't have been the right telegram, yet there was the date, June twenty-seventh, eighteen hundred and ninety-two.

"Ben is still expecting me," I stated, shocked as the words left my mouth. How were they even true?

Vance moved forward, and I fell back a step, and then two, toward the door to my room.

He'd lied to me. Purposefully lied. When he'd said he never would.

"You made it up so I would think I didn't have a choice. So I would *have* to marry you, whether I wanted to or not." I crumpled the paper and threw it at his feet, wishing it were something so much bigger and more hurtful.

"But you did want to—"

"And your lie has made me out to be a liar too. What will they think of me—that I would shirk my responsibilities? That I would so carelessly back out from what I'd promised without a word—without an explanation? And you lied to me when you said you never would."

"I wanted to be sure you'd choose me, Violet. I immediately regretted saying as much after learning such tactics weren't needed, but as we were discussing things, it had seemed the only way to get you to marry me again."

"Of course I wanted to marry you…." Although I'd been quite sure at the train station that I would have chosen Vance, no matter what, now I was too hurt and confused to think straight. Would I have really—and so blatantly—disregarded what I'd promised if it had been my choice?

I clumsily backed into the door to my room.

"I'm sorry I lied. I didn't plan on saying that, but I was desperate for you to marry me, and you seemed unsure, and it just came out—"

"Why? So you could—?" Without meaning to, I glanced toward his impressive, dark wood four-poster bed.

"That isn't why. I needed to marry you because I couldn't stand the thought of never seeing you again, having you live your life apart from me. It made me realize that I love you, Violet. I have for months. I think, even before we were forced into the predicament that produced our original engagement. I just didn't know how to deal with my feelings. They were foreign to me apart from what I was used to wanting...."

His dark eyes, so earnest and filled with emotion matched his words so well, but was it the truth? Did he really love me? Or was he only saying so trying to fix the horrid mess our wedding night had suddenly become?

I didn't know what to believe.

Jostling the doorknob behind me, I managed to open it without turning my back to him. As I stood at the threshold between our rooms, he watched my every move, almost as if he didn't know what to do to stop me.

Without giving him an answer—for I didn't know if I even had one to give—I slammed the door and locked it behind me. I didn't know how to believe him. He'd lied; and he'd told me he never would. So how could I believe anything?

I tried not to care that we'd gone from kissing against that very door, neither one of us wanting anything but each other wholly and completely...to this—to me disappearing back through to my own room in my anger.

But I couldn't go back to those feelings he'd induced in me only minutes before. The emotions that had been surging through me at the merest touch from him were gone, and I didn't know how I'd ever get them back.

Crashing onto my new bed in tears, I wished above all else that I'd never caught sight of that telegram in Vance's waistcoat pocket. For if I didn't know about the lie, then I would have still been in his room, in his arms, letting him love me.

But how could I now?

How could he have founded our marriage on a lie? Didn't he know I would have married him even if Ben had been there at the train station begging for me to reconsider?

I knew this now, as I wept upon my pillows. But I couldn't bring myself to open the door.

He hadn't knocked after I'd shut it in his face. He hadn't said a single word.

It was the scene at the ball, all over again. Except this time after locking myself away from him, he wasn't questioning; he wasn't knocking. And this time he wasn't just a fiancé, but a husband.

The fact that I was more alone than ever, without him, and that he didn't seem to mind—despite his insistence that he indeed had fallen in love with me—caused me to weep until exhaustion overwhelmed me, and I finally decided to turn off the lamps and crawl into my bed.

24

Day One

*"I have been loving you a little more every minute
since this morning."*
—Victor Hugo, *Les Miserables*

T he next morning, I awoke with a start. Half-remembering
everything from the day before—the train station and the
wedding—I sat up.

Then the rest came back to me as well.

The nerves, the kisses, the lie…and Vance loved me?

But I'd locked him out.

I'd locked the door that should never be locked. Oh, what had
I been thinking? I wanted to cry all over again. I'd already utterly
failed at being a wife.

What had caused me to react so violently? Why hadn't I
immediately forgiven him? I'd forgiven him of so much more, and
like he'd said, he'd been scared I wouldn't marry him. And he'd
wanted to marry me so very much, because he loved me.

I groaned and put my face in my hands. I was such a fool.

And now, would he forgive me?

I slowly looked around my room, taking it all in as the sun-
light brightened the walls; as if it were a grand present consisting
of everything I'd always wanted. It really was the most gorgeous
room; the kind of space I'd only ever dreamed of having.

As I examined everything from my bed, I couldn't help from constantly glancing over to the door to Vance's bedroom. I knew I was purposefully stalling, lollygagging in my bed as I was.

Was he there? I glanced at the clock on my nightstand for the first time and realized it was late. But that was good. The servants would expect that, wouldn't they? I certainly didn't want them to know the truth, that I'd locked my new husband out of my room on my wedding night.

My attention shifted to the tray of chocolate-covered fruit still on my other nightstand.

Untouched.

The fact said so much.

I rolled to the edge of my bed and threw the covers back. This would be my breakfast then.

As I fingered the first chocolate-covered strawberry, I glanced to Vance's door again. What if I took the tray to him? Was he even there? Perhaps patiently waiting for me to come to my senses?

I stood, hurried over to the tall mirror over the vanity and took a good look at myself. I'd slept in only my chemise, having taken my dressing gown and corset off for bed, and I considered taking the tray in just as I was, surprising him with my sudden boldness.

But then I lost my nerve and pulled on the dressing gown. I also added the matching slippers. He'd been good enough to gift them to me—something I never would have expected. I wanted him to know that I'd appreciated the thought, and that I came wanting to repair things between us. That would be enough, right?

Turning back to the nightstand, I took up the tray and walked to the door. Propping it against me with one hand, I slowly unlocked and opened the door.

His room was quiet, and remained quiet as I entered. When I finally stood full in the doorway, facing the bed, I realized it was empty. I set the tray down upon a long settee at the foot of Vance's bed and studied the room. The bed was made just as it had been the night before, and I couldn't tell how long he'd been gone; if it had been recently that he'd left, or the night before when I'd turned him away.

On the nightstand next to his bed was the little blue Bible he often had with him. It was opened to a page near the back, and in my curiosity, I glanced at the reference.

The book of Ephesians, chapter three.

I picked it up and took a closer look at the verses—

"That Christ may dwell in your hearts by faith; that ye, being rooted and grounded in love, may be able to comprehend with all saints what is the breadth, and length, and depth, and height; and to know the love of Christ, which passeth knowledge, that ye might be filled with all the fulness of God. Now unto him that is able to do exceeding abundantly above all that we ask or think, according to the power that worketh in us....."

Vance's constant example throughout the months had been inspiring, and I could tell every time he'd ever mentioned Christ or the Bible, it spurred a stronger desire in my heart for more of such things. I had a feeling it was Dr. Wellesley's spiritual mentorship that had prompted such a devoted study of the Scriptures. Vance had been transformed into such a great and godly man, and now I was blessed enough to have him as a husband.

I'd heard once—and I was pretty sure it was also in Ephesians—that husbands were to be spiritual leaders. And there, he'd been doing so throughout our entire engagement without either one of us realizing it.

Putting the Bible down, I caught sight of a note. Unfolding the paper, I found one sentence scrawled in Vance's handwriting: *I'm at Everstone Square.*

And then, instead of seeing the note before me, I focused on the wedding ring Vance had given me—the ring he'd proposed with for real that second time—and his touching words from the ceremony the evening before. With a stronger sense of disappointment in myself than I'd felt before, I sat next to the tray and picked off a few of the chocolate-covered strawberries and slowly ate them. I wasn't hungry now, and I couldn't take another bite after swallowing only a few.

It was useless anyway. It looked pathetically like exactly what it was: my trying to make it look as if we'd spent the evening before indulging in the fruit tray and each other...when neither was true.

And what was the use? No matter when Vance had left, it would have been noticed, and why would he leave his wife at home alone the morning after his wedding, unless things had gone awry?

How would I face the servants now? And what was I to do? Sit in my room all day and wait to find out if he'd ever speak to me again? I didn't even have my writing box. For the first time ever, I'd completely lost track of it. Because I cared about something else so much more now—Vance.

Leaving the tray in his room, I went back to my own, keeping the door between them open in case he came home.

Putting myself together for the day, I put on the least complicated of the gowns Vance had bought me for my wedding trousseau. But I couldn't quite figure out all the ties without Bessy's help, so I muddled it together as best I could and wondered if I'd be able to get her back. I would have to ask Mrs. Jeffries, which meant going downstairs. Alone.

Everthorne seemed exceptionally empty as I walked down the hall and descended the staircase. As I turned from the stairs, Mrs. Jeffries came out of the dining room. She didn't seem nearly as happy as she'd been the night before.

"Good morning, Mrs. Jeffries. I was wondering if you'd make an inquiry for me concerning my previous lady's maid. Her name is Bessy Carmichael, and she was under the Everstone family's employ until about two weeks ago."

"I certainly can do that for you, Mrs. Everstone. Would you like me to offer her the position as your lady's maid once more?"

"Yes, please." I rather selfishly hoped she'd not found a job in the meanwhile and that she would be free to come back to me.

"Mr. Everstone left me a note saying he'd be at Everstone Square most of the day," Mrs. Jeffries added hesitantly.

"I suppose, with the suddenness of the wedding yesterday, he needed to put things in better order before…before…."

"Before you leave for the honeymoon trip next week?

"Yes, that's right," I said with a nervous smile

She didn't actually respond, and went on her way.

With nothing else to do, I decided I'd walk to Hilldreth Manor to visit Miss Abernathy and Roxy. It bothered me that they were still under the impression that Ben would be so thoughtless.

~~~

I walked the few blocks to Hilldreth Manor alone, feeling as though I'd been changed into a new person. But really, there was nothing different about me from the day before besides the fact that I had a new name.

Violet Hazel Everstone.

I practiced saying it, smiling to myself, but then my smile quickly disappeared when I remembered how unlike a wife I'd been in the last twelve hours.

When I came up to Hilldreth Manor's front porch, I climbed the steps and pounded the brass knocker. I hoped they wouldn't think it was odd that I'd come. I really didn't know what else to do with myself.

The butler answered, and I said, "Violet Hazel Everstone," with more confidence than I felt. "To see Miss Abernathy," I hastily added.

He let me in with a smile and had me wait in the hall. When he came back to me and then guided me to the back parlor—a favorite room of Miss Abernathy's, I'd gathered—I immediately realized I wasn't the only visitor.

Aunt Letty and Mabel were there, and even Cal had come.

Of course, because I'd been announced, they'd been fully prepared to see me, and yet they sat so still, looking at me, wide-eyed. They almost seemed stunned. Mabel's gray-blue eyes held questions and even—was it possible?—a hint of *fear?*

Miss Abernathy stood and greeted me, handing her Pomeranian off to Roxy as she did. "Violet, I didn't expect a visit from you this morning!—really, you were only married last night!"

"Vance is at Everstone Square—he hadn't planned to take this week off...he still has so much to do," I answered as quickly as I could. "With the wedding having been moved up, he wasn't quite prepared to leave things as they were for the time while we'll be in Europe." It all sounded so true! Perhaps there really was some credence to my explanations.

"Do come and sit; join your aunt and cousins who have come by for brunch. It has been some time since we've seen them, hasn't it?"

I joined Miss Abernathy on the sofa, choosing not to comment about the lack of communication from my relatives in those last few weeks. It was awkward, to be sure, sitting with them after they'd ignored me for almost a month.

"Congratulations on your wedding, Violet." Aunt Letty smiled bashfully.

"Yes!" Cal added. He almost seemed to fidget with pent-up energy. "We were extremely happy to hear about the elopement. But what are you doing here?"

"I have something I need to tell Roxy—"

"We've heard you've written a few books for children that a publisher is interested in producing?" Aunt Letty glanced nervously at her daughter. "My, that's something you don't hear about often, is it? When did you become interested in—?"

"It's something I've thought about for a long time. I only just decided to focus on doing something about it when my parents passed away last year."

"I'd like to see what you write, Violet." Roxy looked genuinely interested, and I was sorry I'd never mentioned my books to her before.

"I don't have the ones they've contracted, but I have a few others I've been working on since that I can show you. They're at Everthorne."

"What does your husband think of your writing?" Cal asked.

"He was the one who insisted upon showing them to the publisher in the first place. I would have done nothing so bold without his encouragement and belief in me."

"Vance does love you so, Violet. Show Letty and Mabel the ring he bought for you." Miss Abernathy took my hand in hers and extended my arm so they could get a good look at the diamond ring on my finger.

"It's beautiful, Violet," Aunt Letty gasped. "Are you still sailing for Europe next week?"

"Thank you. And yes, that is the plan."

"I'm *so* glad to hear it."

Was she really so anxious to get rid of me? Well then.

"As I said before, Roxy, I came here because I had something I needed to tell you."

"Oh?" she responded.

"Would you mind, perhaps, excusing us to the front parlor, Miss Abernathy?"

"Go ahead, dear. Take your time. I am so glad you didn't leave yesterday for Tennessee." Miss Abernathy reached across the sofa and took her dog from Roxy's hands. "I knew the moment I saw Vance coming up the sidewalk behind you yesterday that you wouldn't be going, no matter what Reverend Whitespire's actions had been." She turned to my aunt and cousins. "You probably don't know the half of what has been going on around here in the last few weeks, but there's no harm in telling you now, since it's all turned out for the best."

"Oh, we'd heard that your engagement to Mr. Everstone had been broken, and we couldn't understand why," Mabel said. "We didn't want to meddle in what wasn't our business."

"We knew you were planning to move to Tennessee," Aunt Letty added. "If it seemed we were distant, dear, it was because we didn't want to bother you."

"You knew? How?" I asked, trying to keep a sudden suspicion out of my tone.

Did that mean Rowen Steele had known about my plans as well? And what if he'd been watching and he now knew I hadn't actually taken the train to Tennessee as I'd planned? But he wouldn't come after me now...not now that I was married to Vance Everstone, *would he?*

"Oh now, how was it, Cal? Didn't you have an acquaintance with someone from the mission society or something?"

"Yes, that was it." Cal shifted his position on the settee, and seemed quite anxious to at least get up, if not just plain leave.

Aunt Letty shot her son a strange, almost threatening look. "We were quite surprised when Claudine told us how your plans had changed again so drastically yesterday; that you'd been reunited and then married to your Mr. Everstone, after all."

"It was one of the most romantic things I've witnessed in my life, let me tell you," Miss Abernathy sighed. "But what Reverend Whitespire did was unforgivable! To tell our sweet Violet that he would marry her—because well, there are quite a few unfounded rumors going about town about your dear niece, Letty—and then to choose to marry some girl he'd met on the train—"

"It isn't quite as bad as we'd been led to believe, actually," I swiftly interrupted.

I didn't want Ben's name as a gentleman to be ruined in Boston, and with the way Miss Abernathy liked to talk, I hoped I wasn't already too late. But surely she hadn't already seen anyone else to tell her opinions to that day.

"What do you mean?" Roxy asked, looking more hopeful than she'd been in weeks.

The audience for my news was larger than I had hoped, but I didn't really have a choice. "Vance made up the part about Ben choosing to marry someone else."

"He did?" Roxy's cheeks went pale.

Miss Abernathy looked less shocked. "Because Vance loves you so very much...I could see him doing that."

"Yes, apparently. But it was a lie, regardless."

"And it is forgivable, I'm sure." Miss Abernathy directed a little grin at me.

"I do forgive him; please don't think—" As I said the words, I felt the truth of them too. All morning I'd been forgiving him, realizing how very much I loved, valued, and admired him despite the lie he'd told.

"Is this what you wanted to tell me—that Reverend Whitespire was still free and looking for someone willing to become his wife?"

"Goodness, what a love triangle—or rather, square—you've been creating in the last few weeks," Mabel laughed.

"It is, Roxy—I'd meant to tell you more privately."

"Why, Miss Blakeley, do you have aspirations to become Mrs. Whitespire? If so, then, I do say, now would be your chance!" Mabel's eyes sparkled knowingly.

"No, of course not...not at all. That would be ridiculous." Roxy seemed to wilt back into her seat.

"You know, Cal has been talking about moving us all up to the area you're from, Violet." Aunt Letty focused all of her attention upon the dog in her lap which looked like a mirror image of Miss Abernathy's puppy, Winston. "I suppose we might be moved by the time you get back from your honeymoon in Europe."

"Why would you do that?" I asked Cal, realizing I really hardly knew him well enough to know why he would or wouldn't do anything. "Do you not like Boston—do you not wish to stay here?"

Vance's words about the connection between Ezra and Cal, between Cal and Rowen Steel echoed in my ears.

"It's my job…" he began, but he didn't finish his thought.

"There is a job he's taken," Mabel continued.

"And it would be better for him to relocate, and it happens to be in the area around Everston," Aunt Letty added, nervously filling in her children's lack of information.

"With this new position, I'll be doing much more good for others. And I'd prefer to keep the family together."

"It will be sad to see you all go." Miss Abernathy scratched Winston's neck. "We'll have to take the train up to visit them, won't we, Violet?"

"Of course," I replied, though my mind was elsewhere.

I stood, intent on finally excusing myself again; convinced that nothing good could come from my staying. And perhaps Vance would come home to Everthorne for lunch…since no one else would be at Everstone Square. "Well, I think I'll be going. Vance might be home for lunch soon—"

"I'm sure he *might*," Aunt Letty said, trying to hide her smile with a lifted finger to her lips. "Poor man, having to go into the office the day after his wedding."

"It is unfortunate," was all I answered. "It shouldn't take long to walk home though; I'll still make it by the time he's likely to be home." I was sure. Because he probably wouldn't actually be there waiting for me. Not after last night.

"Oh no, don't walk home," Cal exclaimed, standing suddenly. "We can take you in our carriage."

I didn't know whether to feel relieved or skeptical. Why this sudden gallantry? Could I trust them to take me home safely, or should I chance the short walk? It really wasn't far, and I hadn't felt that anyone was watching me on the way *to* Hilldreth.

"Were you leaving already too?" Miss Abernathy asked, seemingly perplexed. "Weren't you going to stay for brunch? You just got here."

Aunt Letty and Mabel looked at each other momentarily, but didn't answer right away. All three of my relatives were acting so strangely.

Finally, Mabel stood and said slowly, "We really ought to be going. We'll make it up to you though, Miss Abernathy; in the coming weeks our time will be much less constrictive. We'll have brunch with you then, and definitely before we make the move to Maine."

Aunt Letty followed her daughter to her feet. "Yes, we really ought to take Violet home. I hope you understand."

Even *I* didn't understand. "You don't need to take me home; please stay and enjoy your afternoon with your friends. Don't leave early on account of me."

"If you're worried about Violet walking home alone, it really isn't far, and by the most respectable streets, but I could send her home in my carriage, if that would make you feel better. And I can send Roxy with her for the trip, for I have a feeling they'd still like to have that private conversation we never let them indulge in earlier."

"I would welcome the company, if Roxy feels well enough to join me." I stood at the same time Roxy did, leaving only Miss Abernathy seated. "I would feel much better about not breaking up your time together, especially seeing as it's limited."

"I'd love to come, Violet," Roxy said. "But to be sure, I won't stay a minute at Everthorne—not if your husband is meeting you for lunch."

Miss Abernathy stood to pull the bell next to the doorframe to the next room, and a moment later her butler was at the door.

"Please have the carriage prepared for Miss Blakeley and Miss Hawthorne—I mean, Mrs. Everstone!" She turned to me, "I'm sorry, Violet! You'd think I would remember, as I saw the wedding take place!"

"It's perfectly understandable—it was so suddenly done, after all."

"Please, let's all sit while the carriage is readied." Miss Abernathy suggested as she sat down. Everyone, including me, joined her, and for another twenty minutes of conversation revolving around the most mundane news about the latest parties and engagements, I fought down the voices of doubt that insisted my relatives—my own flesh and blood—were hardly to be trusted.

25

Entrapped

"*The most painful state of being is remembering the future,
particularly the one you'll never have.*"
—Søren Kierkegaard

When Roxy and I made it to Everthorne in Miss Abernathy's carriage, she joined me inside despite her earlier insistence that she wouldn't. I supposed she thought that if Vance were indeed at home, he would have run out of the house at the first sight of our carriage in an amorous display of newlywed bliss.

Which he hadn't, of course. And probably wouldn't have, even if he had been home.

Mrs. Jeffries and Brubaker were mindful not to bother Roxy and me. I was still getting used to having servants, and I guessed that Vance had explained to them that I wouldn't want to be bothered often, for which I was thankful. Roxy and I sat in the main parlor, and I spread my drawings and paintings over the sofa for her to look at.

As she studied them, and then the stories that went with them, she eventually asked, "Do you happen to know where The Boston Inland Mission is, Violet?"

Although I'd had private meetings with members of the mission board at Hilldreth Manor concerning marrying Ben and serving alongside him, I'd actually only ever visited the headquarters once, and that had been to meet the Hatfields. I did have a pamphlet with which contained the address, however, and I dug around my writing box until I found it. I handed it to Roxy without a word.

"May I have this?" Her eyes were wide with excitement, and I wondered just what was going through her mind that made her seem so rejuvenated. She'd seemed sad of late, and I'd guessed it was because her brother and Estella were traveling back to Everston soon, without her, but perhaps it had more to do with Ben than I'd ever imagined.

"I certainly don't need it," I said.

I really didn't want to face anyone at the mission society again, actually. The pamphlet only revived uncomfortable memories. "What are you going to do with it?"

"I'm not certain, but I've heard good things about the organization." She fiddled with the paper in her lap. "I've never done much for anyone else in my life before coming to Boston and being a companion for Miss Abernathy. I know she likes having me around, but she doesn't necessarily need me. She has so many friends already. I feel that I'm simply someone she's been convinced to take along." Roxy produced an impatient little huff. "But there's nothing else for me to do. Dexter and Estella obviously wanted me out of their hair, and living alone with my mother is exhausting."

"I'm sorry. I'm sure that isn't exactly how Dexter and Estella feel. I thought it was considerate of them to bring you along to Boston."

"But now they've gone, and here I am."

"I know. I feel much the same way, actually."

"But you'll be gone within the week, to Europe on your honeymoon." Roxy stood, stuffing the pamphlet into her reticule. "I should go. Thank you for having me in, I'm sure your husband will be back soon and will want all of your attention, so I should get back to Miss Abernathy and her guests."

I stood as well. "About her guests…did you not think they've been acting strangely—avoiding us for so long and then suddenly appearing today—when they'd thought I'd boarded the train to Tennessee yesterday."

"They were rather disconcerted when we told them you were still in Boston."

"Why would they be?" I swiveled around, simply wanting to pace out my frustration. "Why, when they'd originally been so pleased to make my acquaintance, do they now treat me as if the best thing I could do, in their opinion, is move across country and never see them again?"

"I don't know," she answered. "But I did notice that too." She moved toward the door to the hall, looking to the clock on the mantle. "I really should go, I'm sure—"

Mrs. Jeffries entered the room, stopping Roxy's explanation. "I heard you were leaving, Miss Blakeley? I've called for your carriage; it is waiting out back."

"Thank you, Mrs. Jeffries," I said, though a little surprised. Had she been listening to our conversation? "Have you happened to hear from Mr. Everstone yet today?"

"No ma'am. Not a thing."

"Oh."

"Perhaps you would like to walk Miss Blakeley out to her carriage?"

"I suppose I could do that." Oh, how I wished Vance was around! I had no idea how to be with servants!

Mrs. Jeffries excused herself and then Roxy and I made our way to the back of the house, toward the garden where I assumed the carriage would be waiting by the gate. And upon leaving the house, that was exactly what we found.

The groom waited, holding the door to the carriage, ready to help Roxy into the vehicle.

"I'll be sure to see you again before Vance and I leave for Europe next week."

"Thank you. I'd like that."

The groom helped her into the carriage, closed the door, returned to the driver's seat and drove down the path.

I strolled back through the flower garden, not particularly in a hurry to reenter the empty house. Not that there was much to look at by way of flowers, for the weeds had overtaken the space without the careful eye of a faithful gardener to watch over it. There were a few stragglers that had blossomed, but I didn't know much about flowers and could only identify the white peony bushes lining the wrought iron fence.

I walked over and plucked one. I didn't know what had happened to the bloom Miss Abernathy had given me to hold during the wedding the night before; I guess I'd misplaced it. I'd probably left it in Vance's carriage.

The wonderful scent of the peonies brought back memories from the night before…from my wedding.

My last words to Roxy had sounded normal and very married-like, but I still felt uncertain about so many things concerning my new husband. What would Vance do when he came home? What would he say? Would he forgive me for being such a cat?

Or would he ignore me; want to keep his space? What if my actions from the night before had made his walls go back up, and this time there was nothing I could do to get him to bring them down?

I'd truly forgiven him by then, and I really just wanted everything we'd had, before my insufferable reaction to that telegram, to be restored. I felt like there was a piece missing from my life with his disappearance from Everthorne that morning, and that I very well might have permanently ruined everything that had ever been between us.

I suddenly recalled my parents strolling together, arm-in-arm, down a similar path. How much they had loved one another! They had so clearly been one in their devotion to each other. When my father had died, my mother—although she'd been recovering well before that point—deteriorated quickly, as if there were no reason to go on if life didn't include him.

I could imagine.

How I wished my parents could have met Vance, but that would have been impossible if they had lived. My life never would have intersected with Vance Everstone's if I'd not been orphaned the year before.

My family would all still be living at The Hawthorne Inn together, working as a dedicated entity toward our goal—the success of our big brick house turned into an inn.

Perhaps Ezra would have still been my friend—a gentleman, instead of a drunk, a gambler, and a trader of women. The thought of betting my life away in a poker game wouldn't have crossed his mind, once upon a time, and Vance never would have witnessed Rowen Steele's obsession with me. Vance never would have heard of me.

How strange the workings of life were, that God could work so many things together. I was sure God had put Vance and me in each other's paths. It was so obvious the day I'd met him, when Estella had introduced him to me, and revealed to me who she truly was—not a lady's companion, but an heiress much wealthier than most of the wealthy people I'd seen come through the front lobby of Everston.

Vance was different, and for some reason, I'd known from the moment we'd met that he would be more than just another hotel guest. In truth, I really shouldn't have cared one bit about such a man. There shouldn't have been any way in the world that we would ever have been suitable for each other, yet there we were, married. Surely, despite the debacle of the night before, there was grace enough in this world for us to build our marriage to radiate the strength I had witnessed in my parents' life together.

I stood to go into the house with renewed optimism, and heard the squeak of a gate opening behind me. My heart skipped, and then beat faster and faster. Vance had finally come! In a moment I would be in his arms—all wrongs forgiven yet again.

I heard his steps on the path and slowly turned around, relishing the anticipation, yet longing for the moment to culminate.

A man was indeed walking toward me—but it wasn't Vance. His sudden presence sent chills through me, paralyzing me to the ground with fear. I knew him. I recognized the sneer on his face.

It was Rowen Steele.

He looked the same as when I'd thought I'd seen him—when I'd definitely seen him—at The Propylaeum. He was tall, impressively built, and would be able to, without a doubt, overpower me in a moment.

"What are you doing in my garden?" I asked, my voice shaking.

"I've come to collect what is rightfully mine, Miss Hawthorne."

"I'm not yours. If I belong to anyone, it's to my husband, Vance Everstone."

"So it's true. You married him."

"Last night, in fact." I lifted my chin, feigning confidence. Oh, where was Vance? Where was Mrs. Jefferies—Brubaker? "I think you should leave."

"Oh, I will. But you'll be coming with me."

I moved toward the house, and he didn't follow. So I kept walking until I came to the back porch, then the steps, and the door, anxiously wondering if he simply planned to follow me into the house.

But then I tried the knob, jiggling it and pulling against the door. It was locked.

I turned around, looked toward the street where a line of trees created a barrier for privacy. Then I looked at the alleyway and saw a horse hitched to an open-topped surrey, resting near the back gate.

"It seems Mrs. Jeffries has locked you out," Rowen Steele observed.

"How do you know Mrs. Jeffries?"

"How do I know a great many people?" he asked snidely. "I have connections and know plenty of people who either owe me dearly, or at least have a loved one who does. Such as your brother."

"He has no right to promise you anything concerning me."

"I don't care." Rowen came up the steps slowly, one hand now in the pocket of his jacket.

"But I'm married now."

"Again, I don't care. And anyhow, Mrs. Jeffries had some interesting things to tell me this morning. That you slept in your own room alone and that your new husband didn't stay at Everthorne at all last night."

I opened my mouth to answer, shocked he knew so much, but there was nothing to say in response. It was the horrid truth.

"Doesn't sound like a very fulfilling wedding night to me."

I looked in the direction of both ends of the garden again and realized I'd trapped myself by heading to that locked door first. There was nowhere for me to go, and Rowen had begun to ascend the stone porch steps.

"What are you going to do?" I asked.

"You're going to come with me, and I'm going to take you home to Bangor, where you belong."

"Vance will hunt you down," I said with more assurance than I felt.

"Hardly. If Vance knows what's good for him, and you, he'll tell the few people who know about the secret wedding last night, that you'd had a change of heart and had the marriage annulled.

And with Mrs. Jeffries as witness to all that *didn't* happen last night, it will be a likely story." Rowen made it to the porch, and I pressed my back against the door, hoping Brubaker would hear us.

"And when we get to Bangor, you will be my esteemed lady," he sniggered. "Everyone will be eager to be introduced to my new *wife*."

"You don't even know me," I pleaded. "Why do you want me so badly?"

"You know, I'm not certain, exactly." He placed one hand in his pocket and leaned the other on the doorframe above my head, bringing his face close to mine. "Maybe it's the way Ezra flaunted you, taunting us with the idea of you, your hair, your face; how he gave us other women, but kept you from us—from me—for so, so long...."

"You're evil," I choked.

"I won't deny that. Every devil needs an angel." He smiled wickedly. "I can spoil your perfection, though, don't you worry."

That was when I realized he had more than his hand in his pocket. I could see what appeared to be the hollow end of a gun as he pushed it against the brown material of his jacket.

"Now I just need you to get into my surrey." He reached his hand out to me.

The thought of touching him in any way—let alone holding his hand in mine—sent shudders down my spine.

"Come on down now, Violet," he said softly.

I hated hearing my name uttered from his lips. He had no right—

A click from his gun sounded from inside his pocket.

"Come on, let's go. We have places to go, and then a train to catch." As he said this, the back door opened and Brubaker appeared.

Disconcerted by finding me on the porch with a stranger, he asked, "Mrs. Everstone...were you looking to come in—?"

But Rowen yanked his gun out, aimed it directly at Brubaker, and pulled the trigger, sending the butler to the ground. The thunderous echo from the gunshot pounded through my head, and I turned my eyes from the blood that spattered the porch and seeped rapidly from the prostrate butler.

Rowen grabbed me by the elbow, pinching my arm with his big, strong fingers. He pulled me down the stairs and dragged me across the path through the garden toward the alleyway.

I wasn't sure what was a better option, being shot to death while I ran away or waiting to see if I could somehow escape from wherever he would take me.

How could Rowen so easily kill Brubaker? And how could sweet Mrs. Jeffries have been a part of this? Was she desperate? Had he blackmailed her with threats against someone she loved? At least she hadn't told him about me being at Everthorne until that morning, after I'd left for Hilldreth Manor. I wanted to believe that it had been her conscience that had held off giving him the information for so long, but I wished her conscience would have been convincing enough to keep my whereabouts a secret from him indefinitely. She had to know what kind of man Rowen Steele was to blackmail her with whatever information or debt he had in the first place. But to steal me from my new husband just after being married?

How would I ever survive one hour with this awful man?

Once we made it out the wrought iron gate, he stepped closer and pressed the end of his gun into my side, forcing me to climb into the surrey. I still hadn't decided what the best option would be.

He immediately climbed up behind me and then wrapped his free arm around my waist. And that was when I'd finally decided—I would rather run and be shot than possibly endure being the mistress of this man. But as that thought crashed through my mind, his arm buckled around me, and I was forced to sit there uncomfortably with the gun again sticking me in my ribs as the horse pulled us through the alley and out to Dartmouth Street.

"Do try to seem a little more pleased to be in my company, darling. We'll have to convince the couple at the boarding house that we've just been married. I've already shown them your photograph and told them all about you. You're even more beautiful than your photograph, you know; I realized that at The Propylaeum, the first time I ever saw you."

I remained silent, trapped in his arms, his warm breath at the back of my neck making me cower in a constant cringe. Rowen Steele wasn't a bad-looking man—just as the pamphlet I'd first seen his likeness in had suggested—but his heart looked uglier by the moment.

"I wanted to take you right then and there, and I was so close— until Vance showed up."

I registered his assertion. "Mabel knew who you were and that you were there, didn't she?"

"Ah yes, your cousins. I knew about them from Ezra, and once I'd found them and made their acquaintance, it wasn't long before I had found you too. I figured you'd try turning to them while in Boston. And they hardly suspected a thing."

I casually arched my neck to look about the street, in order to determine where we were, but there were no landmarks I recognized.

"Don't think of escaping me. You're my Violet Steele now. Everyone you will know in Bangor will believe it, believe me. There won't be any use in denying it, and if you happen to…well, I'll just make sure the people you care most about pay for your disobedience."

"The Everstones can't be touched by the likes of you."

"What about Vance's brother, Will? I'm sure you've heard by now how he'd been killed not an hour after his wedding last summer, mistaken for Vance himself."

I'd never been told of the details from those days, but the truth was glaring. The Everstones *weren't* untouchable. And poor Vance! The guilt he must have had to deal with!

"And are you forgetting how I so easily infiltrated Everthorne? I could do so much today, if I wanted to. Vance would never know what hit him. And then there's always Wynn, Vance's daughter in Washington. You wouldn't want to see anything happen to her, would you?"

He knew too much. He was too powerful, and I couldn't think of a single thing to do but sit there, trapped, and pray. *God, find me,* I whispered to myself. *Protect those I love. Don't let this man destroy our lives....*

26

The Olde Ram Boarding House

"…a girl with eyes like hers has a will and
is not ruled by anyone but a lover."
—Louisa May Alcott, *A Long Fatal Love Chase*

This will be quick." Rowen let go of me just long enough for both of us to get down from the surrey to the sidewalk. Then he immediately took my hand again, pressing the gun into my side as we walked close, side by side. He hurried me up the street and then stopped in front of a ramshackle of an old wooden house in dire need of a coat of paint and any number of other repairs. The rickety sign above the front porch read, "The Olde Ram Boarding House." I had no idea where in Boston we were, or what kind of place this "boarding house" was. It certainly didn't look very reputable.

"You'll have lunch with the owner's wife—as she'd asked about you this morning and seemed interested in entertaining you while I take care of a few things before we leave. And do try to convince her you're happy to be mine." His tone was light, but his meaning was unmistakable.

"Yes, I recall." My obedience was at the price of safety for the Everstone family.

However, when I thought of Vance, I couldn't help but conspire for a chance to return to him. And I could just imagine him doing all he could for my safe return if he knew of the danger I was in, no matter what had happened last night. He cared for me, more than I ever dreamed he would, and he would try to save me. If he only knew how.

And all I really needed to do was convince this woman that I was there against my will and make her care enough to do something about it. If I had the courage.

Dear God, help me find the right words!

Rowen practically pulled me up the steps to the front porch and threw open the door. "Mrs. Duncan, I'm here and ready to introduce you to my wife!"

We walked into a front entry with a tall straight flight of stairs off to the right, the main room off the hall was wide open to us, but no one was there. We went through that room and into what was obviously the dining room where a few scruffy looking couples sat at tables eating what looked to be soup and bread.

I twisted my sweaty palm against Rowen's hold, but he didn't let go.

"Mrs. Duncan?" Rowen turned to the others seated in the dining room. "She's here, isn't she?"

One of the men nodded. "In the kitchen."

Just as the words were spoken, a middle-aged woman with gray-streaked light blonde hair in a loose bun came into the room through a swinging door. She carried a towel in her hand and worked her fingers against it. She smiled when she saw me.

"Mrs. Duncan—may I present to you my Mrs. Violet Steele?"

I felt hollow inside at Rowen's smooth words—that he thought he could so easily take me from my true husband and pass me off as his own by way of threats. What did he expect life to be like holding a woman against her will? Or would he simply use me for what he wished, for as long as he wished, and then dispose of me? From the way he spoke, I knew any indignity was possible.

"So you're the young lady we've heard so much about," Mrs. Duncan gushed. "You're even prettier in person, I'd say." She tossed the towel over her shoulder. "I have our bread and soup ready and waiting—since Mr. Steele here thinks you need to be on your way north in such a hurry, and he's asked that I watch over you while he attends—"

"That's all very well, Mrs. Duncan, I do realize you've been waiting to meet her, these weeks I've been in Boston wooing her, but my own mother in Bangor has been waiting much, much longer, I promise you." I tried to smile through this entire exchange, but the expression on my face felt more like a grimace.

"Violet, this is Lena Duncan. Her husband, Rufus, owns The Olde Ram." He seemed such a talented actor; that he could somehow gain the admiration of this woman, and that she would look so forward to meeting the young woman he would choose to marry.

"Your cousin Cal was the one to recommend the place in fact," he added quickly. "I don't think I told you that, did I, Violet?"

"No, you hadn't mentioned it." And honestly, I was a bit surprised. It didn't seem like a place my relatives would consider visiting, let alone board at.

I noticed the couple at the table in the corner of the room eyeing my dress and the diamond ring on my left hand. Not that Rowen Steele was dressed shabbily, but I definitely stood out.

"Well, I'll see you in a bit, darling. I need to see two people in particular first, and then I'll return to get my things around before we head to the train station." Rowen grabbed me by the arm and pulled me close to his side. He pressed his lips to my cheek, and I swallowed, forcing myself not to react too harshly; forcing myself not to gag, or scream, or give anything about my real feelings away.

Without waiting for a response, Rowen swiftly walked back through the front room, and out the front door, leaving me there with all of those strangers. I wiped my cheek with my sleeve, disgusted and disheartened. How was I ever supposed to get away?

Could I simply walk out of The Olde Ram while he was gone and hope he was bluffing about harming anyone? But deep down, I knew he wasn't—he'd killed Brubaker without a thought. And that he'd had my own calloused brother bending over backwards—that alone said quite enough.

How I missed Vance! What had I been thinking to hold such a little thing against him? If I'd only forgiven him right away; if I'd only spent the night in his company, we likely would still be there together at Everthorne, closeted away from the world, safe in his bedroom. He likely wouldn't have ever gone to Everstone Square, and he would have been there to protect me.

Would I ever see him again?

Blinking rapidly, I turned off those panicky thoughts. I needed to be alert, not wallowing in what-ifs.

Mrs. Duncan urged me through the kitchen, holding the door open for me to go through. "You can come to the back, deary. I have some private rooms—a private dining room we'll dine in."

I followed her numbly, through the dark and crowded kitchen, and into another section of the house—a small room with another set of stairs; this one much narrower and more plain.

It was odd that he would leave me alone with Mrs. Duncan after going to all the trouble of kidnapping me that morning. It hadn't seemed very well-planned, his coming to Everthorne for me when he did. Perhaps he was just sick enough to think it all a game. He'd made his move, and he was now waiting with cruel amusement for my counter-move.

Mrs. Duncan seemed to stall for a few moments, and then said, "Now, about this cousin of yours, Cal Hawthorne. Do you know why he would have come here after recommending the place to Mr. Steele, to warn me about him?"

"What?" All of my ideas and concerns about Cal came to me at once, confusion clouding all of my past judgements. Why would he—how could he have known? What did it mean?

"I hope I haven't over-stepped my ground in saying...Detective Hawthorne said this Mr. Steele might eventually bring a Miss Violet Hawthorne—his cousin—here with him."

Detective? "Are you telling me that Cal has been trying to help me?"

"Do you *need* help?"

"Yes," I whispered cautiously. Suddenly, I didn't worry about what Rowen's retaliation against anything I did was, now that I knew Cal somehow knew not to trust him, and that he'd gained the confidence of this dear woman on my behalf!

"Your cousin never said anything about you two getting hitched—though Mr. Steele has had plenty to say about it in the last weeks."

"I would never marry a man like him. He just kidnapped me from my home this morning and brought me here. He killed my butler—"

"Oh dear...but thank heavens you've not married him."

"I was just married last night actually, to someone else; my husband is Vance Everstone."

"My, what a last day you must have had then! Married and stolen away in such a short time!—but don't worry, I won't let Mr. Steele haul you off to his mother in Bangor, if that's really his plan. You never know with men like him." Mrs. Duncan tilted her head to the side for a second and put a craggily old finger to her wrinkly lips. "Vance Everstone, did you say?"

"You've heard of him, I'm sure. His family is—"

"No that's not it—I've met the man before. He came here last summer looking for someone. And a little girl, her name was Wynn. I'd helped the poor dear out earlier that winter when her mother died—the someone this Vance Everstone had been looking for—and it seemed Providence had put her in the way of some nice people."

My heart leaped at this news. "Yes, yes, you're referring to Olivia Rosselet and her daughter, Wynn."

"Yes, that were their names."

I decided to skirt the particulars. "Is there a way we can send for help?"

She paced about the small room, staring at the floor. "We need to get you out of here, Miss—excuse me, Mrs. Everstone; but my husband has our carriage—do you happen to know how to ride?"

"I don't, unfortunately."

Mrs. Duncan hurried to a desk along another wall of the little room. She pulled out a chair from a small desk, took a seat, and drummed her fingernails against the wood. "Now, what to do about you. We can't have you simply waiting here for Mr. Steele to come back and take you away. How exactly did he get you here, if not willingly?"

"By gunpoint and threats to harm Vance and his family."

"I suppose that's how he plans to get you to the train station as well—and then to get you to do all sorts of things from then on. What a...." She purposefully let her sentence end there, but I could just imagine the words she would have used were she not, as she supposed, in the company of a lady of refinement.

After rummaging through some things on her desk, she pulled a piece of paper and a pencil from the pile. "You say you married him yesterday? He needs to come right away—oh, I don't know what we'll do to stall Mr. Steele though. And I'm not too sure what he's doing that he needed me to entertain you. I suppose a message will have to do—is your husband very far away?"

"He's at his family's offices...at Everstone Square."

"Good, it isn't far; I've been past it before. We can send a note before us by way of my servant, Thomas, and we'll walk." She held out the pencil and paper for me. "Now, you write your message and Thomas will be sure it gets there in a hurry."

"Mrs. Duncan, I don't know what I'd have done without you!" Before taking the items from her, I quickly hugged the dear lady, hoping that whatever we could do in what time we had would be enough, and that Rowen could be stopped. For if he wasn't stopped, and he figured out our plan, I was convinced that he would only make things worse for all of us in the long run. But it was a chance I needed to take.

And Cal! I wish he'd told me he knew what Rowen Steele was up to, and my poor aunt and cousin; they'd likely been avoiding me to protect me! And I'd had such awful thoughts regarding them all those weeks!

"I can't thank you enough for bringing up my cousin to me! I never would have guessed he knew a thing!"

"From my understanding, he's an undercover detective. I guess you didn't know?"

"I've only met him twice, but that does explain so much!"

Turning back to the table with the pencil and paper, I sat down to write:

Dearest Vance,

Rowen Steele found me in the garden of Everthorne this mid-morning—he shot Brubaker, and Mrs. Jeffries isn't to be trusted! He's taken me to a boarding house called The Olde Ram where a Mrs. Duncan has taken pity on me and let me write to you in hope that you'll be able to help me. We don't know what else to do but to head toward Everstone Square on foot. He isn't here now, but he's threatened me by gunpoint and with threats to harm you and your family. He plans to take me to Bangor by train this afternoon. My cousin Cal can help, that's who warned Mrs. Duncan. Please forgive me for last night. I'm sorry and I love you.

Violet

My last glimpse of Vance as I'd slammed my bedroom door flashed vividly through my mind. I'd been so mean, so heartless. I'd been hurt, and instead of patiently working out my feelings and forgiving him, I'd only wanted to hurt him in return—and the wounded look on his face had told me I'd definitely succeeded.

What would he think when he received the message?

I folded the paper, then wrote the directions to both Everstone Square and Everthorne upon it, and let Mrs. Duncan seal it with a glob of hot red wax.

"Please tell your messenger to only place the missive into Vance's hands."

"I'll tell him; and you can trust my Thomas. He'll reach your husband as quickly as he can, going to Everstone Square first and then to Everthorne only if he doesn't find him there first." She made for the back door. "Well, come with me—being here isn't safe."

I followed her out, and we hurried to the barn where she immediately found her servant, Thomas, and gave him my message to Vance. He'd had his horse ready for some other errand, and was galloping down the street within minutes of speaking with us.

As Mrs. Duncan and I circled around the barn and onto the street, Rowen Steele's surrey drove up, and there were two young women sitting on the open bench seat behind him. He stopped it in a hurry and hopped off. "Dear wife, how nice of you to meet me—couldn't wait to see me again, could you?"

He placed his hand in the pocket with his gun, a silent, yet obvious, threat to me, as he reached out to me with his other arm and half-hugged me. I glanced at Mrs. Duncan who looked like she didn't know what to do, and then to the two young women in the surrey.

"These are the young ladies I've told you all about, darling, who we'll be escorting to Bangor. They've been hired to work at The Grand Hotel." He walked me closer to the surrey and let go of me only to then help them down. Really they weren't much more than girls, perhaps seventeen or eighteen years old. "Miss Philomena Lassiter and Miss Sadie Martindale. This is my wife, Violet Steele."

They each shook my hand accordingly, and my mind buzzed with questions.

What was he up to? But then suddenly, I had an overwhelming feeling that I knew. It was how my own brother had tricked desperate girls looking for respectable work to come to The Hawthorne Inn. He would have them recruited to work at a "hotel", pay for their voyage up from wherever they were from, and then when he'd met them at the train station in Severville.... there was no escaping him.

I still felt sick when I remembered finding out exactly what he'd done; what kind of monster he'd become: the same kind of awful man Rowen Steele was.

It finally dawned on me why he'd been so set on making everything about our "marriage" and our trip to Bangor seem so reputable. It needed to seem that way if he was going to convince these girls to come up with us. And he must have had to pull everything together quickly since discovering my newly married state from Mrs. Jeffries that morning.

I felt the burden of these two hapless girls rest on my shoulders. I couldn't just try to escape and chance leaving these girls with Rowen.

"It's a pleasure to meet you, Miss Lassiter; Miss Martindale," I said, playing along. "Won't you come inside? We can have some tea with the owner of The Olde Ram, Mrs. Duncan," I added quickly and then turned to Rowen. "We have a little time for that, don't we?"

He smiled sheepishly and removed his hand from his pocket. "Well, Miss Lassiter and Miss Martindale can have tea with Mrs. Duncan, but I would prefer to have your help upstairs, Violet."

Mrs. Duncan still looked worried, her arms crossed at her chest, grasping her apron.

"Well, gather your bags, ladies, and let's go inside," I insisted, trying to reassure Mrs. Duncan with my forced smile. I led the way toward the front of the boarding house. "What time is our train leaving again?" I purposefully wouldn't use Rowen's name—I just couldn't bare letting him have the satisfaction of thinking he'd won me over in any way.

Vance would come soon—I was sure of it. He had to.

"I'd like for us to make the one o'clock train, but it's already getting close." With his free hand, he pulled out his pocket watch and popped it open. "It's already noon. We'll need to hurry."

Closing it, and stuffing it back into his pocket, he followed behind Miss Lassiter and Miss Martindale into the boarding house.

Once in the front room, I had the girls take a seat. I studied them both for a moment; they were both pretty. Beautiful, really.

As he'd come in the door last, Rowen took a hold of my hand and corralled me toward the foot of the stairs. "We'll be right down," he said as he stepped forward, making me take the first few stairs up. "Enjoy your tea."

He walked up the stairs close behind me, one hand again in his pocket with the gun and the other now on the railing, blocking me from trying to go back down. After we were about halfway up, Mrs. Duncan followed us.

"I wanted to ask you something, Mr. Steele, before you left. Since you're in such a hurry, I hope you don't mind if I speak to you as you pack."

"I suppose you can, but we don't have much time," he answered impatiently as we made it to head of the stairs. "What is it?"

"Since you seem to have connections with the hotel side of things in Bangor, I wanted to know if you knew anything about the need for boarding houses—I know the town is booming and that there are a lot of lumberjacks passing through looking for work, possibly looking for a place to stay—"

Rowen forced me toward the first room to our left, unlocked it and opened the door. He then turned around to speak to Mrs. Duncan. "Actually I don't have much knowledge of the hotel situation in Bangor; though I do know plenty about the lumberjacks and what they're looking for."

I could tell what Mrs. Duncan was trying to do, keeping me from having to be alone with him for as long as she could. But I could also tell that Rowen wasn't going to put up with her meddling.

"I have a sister who had an inn that burned down last summer, and she still hasn't figured out what to do."

"I'm sure Bangor would be happy to have another inn or boarding house." Rowen blocked the door, standing between Mrs. Duncan and I; his height and wide shoulders completely blocked her from my view. "Now, I'd like to have some private words with my wife while we pack, if you don't mind. I'm sure you understand."

"Can you send her down soon, at least, so she can join the young ladies for tea before you all have to run to catch the train?"

"Sure, we'll see about that, Mrs. Duncan." He slowly closed the door in her face, despite the fact that she'd practically been standing in the doorway. Then he locked it and turned around to face me with a maniacal grin at his lips. "You spoke to her, didn't you? What all did you tell her, exactly?"

I couldn't answer. Upon being pushed into the small bedroom, I was already standing against the footboard of the bed, forcing myself to breathe slowly.

"You don't want to tell me? That's all right. It doesn't matter anyhow, I suppose. She seems to be just as manageable as you've been; and I'm sure I'll be able to find something on her good-for-nothing husband, Rufus, that will keep her quiet."

I wanted so badly to tell him that he'd already lost—that Vance and Cal would be there soon because of the message I'd sent, and that they would rescue me.

Rowen slouched out of his jacket, pulling his pistol from his pocket as he did so. Keeping the gun pointed at me, he then produced a small folded piece of paper with a red wax seal and held it up to me. "Did you happen to lose something?"

27

Unravelled

"I shall do one thing in this life—one thing certain—
that is, love you, and long for you, and keep wanting you till I die."
—Thomas Hardy, *Far from the Maddening Crowd*

How did you—?" I couldn't finish the question, for I could suddenly hardly breathe. All the hope I'd had of Vance coming to my rescue was gone. I didn't even truly care how it had come about. I just wanted to get away. And I couldn't.

Although I felt completely disheartened by the sight of the intercepted message, I was glad that at least Rowen hadn't read it and known that Cal had double-crossed him. Not that it likely mattered now. No matter what Cal had been doing on my behalf without my knowledge, it seemed I'd ruined his plans.

Rowen held the unopened note in my face. "You might not have any experience with doing so, but it's really not that hard to buy the loyalty of others. You just have to offer them enough incentive. Everyone has their price, after all." He stepped closer, pushed the end of his gun into my ribs and handed the note to me. "I'll let you have this as a memento; something to remind you of just how unstoppable I am."

I remembered my written words, and how Vance would likely now always remember me as the wife who'd rejected him and then disappeared.

Would he arrive home soon to find Brubaker shot and bleeding and perhaps dead, and me missing? What would he think happened? Would Mrs. Jeffries lie or had she already run off? He would likely suspect Rowen, but how would he ever find me in time? Was he still at Everstone Square completely ignorant of any trouble?

Boarding the one o'clock to Bangor with Miss Martindale and Miss Lassiter began to seem inevitable.

Rowen moved a little closer, and peered down at me. "You will be mine, and you will like it. If someone like Vance Everstone can make you want to marry him, then it shouldn't be too difficult."

"Vance is nothing like you. He's one of the most admirable gentlemen I've ever met."

His brown eyes narrowed and a grin crept onto his lips. "Well, if that's what he's convinced you of, that's a part I, too, enjoy playing, if you haven't noticed." And then suddenly his smile was gone, replaced by a quick, angry growl. "We simply don't have time for everything I'd like to do—blast those girls downstairs!"

He cupped his big, calloused hand to my cheek, and a pitiful sound escaped my throat. I stared at the wood floor.

"I do wish Mrs. Jeffries had told me you were at Everthorne last night, it would have saved so much trouble for today."

"Don't you need to pack?" I practically whimpered. I didn't look around, but I'd seen plenty of the mess in the room upon being forced to enter.

"Unfortunately, yes." He let go of me harshly and stepped across the room.

I sat on the bed with an inward sigh and watched him slip his gun into a holster tucked at the back of his trousers. Then he opened a drawer to a dresser and tossed its contents onto the bed behind me. He bent forward to grab a suitcase and a few odds and ends from the floor and threw them on the bed as well. While he worked at packing, I closed my eyes, rested my arm on the tall footboard and bowed my head into the crease of my elbow.

The only thing I could think to do was grasp the stolen missive in my clasped hand and pray. *God, please help us! I don't know what else to pray besides—please save us from this awful man's plans. Please return me safely to Vance.*

Rowen grabbed my arm, and pulled me to my feet. Wrapping a firm arm around me, he pressed his hand into my back, pushing me against him. Bringing his face down to mine, he whispered, "Now remember, darling, you love me. Let's don't let the girls downstairs think anything differently—"

A loud crack interrupted his sentence, and I turned toward the door. Another crack, and splinters flew off the doorframe.

Rowen let go of me, reached around his back and pulled his gun from the holster. He took a shot at the door.

"Violet? Are you in there?" a familiar voice shouted from the hall.

"Vance!" I screamed.

With one more crack to the door, it burst open. Vance stepped in first, his eyes blazing with determination and fury. He had a gun drawn, aimed at my captor. And my cousin Cal was right behind him with a gun drawn, as well.

I dropped to the floor and crawled away from Rowen's reach for fear of his grabbing me and holding me hostage. But I couldn't go far, only around to the side of the bed where I was prevented from seeing anything that was going on. Realizing I still held the note I'd earlier written for Vance in my hand, I quickly stowed it away into the hidden pocket of my gown.

"Rowen, put your gun down," I heard Vance say slowly, his voice calm, yet harsh and angry. "Toss it on the bed."

"What are you doing here?" Rowen asked, visibly unnerved at seeing Cal with Vance.

"I'm here to arrest you," Cal answered from the doorway. "For the murder of Harry Brubaker, for kidnapping my cousin Violet, and for the coercion of the two young ladies downstairs."

"What do you mean? What are you, the police?" Rowen asked.

I was quite certain Rowen still had his gun aimed at them.

"As a matter of fact, I am," Cal answered.

Still hiding behind the bed, I heard a scuffle of feet on the wood floor, and I had a feeling it was Rowen launching himself at Vance. But then it seemed all three of them were wrestling each other. I stayed hidden on the floor behind the bed praying Rowen would be defeated.

Suddenly a gunshot echoed through the room, another one quickly after it, and then the unmistakable sound of glass shattering and a loud cry, followed by a thud.

I peeked over the edge of the bed to see that the window had indeed been broken through, and that Vance and Cal were still both in the room. Rowen Steele was nowhere to be seen.

"No, go to her. Violet needs you—" I heard Cal mutter.

Before I knew it, Vance was around the bed, his knees hitting the wood floor beside me. "Violet, you're safe now." His arms came around me and held me tight, stroking my hair, his cheek pressed to mine. "I'm so sorry, Violet. I am so sorry for leaving you alone today, for lying to you yesterday."

I couldn't utter a word, and instead simply put one arm around my husband and buried my face into his shoulder. I wanted to weep, but the tears wouldn't come. How was he there? Was he real? I could hardly think beyond the fact that his arms *felt* real around me. I leaned in heavily against his chest, savoring his presence. I'd been so close to never seeing him again, so close to having been whisked away by that vile man....

"He's dead, Violet."

Relief washed over me, and I began to tremble uncontrollably.

Vance turned me to face him and looked me in the eyes. "There's no more need to fear."

For as much as I wanted to hear those words, I was too shocked by everything that had just happened. I could only crash against his chest, weeping, grateful that Vance was there holding me again. As I did so, a cloud seemed to lift from me, creating an overwhelming sense of clarity. All that had really just happened, and I was now free when I'd been so sure I never would be. "How are you here?"

"We'll get to all that later, right now we need to attend to your cousin. He's been shot."

"Oh, is he—?"

"No need to worry, Violet," Cal groaned from the floor on the other side of the bed.

Vance and I stood together and found Cal leaned against the wall, pressing a wadded up blanket to the side of his thigh.

"It's just a deep graze. All the blood makes it seem worse than it is," Cal insisted, his face pale and contorted from pain.

Vance immediately stooped to gather Cal from the floor and laid him on the bed. "Violet, please go get Mrs. Duncan, he needs a doctor." He ripped Cal's trousers all the way up to his thigh, and I turned away at the sight of the bloody wound.

At the same time, the door to the hall opened and Mrs. Duncan stood staring in, Miss Martindale and Miss Lassiter behind her.

"We heard what happened. I went out back to be sure he was dead, and he most certainly is." Mrs. Duncan entered the room, gave me a hurried hug. "I tried my best to stay with you, Violet. I'm sorry I failed. I hope he didn't hurt—"

"He didn't," I assured her.

She let go when she caught a glimpse of Cal lying on the bed, grimacing with pain, blood everywhere. "Oh, your cousin!"

"It looks bad, but Cal says his leg was only grazed by the bullet." I steered her back to the hall, hoping to keep the girls from seeing what Mrs. Duncan and I had seen of Cal's leg. "Do you happen to have someone—besides Thomas—that you can send for a doctor? Thomas isn't to be trusted. At least he wasn't trusted with this." I fished the note we'd sent with him out of my pocket.

"Oh no! That boy! But how then did your husband and cousin know to come?"

I quickly stuffed my note to Vance back into the pocket of my dress. "I don't know. I suppose because of Cal's original recommendation to Rowen, he must have figured this was where we might be."

"Goodness," was all Mrs. Duncan uttered, and then turned to the two girls waiting in the hall. "Will one of you get a pot of water boiling in the kitchen, please?"

"I can do that," Miss Lassiter answered, and then both girls disappeared down the stairs.

"I'll go for the doctor myself." And without another word, Mrs. Duncan was down the staircase and out the door, intent on accomplishing her important mission.

I walked back to the bedroom where Vance attended to Cal, a little wary of getting too close a look at the wound again. But Vance had a wadded-up sheet pressed to Cal's leg to help staunch the bleeding.

"Violet, will you take over here for a few minutes?"

As I came closer, I realized my cousin had passed out, and that all of my questions for him would have to wait. I pressed my hands onto the sheet, next to Vance's.

He didn't move for a moment, staying close to me. "I'm glad you're safe, Violet. For the time it took Cal and me to get here...I wasn't certain what I was going to do."

I had too much gratefulness bursting from my heart to speak right away, but I did cover Vance's hands with one of mine in silent answer.

Cal stirred and Vance let go, allowing me to take over.

After a minute, Vance came back and I stood back as he carefully worked a shoelace around Cal's upper left thigh. "Who were those young ladies? Were they involved somehow?"

"They thought that we—supposedly a respectable married couple—were taking them up to work at a hotel in Bangor, when really, I suspect, they were actually headed to some place more like The Hawthorne Inn."

"He was recruiting young women to become prostitutes—only without their knowledge."

"Exactly." I stood close to Vance, studying the cousin I hardly knew, who'd done so much for me in the last few months without my knowledge.

"The water is warming," Miss Lassiter announced as she came to the head of the stairs.

Vance and I put a respectable distance between us before she reached the doorway of the bedroom, neither of us yet accustomed to the fact that we were married and perfectly allowed to be anywhere we wanted…quite alone.

"The detective has passed out, has he?" She stood before Cal, and then took a long look at us. "This is your husband then?"

"Yes, this is Mr. Everstone, my husband." I smiled, taking immense delight in saying the words.

"Mrs. Duncan explained to us what happened," she said sadly. "I've served in a hospital before, under the guidance of my mother, who is a nurse. I don't mind watching over the detective until the doctor gets here…if you'd like some time alone after such a morning."

"Thank you, Miss Lassiter. That would be wonderful.…" Vance took my hand in his as we walked out to the landing, not too far from Miss Lassiter and my cousin, for the sake of propriety. Vance cautiously put his left arm around my shoulders. He spoke quietly as he went on to say, "Cal will be fine, Violet, don't worry."

"I feel absolutely terrible for the things I've believed of my relatives." I hoped that I would still be able to form a meaningful relationship with them before they moved to Maine—if Cal truly would be alright, and that was still their plan. "I'd almost been able to escape with the help of Mrs. Duncan while Rowen had left me in her company to collect Miss Lassiter and Miss Martindale. He didn't realize, of course, that Cal had warned her about him, and that he might eventually bring me here."

"We have much to thank him for, don't we? We grossly misjudged him."

"I hope they forgive me," I said, turning my face to Vance's neck, wanting desperately to lean into him. But I couldn't. Not yet—not without first apologizing and gaining his forgiveness too.

"Rowen was trying his best to make everyone believe we were married and that he was a gentleman, but never acted like one to me. He was horridly unpleasant."

Vance squeezed closer, but then leaned me back to look me in the face. "Is that all?" he choked out, his eyes filled with fear that so much more had actually happened.

"He never had a chance to do anything," I insisted. "I'm not lying to you. It's the truth. The first time he had me alone, besides at the garden at Everthorne where he'd found me, and in the surrey on the way here, was just as you and Cal showed up and burst into the room." I shivered at the realization of what all could have happened.

Vance pulled me close again, not saying anything for some time, until he uttered, "I don't have the words for how relieved I am—"

We heard the front door of the house open and a few people enter the house. Hoping it wasn't just some boarders of Mrs. Duncan's, we went to the head of the staircase and looked down to the front entry. It was Mrs. Duncan herself, and she'd brought the doctor with her. A police officer had apparently arrived at the same time.

They all three came up the stairs, followed by Miss Lassiter and Miss Martindale who brought the small pot of hot water just as it was needed.

I heard Cal's weak voice as the officer entered the small room. "Sergeant Taulbee, it's so good to see you...."

28

With You

"God has set his intentions in the flowers,
In the dawn, in the spring—
It is his will that we should love."
—Victor Hugo, *Toilers of the Sea*

After Sergeant Taulbee collected information from everyone involved about the events of the morning, Vance and I were finally freed to go home.

Once the doctor situated Cal comfortably into Vance's carriage, taking up an entire bench seat, we entered the vehicle to escort him home, seated together, facing him. Vance kept a tight hold on my hand, lending me strength.

As soon as the carriage door was closed, Cal said, "I knew Rowen had been trying to get close to you through me, and eventually my mother and sister lately…. I'm sorry we didn't tell you. We thought it was best that way."

"I now see that their concern was the reason for their sudden coldness, and why you all didn't attend Vance's father's wedding," I said, so glad to finally put the puzzle pieces together.

"I'd been trying to arrest Steele for anything I could ever since your brother came to town to tell me how he'd lost you in a poker bet. He also told me about chopping your hair off and the way he'd sabotaged you into getting engaged to Vance a lot sooner than planned."

Than planned. I smiled and squeezed Vance's hand. Without Ezra's meddling, there probably never would have been an engagement between us.

"Ezra didn't know I was a plainclothes police detective, which was probably for the best. That was how I discovered the plans regarding Miss Lassiter and Miss Martindale, from digging into anything and everything I could on both Steele and your brother."

"Oh, so you know about Ezra...."

"I'm not going to hold your brother's sins against you." Cal pulled a face as the carriage wheels hit an extra bumpy section of the road. "You're nothing like him, I can tell—and so can mother and Mabel."

"Thank you—"

"It does say something for him that he was doing all he could to keep Steele from collecting on his careless bet though." Cal closed his eyes, as if the pain was making speech difficult.

"I still wouldn't consider him a beloved brother—no matter what he's done to try to help," Vance added.

"No, definitely not...but he *did* find a way to keep Violet relatively safe in Boston, by being engaged to you, and therefore having her so completely surrounded by your powerful family. However, when your father's wedding took place...I didn't realize that everyone would be leaving town. Once they left, I didn't feel quite as confident about Rowen keeping his distance." Cal opened his eyes and looked to me specifically. "But fortunately, Steele had apparently lost track of you after your move to Hilldreth, and although your temporarily broken engagement and new plans to travel to Roan Mountain Station weren't public, it wasn't too difficult for an undercover detective to figure out." He smiled to himself, although his eyes were again closed.

"So you thought I was safely tucked away on a train headed to Tennessee this morning when Miss Abernathy told you that I hadn't, in fact, left as planned, but that I'd instead stayed and married Vance after all...."

"That was definitely unexpected, I can assure you."

Vance didn't add anything, but he took our entwined fingers to his lips and silently kissed my hand.

"And then you showed up at Hilldreth—which was even more unexpected. And walking about Back Bay all on your own—I didn't know what to do with myself!"

Vance sat up, turning me to him. "You walked to Hilldreth on your own this morning?"

"I needed to tell Roxy and Miss Abernathy that what you'd said of Ben was false."

"I'd been fairly confident you would be safe riding home to Everthorne with Miss Blakeley," Cal added, suddenly looking a bit piqued. "Especially since you insinuated Vance would be home for lunch."

"Hoping, were you?" Vance asked in my ear. I could hear the smile in his voice.

"However, when Miss Blakeley didn't return right away as she'd said she would, I began to worry. I left mother and Mabel at Hilldreth and went straight to Everthorne to investigate." Cal had remained alert for most of the ride, but at this point in the story, he spoke slower and slower and became more lethargic. "That was when I'd found your butler had been shot and killed. I notified the police at that point, and that's when I stopped at Everstone Square—since it was right on the way—and told Vance what I suspected had happened."

The doctor had said Cal's body would eventually tire from the loss of blood and it seemed as if his confession of everything that had been going on without my knowledge had also helped to wear him out, for soon after he'd said this, he fell unconscious and didn't wake up when the carriage stopped in front of his mother's house, or as Vance picked him up and carried him in to be cared for by his loving mother and sister.

When Vance returned to the carriage to head home to Everthorne, he sat beside me on the frontward facing seat. He made no remark, and I wondered what he was thinking—though having his arms securely around my waist gave me a good idea. He certainly didn't seem mad at me for what I'd done the night before, but I knew I still needed to apologize.

I really didn't know how to begin, so I simply said, "It's time to go home."

Glancing up at him, I found him simply staring down at me, something dangerously heated kindling behind his black eyes. "That sounds like an excellent idea."

Not knowing what else to do or say in response, I recalled how I'd written out my apology to him in the message Rowen had given back to me. "I wrote you something today...." I pulled the still-sealed note from my pocket and handed it to him, the wax seal faced up.

He immediately flipped it over and read the two addresses I'd written—Everstone Square, and then below that, the street address of Everthorne. "What is this?" he asked skeptically.

It must have seemed strange, to be sure.

"It's the reason I'd lost all hope that you would come in time... just before you did." I smiled bashfully remembering how he'd held me in his arms and wouldn't let me go once he'd found me in that tiny bedroom. "It's a message I'd tried to send to you, but Rowen intercepted it."

Taking his arms from around me, Vance broke open the seal and then slowly read my words. I watched as his beautiful black eyes roved over the page. He didn't look up from the paper for much longer than it had to have taken for him to read the few sentences that were there. And then after studying them quite intently, he only smiled—a much bigger smile than I'd ever seen stretch across his cheeks.

I smiled back, but I couldn't help my gaze from dropping to the floor of the carriage. "Would you like to begin our marriage, again? And will you please forgive me for how I behaved last night?"

When he didn't answer right away, I looked up and found him staring down at me.

"Now, you know I haven't been the best at new beginnings, though I've tried my best." He had a playful smirk on his face, but I could tell there was much truth behind his words.

"You never give yourself enough credit—"

Vance placed a finger at my lips, and suddenly I didn't exactly care to say anything more—I just wanted him to kiss me.

"But this," he held up the letter, "—this is rather compelling. It makes me want to try, again and again." He moved closer and wrapped an arm about my waist. "Especially because of that last part."

"The part where I said…I love you?"

"Yes, that part, exactly." He brought his other hand to my neck and fingered the strands of my short hair hanging over my ear. "Because in case you missed it in yesterday's late-night discussion, the reason I wanted to marry you so badly was that I'd fallen in love with you too."

"We're both fools, Vance," I said softly, "hurting each other so clumsily. I've been sorry for how I reacted; especially this morning. And then all this happened, and all I could think about was how I'd possibly never see you again, or ever be able to gain your forgiveness. I've regretted my haste in shutting you out last night." I lowered my eyes to my lap. "Will you forgive me…and allow me to make things right?"

"Oh, I don't think that will be too difficult." Vance's arm tightened around my waist, bringing me much closer than he had since when we were last together alone, the night before in his bedroom.

I couldn't help but look up into his gorgeous, black, serious eyes. I also couldn't help but smile shyly.

"Now that I'm holding you again and have these words to treasure...." He held the letter I'd so frantically written earlier, gently caressing the corner of it across my cheek. He then followed its trail with a kiss, until his lips were just barely pressed against mine. "I think it will be quite easy, in fact, my sweet wife."

About the Author

Dawn Crandall is an ACFW Carol Award-nominated author of the award-winning series The Everstone Chronicles, which currently consists of: *The Hesitant Heiress*, *The Bound Heart* and *The Captive Imposter*. *The Cautious Maiden* is her fourth book.

Apart from writing, Dawn is also a mom of two very little boys and serves with her husband in a premarital mentorship program at their local church in Fort Wayne, Indiana.

A graduate of Taylor University with a degree in Christian education and a former bookseller at Barnes & Noble, Dawn Crandall has always loved books but didn't begin writing until 2010 when her husband found out about her long-buried dream. It didn't take her long to realize that writing books was what she was made to do.

Dawn is a member of the American Christian Fiction Writers, the secretary for the Indiana ACFW Chapter (Hoosier Ink), and an associate member of the Great Lakes ACFW Chapter. She is represented by Joyce Hart of Hartline Literary Agency.

Connect with Dawn Crandall online…
Facebook: www.facebook.com/DawnCrandallWritesFirst
Twitter: @dawnwritesfirst
GoodReads: www.goodreads.com/dawn_crandall
Blog: www.dawncrandall.blogspot.com